BLACK GOLD

Frank Palmer

Constable · London

First published in Great Britain 1998 by Constable & Company Ltd,
3 The Lanchesters, 162 Fulham Palace Road, London W6 9ER
Copyright © 1998 Frank Palmer
The right of Frank Palmer to be identified as the author of this work
has been asserted by him in accordance with the Copyright,
Designs and Patents Act 1988
ISBN 0 09 478650 X
Set in Palatino 10pt by SetSystems Ltd, Saffron Walden, Essex
Printed and bound in Great Britain by
MPG Books Ltd, Bodmin, Cornwall

A CIP catalogue record for this book
is available from the British Library

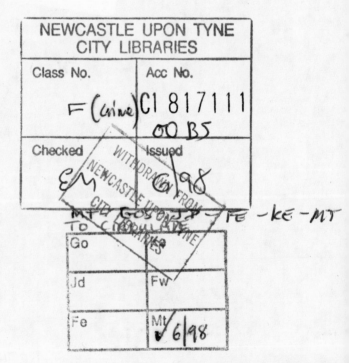

The East Midlands Combined Constabulary is fictional.
So, too, are all the characters and companies in its cases.

For our grandchildren

1

Another paragraph or two and it's done and dusted.

Not one of those two-hundred-page slogs, this job, a major investigation entailing weeks of work, i's dotted, t's crossed on a dossier to be read by everybody from the Chief Constable up to the Director of Public Prosecutions.

This is a short story; short, simple and sad.

I scroll back what's already in draft on my dinky little office-issue laptop; just a two-sheet summary.

Abe Myles was arrested on suspicion of a smash and grab at a back-street jeweller's – reasonable suspicion bearing in mind that the first police officer on the scene found him standing in front of the shattered shop window, ranting in a foreign tongue above a jangling burglar alarm.

'It's family' was all he'd said when he reverted to his long-adopted English on arrival at the station. And so it proved, as the detective inspector assigned to the inquiry soon established.

Myles had taken over the jewellery business from his refugee father. Years on, he handed it down to his own son, who had modernised and expanded into a chain with its own distribution depot. They had fallen out over changing the name from 'Myles and Son' to the more upmarket 'Milestones'.

He'd readily admitted he'd smashed the window of his old premises where the business had started in the immediate post-war years. 'As a protest,' he'd added. He refused to explain about what.

In his cell, he saw a solicitor, but didn't request a visit from his estranged son. The inspector, a woman, phoned him anyway.

The old man had not been himself since mother died, Myles Junior told her. He was ill and lonely, nothing to occupy him, no interests outside the synagogue and doing his bit for charity.

He'd been talking about resuming work, but, as he was poorly with prostate problems and well past retirement age, the idea had been vetoed. The son gave the name of the family solicitor, but didn't turn out himself to see his father.

The reference to illness and the phrase 'not been himself' alerted the inspector. Playing safe, she summoned the police surgeon. He arrived about the same time as the lawyer. Both saw old Abe briefly and separately.

The solicitor reported his client had been uncooperative. He had left him with pen and pencil to write out his account of events in his own time. The lawyer made no complaint about his treatment in custody and said the family didn't want the old man charged and brought to court.

The doctor diagnosed Abe fit for continued detention while a decision was made.

Being new to and inexperienced in CID, the inspector consulted a veteran custody officer. 'Stick a holding charge on him of maliciously damaging the window,' he advised, 'and let him go on bail to give you time to sort it out.'

She went back to the cell to set Abe free, couldn't see him through the peephole or the serving hatch, couldn't open the door at first.

The custody officer helped her shove it back. On the tiled floor behind the door they found him. From the front of his shirt, he'd torn off the double thickness strip for button holes, looped one end round his neck, tied the other to the brass knob on the serving hatch and hanged himself.

They tried mouth-to-mouth and pumping his chest while the doctor was recalled. He pronounced Abe dead.

On his bunk was the shortest of suicide notes: 'Exodus.'

A knock comes on the door of this borrowed office. The station sergeant shows in Peter Myles for his 11 a.m. appointment.

'Thanks for coming in,' I say, half rising, not shaking his hand, having spent an hour with him at his comfortable flat yesterday.

A dark, dapper man in his mid-forties, he sits across the desk.

I slide the one word note towards him. 'There's just one formality.' I nod at the note. 'Can you positively identify that as your father's handwriting?'

Sombre-faced, he studies it for longer than seems necessary. 'Yes,' he finally answers.

I hand him his statement, prepared yesterday, which will join the other witnesses' in a fairy thin file. Head down as he signs, he asks in a light, cultured voice, 'What happens now?'

'There'll be an inquest, of course,' I tell him.

His head comes up. 'With a suicide verdict a foregone conclusion, I assume?'

He has given me an opening. Deaths in police custody have caused riots in the streets before now with allegations of cover-ups of police brutality.

Even suicides of sad, sick souls in station cells can bring out pickets from busybody organisations like 'Custodywatch' whose placards turn routine inquests into media circuses with grieving relatives pushed before cameras and notebooks to give the usual newsbite. 'He'd still be alive if they'd taken better care of him.'

Had the subject of the inquest killed himself at home, there'd be only deep condolences all round, of course; comforting words like, 'Don't blame yourself. No one could possibly have foreseen such a tragedy.'

But, whenever a life ends at a State-run care-of address, then the heartless State should have anticipated the outcome, so it's all our fault and we must be made to pay because everyone, grieving relatives especially, has their snout in the compensation trough these days.

Gratefully, I accept the opening. 'Unless you're not satisfied with the way he was treated in here.'

'Oh, no.' He looks mildly surprised, as if the thought had never crossed his mind. 'Everything possible was done.'

A ticklish task now. Both the police doctor and the detective inspector are Asian, Muslims for all I know or care. Abe was Jewish, not Wailing Wall Orthodox but certainly a regular worshipper.

Now the East Midlands isn't the Middle East, but, then again, some Catholics and Protestants you see on TV frothing at the mouth about Ulster might as well still be living in the days of the dissolution of the monasteries.

In this job, you just never know where the next whinge about religious or racial intolerance might spring from. I can't very well ask point-blank: 'No objections to Islamic lips trying the kiss-of-life on your Yiddisher poppa?' So, instead, 'And you're satisfied with the conduct of the doctor and the officer in charge?'

11

'Absolutely.' He looked quite shocked. 'Both did their very best.'

A satisfied customer, I think, thankfully.

'No complaints from next of kin' is typed with two fingers on the keyboard, rounding off the summary. 'Recommend no further . . .'

A tap comes on the door and I look up to see the sergeant again. 'May have another one for you, sir.'

2

There must be a look of abject and undisguised horror on my face, because, even with an ever-increasing prison population, this is no way to solve the problem of overcrowded cells.

Somewhat crudely, he adds, 'Not a cell topping this time. In a police pursuit.'

He shuffles uncomfortably from one foot to the other. 'She's not dead. Not quite. But I thought you ought to know since you're here.'

I ought to know because I run the Complaints and Discipline Department. Into my in-tray at HQ comes every moan about police officers in this force – from incivility to brutality, and including deaths in custody and arising out of police chases.

It's not much of a job. Apart from one assignment, semi-undercover on a bogged-down murder case just before Christmas, it's boring.

A bit premature, I think, mawkish really, to launch a fatal accident inquiry before the subject of it is dead, but since I'm here with half a day to spare, well, yes, I'd better get the feel of it, view the scene, make the odd preliminary check and, first of all, speak to the hospital.

*

Stripped of medical mumbo-jumbo, what I'm hearing over the phone confirms what the sergeant said: She isn't quite dead. But she will be. Soon.

'Sorry,' he adds.

Why the hospital social worker should say sorry to me isn't clear. I don't know the woman, not even her name. As yet, it appears, no one does because she was carrying no documents.

She's Asian, about thirty, he goes on, black hair tied in a bun, wearing a floral sari and thick, black short coat. 'Deeply unconscious,' he adds.

He's sorry I'll never get to talk to her, I suppose, get her side of the story.

I say 'Thanks', return the phone to its cradle, get up, retrieve my brown raincoat from its stand and my dirty Volvo from the courtyard at the centre of this splendid station.

It's splendid because it's distinguished, white stone in neo-classical design, with tasteful extensions, not like so many nicks that all look the same.

It's a short drive down Charles Street, after which the station takes its name, right at a roundabout, over a flyover and into Belgrave Road which runs into Melton Road.

In summer, no other street on my patch stirs so many senses. All the colours of the rainbow, and many in between, come from the saris worn by Asian women, from windows filled with fruit and veg, posters in travel agencies for exotic destinations and for films on show at a cinema called Bollywood or on sale at video shops.

The glitter comes from gold displayed by jewellers, so many of them that they call this street the Golden Mile.

The sounds of eastern music float from record and clothes shops. Enticing smells drift from spice stalls and restaurants.

But, on a misty winter's day like today, dull, heavy western coats cover the saris and all doors are shut against the cold. It's like dropping into a cricket ground out-of-season. It loses its attraction.

Besides which, I've travelled up and down it several times for two days running, both on my way to and from home and calling in the back streets off it on Abe Myles's case.

So I don't look around me when traffic at the north end slows to a stuttering crawl, just wish I'd commandeered a squad car with flashing light and siren.

On the outskirts of the city, the road changes from a name to a number and into dual carriageway. Vehicles with headlights dipped drive slowly through the February murk on the other side of the central reservation.

The accident investigator, sitting in the passenger seat next to me, looks through the windscreen at a red Mazda, its bonnet embedded in a concrete lamp standard. He points to its rear hatch door which is up. 'The paramedics got her out that way,' he says. 'Terrible head injury, I'm afraid.'

Now he nods to tyre marks clearly visible on the greasy road surface, that filthy film which fog always leaves behind. 'She was driving too fast without lights. All the independent witnesses say so. It's a nippy motor. I guess she wasn't used to it. She lost control and hit the lamp post.'

'Who's the vehicle registered to?' I ask.

'A local businessman. Not reported stolen. Not yet anyway.' He shrugs. 'Maybe she borrowed it.'

The skid marks, I note, stretch a long way from the outside lane across the inside and stop at the rear wheels of the crashed car. It was such a dreadful piece of driving in poor visibility that at midnight you'd be looking for a drink motive.

But over the top at midday? Just doesn't ring true. A white woman driver in late, neglected middle age, I just might buy, but not an Asian woman, aged about thirty. Unless, of course, she'd become westernised.

Ah, well, I think. Her name will give you her background. The hospital will give you her blood-alcohol content.

A muffled rap close to my right ear turns my head. My eyes go from gloved fist to the pinched face of a traffic officer. I wind down my window a couple of inches, letting in the cold. 'OK if we move it now, sir?' he asks through mist of iced breath. 'Only there's a big build-up back towards the city centre.'

Don't I know it, I think. 'Has the photographer been?'

'And gone,' he billows in another small white cloud.

'OK,' I say.

On the way back to the station, I toy with the idea of pulling in at one of the many curry houses for a quick worker's lunch. Only the fact that there's a hot meal lined up at home tonight drives me on.

A couple more sheets and this account is done and dusted, too; a good day's work.

I scroll back over what's already in draft. Road and weather conditions, an hour before the end of a busy five-to-one shift for the crew of Local Police Unit 10.

Even the most sceptical supervisor in the independent Complaints Authority, to whom I have to report, should be able to catch the unwritten drift that they'd hardly be looking for an arrest and the paperwork that goes with it when home and a hot meal beckoned.

Over sausage sandwiches in the canteen, the driver of the LPU 10 had been honest enough to admit he'd stopped in a pub forecourt for a smoke with window wound down. I've not mentioned that, just tutted when he gave his statement.

A red Mazda hatchback whizzed by, a woman with shawled head at the wheel, going far too fast in the conditions. Out the window went the tab end. On went the blue lights.

Seventy was touched heading north-east away from the city, getting close enough for the observer to read off the number plate over the radio to the information room. Not reported stolen, the controller responded after a computer check.

The driver slackened to sixty. Further up the A607, where the dual carriageway meets the new bypass and becomes the A46 Fosseway, a high-speed Immediate Response Vehicle was stationed, Control informed him.

They were being alerted to intercept. Between them they'd catch up with her, look at her documents, give her a breath test if she smelt of booze and, whatever the result of that, book her for reckless driving.

From up ahead they heard the squeal of brakes and the blare of horns and reported it over the radio. Even before the observer got out of the patrol car the driver was summoning up an ambulance.

The time between calls to Control was twenty seconds. At 60 m.p.h., that means the police car was a third of a mile behind.

Forensics confirm the skid marks on the road surface were from the crashed car. None were made by the police patrol; hardly hot pursuit.

Vehicle examiners found that the index and the chassis numbers matched. The car had not been stolen or given false plates. The registered owner, one Ravid Mal, had still not reported it missing.

Open and shut. No suspensions or transfers are called for. The crew can have the weekend off and I'm going to suggest that they return to normal duty next week.

That's the final paragraph decided then: 'No further action recommended.' Then my signature block will go above a short list of enclosed statements.

I'll not clean it up and print it out tonight, or tomorrow, a long-booked day off. Over the weekend, perhaps, when I'm senior duty officer, if she dies between now and then.

God, that's macabre, you insensitive sod, I rebuke myself sternly. But practical forward planning, I have to admit.

Home now for that promised moussaka.

Another bit of office-issue technology is bleeping in my pen pocket: a pager with a panel which displays telegram-type messages.

One superintendent is alleged to be conducting a lengthy, passionate and extremely expensive (to the taxpayer) correspondence on his with a woman inspector from North Wales he met on a training course.

Such misuse of equipment is the concern of my department, but I don't think I'll investigate it. The only outcome would be a ban on all private messages.

'Call home' dances across the small screen. 'Catering cock-up.'

'Forgot to defrost the minced lamb,' Em confesses when I make the call.

'What about the microwave?' I ask.

'Forgot to get the bloody thing repaired.'

No great disappointment, this news. Her moussaka always tastes like gran's shepherd's pie used to. I wouldn't break the speed limit to get home for either.

My Em always has to alibi an error. Nothing is ever entirely her fault. Usually our delightfully mischievous daughter, eighteen months old now, gets the blame. The excuse this time is that she'd been distracted by workmen refelting and tarring the flat roof over the garage. 'Cash, by the way,' she adds, dully.

To save the contractor paying income tax and us VAT, I realise with the sort of twist of guilt that comes with driving with a glass of wine too many or secretly studying other ladies' legs. You shouldn't be doing it, you know, I always tell myself, and then ignore myself.

I start putting the paperwork scattered about the desk in order with my free hand while hearing that Laura, our daughter, has a little friend in and they're making a din with old Tupperware pots in preference to playing with stacks of expensive toys.

'So . . .' Em's voice trails.

The photos of the crash scene are in, I note, but there's no hospital report yet. Nothing in writing indicates that the owner of the car has been informed that it's been recovered, albeit written off, before he even knew it was missing. And a media appeal with description has not come up with any lead to the identity of the unknown woman driver.

'So?' she says more stridently, about to accuse me of not listening, a frequent complaint when nagging loose ends enter my mind.

'So I'll bring in take-out,' I offer.

'What time roughly?'

I always lie, barefaced and unashamedly, to Em about my estimated time of arrival home, often add an hour so that if something unexpected turns up she won't worry. If not, she's pleasantly surprised when I'm early.

I tell her about my afternoon case. 'We haven't ID-ed the victim yet.' Belatedly, I realise I should have said 'casualty'. It wasn't quite as bad as 'fatality' but, even so, I shouldn't be killing her off just yet.

As if to make amends, I tell her about the doubt that crossed my mind at the scene. 'Driving, let alone drink driving, isn't part of the culture of Asian womenfolk.'

'You of all people will get into hot water talking about cultural offences,' she chides.

She's not quite correct. It's OK to talk publicly about armed

17

blaggings being a white thug's crime, but not muggings being a black's. I fall back on the new in-word. 'Doesn't fit the profile then.'

'In what way?'

'Well, you get lonely middle-class white wives hitting the bottle for breakfast and driving to the off-licence at lunchtime to buy another but . . .'

'Like me soon,' she says with what I know is feigned forlornness.

Never, I vow to myself, will this job come between me and my family. And this particular job will certainly keep.

Stick someone from the coroner's department on the ID, I instruct myself. Or give the media appeal another twenty-four hours. By then Fingerprints or Missing Persons may well have come up with a name. Take your planned day off tomorrow, finish the routine by phone over the weekend. 'Eight at the latest, I promise,' I tell her.

'Chinese or Indian?' she wants to know.

The mere thought of a curry sometimes literally makes my mouth water, all the more so with the knowledge that I'll be driving back down the Belgrave and Melton Roads with no need to resist the temptation tonight.

'I could murder an Indian,' I say, almost salivating.

'Tut-tut,' she clucks. 'One of these days your political incorrectness is really going to drop you in it.'

The pager bleeps again while I have the shift inspector on the carpet in front of my tidied-up desk. 'Phone ICU, LRI' rolls out on the screen. 'Urgent.'

Not so urgent that I'm not going to finish this bit of a bollocking first. 'Phoned four times,' the inspector has already protested. 'Left messages on his machine at home.'

'Tried his office?' I inquire, looking down, re-stowing the pager in its pocket.

'Can't locate one. Works alone from home, it seems.'

I look up at him. 'Have you sent a car round?'

'About two-ish.'

That, I point out stiffly, was three hours ago.

He trots out the reason every police officer above the rank of constable uses in these hard-up days for doing next to nothing. 'No spare bodies.'

Lack of resources is an excuse that every officer above the rank of constable is supposed to accept without question, so he's visibly taken aback when I ask, 'Why?'

His chin comes up and the outer veins on his neck stiffen. 'Multi pile-up on the M1, diversions half the day.'

Detach someone to knock on Ravid Mal's door again, break the news about his car and find out who was at the wheel, I order. If there's still no reply, canvass neighbours. 'Or go yourself,' I conclude. Deskmen don't like going out in the cold, so that should get some action, I think, picking up the phone as he departs.

'This RTA on the A607.' The doctor in ICU (Intensive Care Unit) at the LRI (Leicester Royal Infirmary) has worked with cops for so long he now talks PIS (Police Initial Speak).

'Well.' He draws a long breath. 'She is a he.'

I'm not going to draw breath or say 'Sorry?'

'Sorry.' He says it for me. 'Should have got back sooner.' They had an emergency ward full of road traffic casualties, he goes on. 'In any case, we were concentrating on the head injuries.'

That's ruined the already-released media bulletin, I think selfishly. How am I going to publicly explain we got a man confused with a woman? 'A cross-dresser?' I ask tentatively.

'Obviously, but not a drag artiste or female impersonator or anything like that.' Pause. 'He's no transsexual in that there's been no sex change operation – at least not in the accepted sense.'

Now I'm forced into 'Sorry?'

'He's a eunuch.'

And I do draw breath. 'Castrated?'

'Never come across anything like it before,' he goes on, rather plaintively.

I'll second that, I think.

'Cauterisation is years old, very crude,' he continues. 'The wound is just a deep dark scar and some pubes have regrown so . . .' So they missed it on admission, he doesn't quite say. 'This operation, if you can call it that, took place, oh, I estimate, in his teens.'

Too late for a bit of John Wayne Bobbitt-style micro-surgery, I think. I sigh out some sympathy. 'Poor little bugger.'

'Well, since you mention it, there are signs of some anal activity, though not of recent origin.'

A bum boy, he means, but not operational over the last few nights. 'Any signs of booze?' I ask, thinking of his dreadful driving.

'Not on preliminary examination, but blood tests will tell us. Definitely of Asian origin. Long dark hair tied into a bun. Long painted nails. Otherwise, a fit, rather plump, masculine physique. No bust implants or oestrogen enhancement. Indeed, there's now a distinct five o'clock shadow on his face.'

His voice drops a note. 'We're not talking accident of birth here, hermaphrodite or . . .' I think he says something like 'git'.

'What's that?'

'Gender Identity Disorder . . .'

Must be GID or GIDD, I realise.

'. . . you know, registered as one thing at birth when, because of a rectifiable medical problem downstairs, they are, in fact, the opposite sex.'

Since I'm displaying my ignorance, I might as well ask, 'Define hermaphrodite.'

'Someone with the sexual organs of both male and female. It's not that, either. He was born a man but he's had his manhood entirely removed, cue, balls, the lot.'

I shudder. 'And you've never come across it before?'

'Personally, no. I've asked around, naturally, and I'm told that in certain parts of Asia – India, I think – they go in for this emasculation – and that's what it is – in the way that beggars sometimes chop off bits and pieces.'

A queasy feeling is running through me. 'To earn money, you mean?'

'Seems so,' he says doubtfully.

Someone back at HQ when they read this report will jokingly ask if he's on a male or female ward, but not me. Suddenly I'm off tasteless asides, even private ones. 'Anything else?'

'Well . . .' Slowly, as if thinking. '. . . was he thrown against a tree or anything?'

I picture the scene. 'The car hit a lamp standard, but he wasn't thrown out of it, no. Why?'

'There's odd marks on his face and neck. Very superficial compared to his, well, to be frank, terminal head injuries.'

'What sort of marks?'

'Scratches and little pricks.'

No pun intended, I'm certain. Because this conversation is entirely devoid of laughs.

'You expect to find them when a patient has come into contact with heavy vegetation, ploughing into a wood or head first into thick shrubbery; something like that.'

'No,' I say, frantically trying to think of an explanation – and failing.

'Sadly,' he says, very sadly, 'we're not going to be able to ask him about them or, indeed, anything. It's a very deep coma.' Then, sadder still, 'We'll need next of kin here a.s.a.p.'

To consent to the switch-off, he's telling me, and I groan inwardly.

3

Mr Ravid Mal can't take my call right now, the answering machine informs me in a light, rather reedy, male voice. I don't take up the invitation to leave a message.

Another major shunt on the M1, the harassed shift inspector reports when I drop into his humming office as I head along a warm, wide corridor for the stairs down to the courtyard and my car.

Not to worry, I tell him. Mr Mal's house is on my way home. Not quite true, but, as my dear old gran used to say, if you want a job doing properly, do it yourself.

Sometimes, I wish I'd never listened so closely to my old gran, I sigh to myself, wondering what to do now.

Mr Mal's house is on one of those newish, too-neat estates that have eaten up green belt around every city; executive estates they call them. One well-lit narrow straight road after another with small cul-de-sacs leading from them. Every dwelling has differently designed brickwork, but all manage to look the same: not really lived in, Mr Mal's especially.

Each house has a single garage with red Tarmac in the shape of a horseshoe in every front garden. Most accommodate a second and, here and there, a third car. There are no garden walls, so they can get in and out without taking off a coping stone. No vehicle stands on Mr Mal's driveway.

Most houses have small semicircular lawns between the public footpath and driveway. His has thick shrubs set among loose bark that screen the front door from neighbours.

None is tall enough to offer shelter as I back away from the carved teak door, the chimes unanswered.

Dusk now, though it has seemed like it all day. The mist is beginning to thicken into fog, bringing with it fine drops of moisture that hardly amount to rain.

I fish in my raincoat for an olive green waterproof bush hat. It is so floppy it can be shaped roughly into almost any style of headwear from bowler to deerstalker. I've run through the whole range for little Laura, whose Christmas present to her daddy it is. She likes sou'wester style best. Tonight I pull it firmly over my blond hair and snap down the brim, trilby fashion.

No lights shine behind a large leaded window downstairs or three smaller windows above, the centre one of which has closed vertical blinds.

This is a job for the community crew, not a chief superintendent i/c Complaints and Discipline, I fume, irked with myself and, more especially, my late gran.

They become part of your conscience, don't they, departed loved ones? They influence your dos and don'ts. A warm feeling when you're doing, saying, even thinking, the right thing because you know they'd approve; a heavy heart when you do the opposite. They can be a bloody nuisance sometimes, like now.

Go back to the car and use its phone to order the shift inspector to send an LPU round in an hour or two, I decide. Go home and let them do the worrying.

'Trouble?' A male voice behind me.

I turn to face a small, bespectacled man standing close to my parked car. He has a dark, waxed jacket thrown casually over his shoulders. 'Police,' I say, walking slowly towards him across the red Tarmac.

'May I see your credentials?' he asks politely when I reach him.

It's not a request that's often made and I study him as I rummage beyond my raincoat into the inside pocket of the jacket of my dark green suit. He's about sixty, slightly built with brown thinning hair.

In the bright orange light from the street lamp he peers at my card while I explain I want to see Mr Mal about his car.

'Funny,' he says with a perplexed face. 'You're the third policeman to come round today.'

Third? I think. Funny. I know the shift inspector ordered one call about two o'clock. Maybe, after that mild bollocking, he's had a second go.

He introduces himself as the local Neighbourhood Watch co-ordinator, Len Norris. 'Live there,' he adds with a hoick of his head across the cul-de-sac.

Since Neighbourhood Watch is an ally in the war on crime, I tell him about the fate of Mr Mal's car.

'Odd,' he says. 'Saw it this morning.'

Mr Mal was backing it out of the garage when Mr Norris took his dog for a walk about ten thirty. They gave each other a wave. An hour or so later, while he was cleaning inside the upstairs front windows, he saw the red hatchback had returned.

When he drove his own car out to go to the shops just before noon, the Mazda had gone. A blue Escort stood in its place.

Nothing unusual in that, he says. Mr Mal worked from home and often had callers. 'An importer/exporter, you know.'

What was unusual was that a young, tall, fair man walked from the Escort with his hand held up. Mr Norris braked.

'See which way that red Mazda went?' asked the man.

'Why?' asked Mr Norris.

'I'm CID and he's supposed to be leading me to Soar Valley,' the man from the Escort explained.

I go back, cross-checking. 'This plainclothes officer . . .' I am still too far ahead. 'He was in civvies, was he?'

'He wasn't in uniform . . .' Mr Norris thinks carefully before going on. 'He was wearing a dark jerkin. He was very tall.'

I resume, 'This officer called here before noon, you say?'

Mr Norris nods.

23

'Sure?'

Another nod, firmer. 'Absolutely.'

Before the crash, I tell myself. So what was the purpose of the call? Something's wrong somewhere. Unable to work out what, I go quiet.

Mr Norris reveals that he had told him, 'Sorry. No.' He gave him quick directions to Soar Valley.

A copper asking the way? I ask myself. Something is definitely wrong. I open the hand that still clutches my warrant card. 'Did you ask to see this?'

'No time. He just turned and walked back to his car. Another man was sitting in the passenger seat.'

'What did he look like?'

He motions to the thick shrubs. 'They obscure the view. Just made out the outline, that's all.'

Round about two this afternoon a police car called, according to his wife, but he personally hadn't seen it as he was dozing after lunch.

That, at least, ties in with what I know. The rest will have to be checked on the control room logs.

Mr Norris is wearing a worried expression. 'He travels abroad a lot, does Rav, just quick trips, but he always tells me when he's going away for any length of time.'

Mr Mal lives alone, he explains. His wife died just over a year ago. He took her to their native Bombay for the funeral and stayed for three months. For another three months he'd been very low. He'd got down to business again, but still has bouts of deep depression.

'Fun . . .' he beings to say. He changes it to: 'Peculiar.'

Everything seems funny, odd or peculiar to Mr Norris which must make him an eagle-eyed Neighbourhood Watch look-out. He has lapsed into silence so I ask him what's peculiar.

'What about Laz?' he says mysteriously.

'What about Laz?' I responded automatically.

Laz, he says with a fond smile, is the cat Mr Mal adopted after his wife died – company for him and a home for the cat, which, according to the animal shelter, had used up all nine lives and a couple more on top. Hence its name, a shortened version of the biblical Lazarus.

'If he's been called away unexpectedly, who's feeding and

letting Laz in and out? It's a bit late for its tea.' He frowns and finally comes out with what's on his mind. 'It's a bit worrying; strange.'

That's good enough for me. You can always get away with unauthorised entry when a neighbour expresses concern. 'Do you have a key?'

No, he replies. Mr Mal always dropped off a spare when he was going away overnight. A cleaner who came one morning a week had a front door key. He begins to explain where she lives on what he calls 'the old council estate', then suddenly stops. 'There's a way in via the garage if it's not locked.'

Having already studied the outside, I point to a white box burglar alarm between the eaves and the upstairs window with the closed blinds. 'Won't that go off?'

'It's just a case. For show. There's no control panel inside.'

We walk to the garage, Mr Norris chuntering on about the number of times he's urged Mr Mal to instal a working alarm.

A twist and tug on the chrome handle on an up and under door, metal panels painted maroon, and it rises. There's no vehicle inside and no oil stains on the concrete floor, an indication that Mr Mal always has well-maintained vehicles, unlike mine which is well overdue for a service.

It's a long garage with room at the back for appliances usually found in a kitchen. Between a chest freezer and a washing machine is a half-glass door. Through it shines faint light.

As we walk through the garage, Mr Norris says with expertise presumably gained at crime prevention meetings, 'I told him two or three times this was a potential breach in his security. He sometimes has ready cash here, you know.'

The rear door opens into a small tiled porch with three more doors. There's stronger light in here. The first door on the right is slightly ajar and leads to a basic toilet, no plaster on the bricks. The second – 'To the back garden,' Mr Norris says over my shoulder – is locked.

I pull down the handle of the third door on the left, again half-glass, push it open and step into a sizeable kitchen with double stainless steel drainers, a breakfast bar with four stools, lots of work tops, cabinets above and below them. One of two strip lights in the cream ceiling is on.

Two fluted glass doors lead from the kitchen; one closed, the other open on to a dim hallway.

From beyond it come faint thumps, too heavy and irregular to be heartbeats, and the tinkling sound of a tiny bell.

I pray we're not interrupting Mr Mal making his devotions to some eastern god.

Through the door pads a black cat with a short, shiny coat. It is wearing a red collar with a tiny golden bell to warn birds and intruders like us of its approach.

Behind it, across the fawn foam-backed carpet, it trails blood-stained pawprints, growing fainter with every step.

'Lord,' groans Mr Norris, stooping to stroke Laz, the cat, purring around his feet.

'Don't touch it,' I snap, agitated, feeling my blood pressure rise. 'Don't feed it. Don't let it out. Don't move from where you're standing.'

Get a grip, I command myself.

I follow the pawprints through the hall, flicking on a wall switch which lights up the landing over a set of open plan, polished wooden stairs. Every step has dark, double smudges where the cat has hopped down to greet us.

I climb up to a square platform with two more steps on each side. To the right is a closed door to a room above the garage. To the left, the landing has four doors. Two are open. One leads to a bathroom. The other has more, very thick pawprints on the fawn carpet emerging from it.

Three or four short strides alongside them is all it takes to look inside a small room.

With the blinds closed against the street lamp and in the half-light from the landing I don't take in any view other than a small tubby man leaning forward out of a high-backed swivel chair with his head on a desk.

The back of his head is a mangle of grey hair, white bone splints and blood which has seeped down his neck and cheeks and spread on to the papers on either side of him.

On the papers are thick pawprints where the cat had tried to rouse him for its five o'clock tea.

Oh God, I think, chilled, someone has murdered an Indian.

4

On finding a dead body in suspicious circumstances, a real-life detective doesn't do what they do in TV films – poke a pencil down the barrel of a smoking gun, if any, or sample on the tip of his tongue any white powder that happens to be about or aimlessly trample all over the scene. Not if he wants to remain a detective, he doesn't.

He retreats, carefully picking each step, back the way he came and summons the specialists, which is what I've just done on my car phone, taking an ashen-faced Mr Norris with me, leaving Laz, the cat, shut in the back porch, miaowing pitifully with hunger.

'Is he dead?' Mr Norris had asked as we walked to my Volvo parked in front of the driveway.

'Put it this way,' I'd replied. 'Someone up there has no pulse.'

I'm cautious because, fairly soon, this cul-de-sac will be packed with reporters, knocking on every door. You can ask, but not order, a witness not to talk to them. Some find the prospect of their name in the paper or, increasingly these days, an appearance on TV totally irresistible and blab everything. So it's best that they can't reveal too much.

'Oh dear, how appalling,' he'd said.

Now that I have reported the discovery, we are sitting side by side in the front seats of the car. 'Can I nip home a minute?' he asks.

It's a perfectly reasonable request, because wives worry about absent husbands, but I don't grant it. Instead, I hand him the phone and suggest that he tells her he's been delayed on Neighbourhood Watch business and no more.

He does as he's told, fobbing off her questions, and hands the phone back for me to rehook. He's silent for a while, then natural curiosity overcomes him. 'What will happen now?'

Well, first, the nearest patrol cars will speed up, blue lights revolving. Their crews will tape off the house and maybe this whole side road. Then, in no particular order, the divisional police surgeon, the CID and the Forensic specialists will arrive, don white overalls and go inside.

The doctor will pronounce death which means the body doesn't have to be moved to hospital and the scenes-of-crime photographers will take all the time they need over their grim pictorial record.

Similarly attired scientists will comb carpets for fibres and surfaces for fingerprints, take Laz to their laboratory and vacuum its coat. They will bag anything that takes their fancy and certainly pack up the papers in the study for further examination. Meantime, officers from Major Crimes will fan out in a neighbourhood canvass.

It's a costly and time-consuming operation.

Oh, and yes, Good News Goodman, Assistant Chief Constable (West) will turn up. He'll claim to the officer he puts in charge that he's only here to make sure he has all the logistical support required, but really he wants to do the TV interviews.

He's addicted to them, totally hooked, appears on the screen as regularly as, oh, let's see now ... Ruby Wax, of whom, being short and plump with a motor for a mouth, he reminds me.

All I tell Mr Norris is that they'll need our shoes for elimination purposes. I get out, go to the boot, take out a Sainsbury's plastic shopping bag and my white golf shoes which, fortunately, have pimpled soles rather than metal spikes.

It's occurring to me that pretty soon I'll have to phone home to cancel that take-out supper and get Em to ring my partner to call off tomorrow's golf.

Back in the driving seat, I swap footwear. Mr Norris's shoes follow mine into the bag. We wait, interior light on, the engine running, heater humming, to keep his stockinged feet warm.

I take off my rain hat, fold it and put it back in a pocket.

He looks at me with a glum face and, completely out of context, says, 'Same coloured hair as you, only cut much shorter.' He pauses. 'That plainclothes bobby who called.'

I nod, suspecting he could be in shock.

He looks straight ahead out of the misted windscreen. 'A smashing chap, you know, Rav,' he says with a heavy sigh. 'A gentleman.'

For something to do, I encourage more.

Mr Mal was about his age, Mr Norris begins. 'Sixtyish, small, portly, silver-haired,' he adds. 'Is it him?' His head turns and his eyes travel up to the closed blinds.

I keep my head still.

He'd lived opposite for five years, in England for half his life, he continues. 'No children. A brother in Bombay.'

Mr Norris isn't quite sure how his business worked. 'He's a sort of buyer and seller.' Some foreign company, often in the Third World, would order, say phials for medical purposes. He'd use his worldwide contacts to find them at the lowest price. He'd order the phials to be dispatched direct to the purchaser. 'All done on paper 'cos nothing's ever delivered here and there's no warehouse that I know of.'

'You said that sometimes there's cash about the house,' I remind him.

'Dollars, mostly. His commission, I suppose.'

Why not settle accounts by cheque? I ask myself. A tax fiddle is the cynical answer I give myself.

'Very religious.' He sighs. 'Zoroastrian.'

Zorro with his flashing sword I remember, of course, from those Saturday morning matinées at the Ritz at Matlock, but that's not a name or a religion I've come across.

He wasn't a regular attender, Mr Norris goes on, because there isn't a place of worship round here, which explains why he took his dead wife back to India, but he was active in other ways.

'Such as?' I ask.

'A big supporter of Pillars.'

I cock my head, quizzically.

'Haven't you read about it in the *Mercury*?'

I tell him I live outside its circulation area.

'Pillars of Faith. Mercy missions to places like Eastern Europe and Bosnia. He paid for one of the trucks, a memorial to his late wife, a lovely lady, and provided some of the medical supplies.'

I toy with the idea of seeking more about the CID caller here before noon. He and his companion must be on an inquiry entirely unconnected to the car, which hadn't crashed by then.

But I don't want to dwell on the fact that we've visited this place twice before. If Norris eventually talks to the press he might inadvertently provide them with an unfortunate headline on the lines of: 'Police called twice, but missed body'. Instead I dwell on his charity work.

29

'Oh, yes,' says Mr Norris. 'Worked very hard for Pillars. Both of them.' It's an all-creeds charity founded four years ago, he explains.

Once a quarter they fill a truck with items of aid and dispatch it to territories that have been ravaged by war or famine.

Mrs Mal had been a member from the outset and, when she died, her husband bought a brand new Mazda diesel van to replace the original vehicle which had become clapped out.

No change out of ten to twelve grand for that, I estimate.

And I toss every appeal that comes through the letterbox into the kitchen bin with the junk mail, I brood with a feeling of shame.

Good News Goodman has turned up, just ahead of the first TV camera crew waiting behind the blue and white tapes at the entrance to the cul-de-sac.

I got out of my car to brief him away from Mr Norris about the inquiries into the crash of Mal's Mazda and its driver which led to finding the body upstairs. He nodded here and there, asked few questions.

Now he is standing at the heavy front door which a scenes-of-crime man opened more than half an hour ago after I told him how to get in via the garage.

Goodman puts on cellophane footwear and gloves and disappears from view.

Half a dozen experts are already inside, including the police surgeon, Dr Dilip Service, a thin, dark-skinned Asian, fortyish, the last person to see Abe Myles alive.

He didn't acknowledge me as he arrived, either because he didn't notice me sitting in my car, now surrounded by several more vehicles, or because he's still annoyed with me.

When I took his statement yesterday about his consultation with old man Myles in the cell, he gave the impression that he thought I was questioning his medical competence. I got the impression he's a prickly character.

He won't be inside the house for long. Every division has a doctor on standby to call out in an emergency. They examine prisoners taken ill in cells (mostly from drugs withdrawal these days) or certify deaths at crime scenes. They do the prelim, that's all. The real work is done by the pathologist when the body finally gets to the hospital mortuary.

They also give second opinions on police officers whose GPs have signed them off sick. Some, in my view, are skiving until they qualify for their pensions. A few, I'm sure, con the medics to avoid disciplinary proceedings so they can quit on health grounds before I can sack them.

It's a scandal I'm determined to stamp out and my persistent chasing of police doctors over sick notes has upset them. Not many like me.

A woman I didn't see arrive in the general mêlée joins the re-emerging Goodman on the doorstep. I recognise her immediately: Detective Inspector Chand, the officer in charge of the original Myles investigation, now being investigated herself.

She has an attractive face with high cheekbones, quite light-skinned, and an attractive first name I never used in our formal interview: Primilia.

It's a bit of a surprise to see ethnic minorities so well represented on this job. Almost a quarter of this city's population (more than a quarter of a million) are from, or their folks were from, the sub-continent. Only four per cent of our officers are: another scandal for which each and every one of us is to blame. None of us, me included, spoke up against racism that was part of our culture when we joined, in my case, twenty years ago. Now we recruit about as many blacks and Asians as the armed services – abysmal.

Goodman nods towards my car and goes back inside.

Inspector Chand peels off a white boilersuit to reveal a sharp, well-fitted dark suit. She crouches to remove her protective footwear, cupping each leg alternatively at the knee, making her skirt ride up. I can't help but notice she has attractive legs too.

She walks unhurriedly across the red Tarmac. She smiles cautiously. 'Good evening, sir.' She has a beautiful accent – musical, almost Welsh.

I run through it all again for her, gesturing behind me to Mr Norris, still sitting in the passenger seat. 'If you can't trace next of kin, he can ID the body.'

'There is no need,' she says crisply. 'The doctor knew him reasonably well. They were on the phone to each other only this morning.'

She motions towards Mr Norris whose facial expression has faded from curiosity to boredom; generally the case with amateur sleuths when they finally find out how tedious police procedures really are. 'Would you mind if I took a formal statement from him?'

'Help yourself, please,' I enthuse, not looking for paperwork.

She makes no move, standing there, rather awkwardly. 'I hope you do not mind my asking, but was everything to your satisfaction on the Myles case?'

An understandable question, I acknowledge. Every officer agonises about the outcome of an internal probe for the Complaints Authority; promotion and pension can ride on it.

'Perfectly.' I give her a reassuring smile. 'His family have no complaints either.'

'Thank you.' Her smile is very relieved now. She turns and walks to the passenger door, opens it and invites Mr Norris out, explaining what she wants. He leads the way in his stockinged feet across the wet road towards his home.

I hang around in the still mist, stamping my white golf shoes on the herringbone brick path, to try to keep my feet warm.

Eventually the doctor walks out, black briefcase in one hand, navy blue raincoat collar half-way up the black hair at the back of his neck. He looks perished.

I resolve not to repeat the mistake my old gran made in the last year of her life when a stand-in GP – 'coloured', she described him as – paid a house call one bitter winter's day.

'You must find it very cold here,' she sympathised.

'Actually, I was born here,' he replied starchily.

His reaction clearly upset her, because she told the story more than once. 'I was only trying to be chatty, friendly like,' she said regretfully.

I step forward, blocking his way. 'Can I pick your brains, doc?'

'Again?' Dr Service looked irritated. 'I've already told Mr Goodman.' He sighs, anxious to get off, I presume, now he's earned his fee. 'Head injuries. Blunt instrument. Dead six to twelve hours. Can't be more specific.'

I tell him about Mal's car and the unidentified driver in

hospital. 'I was wondering if from your knowledge of the sub-continent . . .'

He interrupts: 'Been here twenty years.' I'm used to stroppy doctors and lawyers but why is it they seem all the stroppier when they're not white? I wonder.

'. . . your knowledge, either first or second-hand, if you've heard of men who not only dress as women but have actually been castrated?'

'Heage-rahs,' he says immediately. 'Neither male nor female.'

'Why do they do it?' is all I can think of.

He smiles somewhat condescendingly. 'What do you know about India, Mr Todd?'

Let's see, I muse. Not much, never having taken the saffron robes of Hare Krishna in my college days or got round to reading the Kama Sutra. Which leaves arranged marriages, dowries and castes. Gavaskar and Gandhi, Tendulkar and Mother Teresa, Bishan Bedi and Bollywood, the last only because I've dipped briefly into some bizarre films surfing the TV channels late at night. They were no better or worse than old George Formbys or Norman Wisdoms.

'I think,' I say stiffly, speaking from the heart as a bored spectator, 'that if they'd got on with it a bit on the second day at Trent Bridge last summer they might have tied the Test series.'

He doesn't smile, much less laugh, so he's no cricket fan, and I doubt if we'll ever find common ground.

'No use looking at everything through western eyes,' he says, pompously. 'There's lots of extreme poverty, desperate people who must earn money or starve. They become dancers in the streets, or at weddings or birth celebrations. They claim powers to bless or curse, if you understand me.'

I do, as a matter of fact. My gran always paid over the odds for clothes pegs being hawked from door to door by gypsies rather than risk a foul-mouthed curse, but I'm not going to share precious memories with this prickly prat. 'But why the operation?'

Goodman strolls up with the Forensics man as the doctor replies, 'They're a kind of cult, followers of some mother god-dess. They believe that the sacrifice of their manhood enhances their powers.'

I go silent, thinking: Thank Christ or Allah or Zorowhomsoever I wasn't enrolled in their Sunday school.

'Of course,' the doctor goes on, 'some finish up as male prostitutes down the Falkland Road.' He doesn't explain, so I can only guess at a big city red light district.

'What the devil are you talking about?' a startled Goodman butts in.

'A heage-rah.' Obligingly and without sighs, Dr Service repeats his quick rundown on them.

'Spell that,' says Goodman curtly.

The doctor appears to have more patience with Goodman than me, presumably because he pays the bills, and he does so, slowly. 'H-i-j-r-a.'

'Good grief,' Goodman exclaims in triumph. 'Wasn't that the name we couldn't make out on his kitchen calendar?'

'Something like that,' says the Forensics man uncertainly.

Goodman rubs his hands together, in glee, not from cold. 'We've got a diary date with a homo and a transvestite in the victim's crashed car. Hmmmmm. Good stuff.'

I can tell he's beginning to write it off as solved already.

'Well, Mr Todd.' He beams at me. 'Fax me a full signed statement. We'll take it from there, shall we?'

Here I stand, cold, damp and beginning to get hungry, having done everything right, and he's dismissing me. I don't want to work through the night, thanks very much, but I'm not going to be dropped like some bloody cadet. 'What about putting a name to the dying driver?'

He thinks, doesn't respond.

'I need it for my report to the Complaints Authority,' I point out, knowing that nobody, not even a bumptious little ACC, will put further promotion to the Chief's chair on the line by interfering with a complaints inquiry.

'We'll liaise on that aspect, shall we?' He emphasises 'that' to underline that the murder part of the inquiry is his department's.

I open the car door, take out and hand over the bag with the two pairs of shoes to the Forensics man, explaining the need to eliminate them.

It takes only a moment or two, but in that time Goodman saunters away, without a goodnight or thank you. So does Dr

Service, giving me no chance to tell him about the outcome of the Myles inquiry.

Back in the driving seat, I watch through the windscreen as Goodman parts from Dr Service and heads for the blue and white tapes, smoothing back his hair and striding out from a stroll into a brisk walk that's almost a march.

TV arc lamps switch on to bathe him in a yellowish white glow, heralding the approach of the master of the media.

I phone home to tell Em I'll be about an hour late. Still unaccountably troubled by that flip remark when last we spoke, I add that I'll be bringing home Chinese, not Indian.

5

Just toast and marmalade this morning, not really hungry after sharing three Cantonese dishes with prawn crackers last night. Anyway, it leaves room for a large lunch.

Em and Laura opt for Weetabix with milk. 'What time are you being picked up?' asks Em.

'In half an hour,' I reply from behind the *Daily Telegraph* which isn't carrying anything on Mal's murder.

We're off, my partner and I, at eight-thirty, in the second fourball. I'm already dressed in baggy blue slacks and yellow polo neck sweater which double as golfing and gardening garb. A change of clothes and waterproofs are packed in a canvas sports bag by the front door. Folded on top is my raincoat with floppy hat tucked into a pocket. The white shoes are next to it on the carpet.

She turns her head towards the kitchen window. 'You might be lucky with the weather.'

My eyes leave the newspaper and follow hers. Woefully weak sunlight is battling against lingering mist.

While I was shaving, I'd heard the radio forecast fog in the north and a spring-like day in the south. Living half-way up the country, it's hard to tell what we will get. 'Bound to be. It's all free.'

'The Old Farts Club?' It's her term for members of the Police Pensioners' Sports Association; an irreverent, but often accurate, description. 'How can they afford it?'

'It's being sponsored,' I explain.

'Who by?'

I name a big communications company.

'Who', she says with a disapproving face, 'no doubt installed all your new tech.'

She's right of course, I accept, head back behind the paper, and I can't claim I've never looked at it this way before.

Free days out like today's are either thank yous for lucrative orders or bids for future business or both. I wonder how many senior officers (or members of the regional police authority, for that matter) were taken to lunch or on fact-finding all-expenses-paid trips to sunnier places before the contract for all these new gadgets was struck.

Now the company has banked the taxpayers' money they are going to offset a few grand of their profit before the Inland Revenue gets hold of it.

They could not, of course, pay for a day out for HQ staff without running the risk of attracting questions from leftie members of the authority and even more awkward publicity, so they are using the Old Farts Club as cover, making it seem like an act of charity. At best it's tax avoidance. At worst it's a kind of kickback.

Em is a journalist who rails against this sort of perk in her own profession, like free holidays for two in return for a plug for the generous host from the travel writer. Or new cars on never-ending road tests by the motoring correspondent. Then there's tools for the gardening columnist to try out that are never returned. And books that wind up on cut price sale in second-hand shops, the publishers' 'for favour of review' slip still inside the hard covers because the critic never opened them, let alone read them, before flogging them on. All nice, tax-free little earners.

Em is also joint mortgagee of this warm, solid, between-the-wars house with spacious walled garden, who yesterday paid cash in hand for a replacement roof to avoid VAT, but I'll not point that out.

I fold the paper and, to change the subject, I tell her a bit more about last night.

'And, having found the corpse, they didn't keep you on the case,' she says.

Good News wants his own team on it, I answer moodily.

Goodman didn't, in fact, earn his nickname because of his mania for the media. They call him Good News because that's all he wants to hear. He's top of the league for crime clear-ups and bottom for spending.

He achieves this by dispatching his officers round prisons chatting up recently convicted offenders. The invitation is pitched like this: 'Have a day out, a slap-up spread on us. Cough to a few of our undetected crimes. On your way back, we'll drop you in at home. You can have a private hour with your missus.' The takers are not so sex starved, however, that they don't seek and get immunity against further prosecution.

A week or so later lots of burgled householders receive a letter from Goodman who is happy to tell them that the criminal who raided and ransacked their premises is in prison in connection with a similar offence, but, sadly, their missing property remains untraced.

By then most of the householders have had their insurance pay-offs and, especially if they have bumped up their claims, they don't ask too many questions, like: Did the burglar plead guilty in an open court or, failing that, was the break-in at my place taken into consideration by the judge in sentencing him?

The answer to both is: No. He probably didn't do it, merely claimed responsibility in return for his day out. The Chief Constable or the Home Secretary don't press too hard either because they want to be able to crow: 'Look at our figures for crime clear-ups. We're winning the war.'

It's bullshit, a fraud of the taxpaying public, but that's what you get with league tables in any public service.

'Do you wish you'd been kept on it?' Em asks with a serious face.

A difficult question, that, and I pick up the paper again as I ponder it.

I was in CID and Special Ops, out and about, one of the boys, for years. Then I got badly shot in the leg and am fortunate, I suppose, to be here in the bosom of my family, let alone kept on in the force.

The postings they've found me – first Special Branch and now Complaints – aren't what I joined up to do. They're lonely as well as boring. I miss being part of a team, the thrill of the chase.

The one great compensation is that, in the main, I work office hours which means lots of lovely time at home, like now, just idly chatting with Em and playing peekaboo behind the *Telegraph* with Laura.

'Boo,' I boo, leaning forward suddenly.

'Again,' Laura chuckles.

In that split second I make up my mind. 'No,' I finally answer.

'Your father is a fibber,' Em tells Laura with a wry smile.

Eighteen points to the turn, par for Stableford, not bad for a player with a handicap in the high teens, partnered by a duffer off the maximum.

So deep is my concentration I haven't really noticed the sun losing its battle and the morning becoming increasingly grey.

Crossing the gravelled car-park of the Fosse Golf Club, a pleasant parklands course behind HQ, I pass close to Good News Goodman just setting out with a fourball which includes the Chief Constable.

'Any name yet for your hermaphrodite?' he calls heartily enough for the Chief to hear.

This, I know, is his idea of liaison, the point-scoring creep. I shake my head. 'Making progress on my body?' I underline 'my' loudly.

'Very well, indeed,' he rejoins. The Chief smiles thinly.

For the first time since breakfast I am thinking of last night; a mistake.

'You have to play this daft game with a totally blank mind,' I tell my team-mate as we watch my sliced drive on the tenth dribble into a deep sand bunker.

'I'm surprised you're not off scratch then,' he replies cheerfully.

In the rough of the twelfth, my replacement shoes, leather cracked from neglect in the car boot, begin to leak as I trudge through saturated long grass in search of another wayward shot.

The long par five thirteenth takes an age. The spring in my step that's always there when I'm playing well has gone. My gammy leg beginning to drag. The best we can manage between us is a net seven for yet another single point.

I'm wishing now I'd never accepted this invitation. It's not just the dampness that's seeping under the collar of my waterproofs, reminding me of the back of Mr Mal's neck. It's not my cold hands that can barely grip a club. Nor is it my ever-stiffening leg.

It's the thought of the prize table back in the clubhouse packed with pairs of portable phones, answering machines, electronic contact books; all sorts of gizmos. It's the thought of the four course meal to follow, three choices per course. My mouth isn't watering at all. It's graft. It's wrong.

Most of the top brass have wangled invitations, snouts in the trough, like writ-happy compensation seekers.

My grandfather, my guiding light, would not approve. 'You shouldn't be here, freeloading,' I can almost hear him saying. 'You should be back in Leicester.'

There's a hold-up on the next, a short hole and no shelter on the long, narrow tee, just a plank bench out in the open. We sit on it, waiting for the green to clear.

'You're playing like a big soft girl,' says 'Jacko' Jackson, my host, lighting up his regulation cigarette per hole.

He may not be strong on political correctness but he's high on courage. He was with me, his final job before retirement, on the day I got this leg shot. Without him at my side my head would have looked like Mr Mal's.

I tell Jacko about last night; another mistake.

In retirement, he is writing crime novels. His first series was based loosely on his own experiences, the second series on mine which I put down on tape for him, the least I can do for saving my life.

The arrangement – 'the deal', Jacko calls it – is that he changes all the names and locations and invites me to dos like this, worse luck.

His mouth drops open when I impart what little I've learned about hijras. 'Oh, Sweeney,' he coos, using a nickname I hate. 'What a yarn.'

He goes silent, pondering. 'Never knew about 'em,' he resumes, eyes watering behind metal-framed bifocals. And, he goes on, he'd been having a binge on Indian novels, the current rage. 'Given 'em up, because they end so sadly.' Jacko likes happy endings.

He becomes almost dreamy about the potential of the story. 'It's got everything; a mystic mystery.'

'It's got nothing.' I'm shaking my head firmly. 'No hue and cry. No race against a deadline. Nothing for you anyway.' Sulkily, I add. 'Besides, I'm off the case.'

The raised green ahead empties. His mind miles away – on the crime writers' Golden Dagger award that will never come, I speculate privately – he steps up to his ball, nonchalantly flicks his cigarette end away, swings stiffly and misses the flag stick by the length of a soccer pitch. He takes off his specs and theatrically wipes away non-existent dirt; his excuse for missing the target.

Back in the clubhouse, we sign a crumpled card for twenty-six points; hopeless. Then we strip off damp clothing and shower. I put on a white shirt and grey trousers. I pull out the pager from the pen pocket of my thick blue jacket. The screen is displaying: 'Please call DI Chand.' The number of Charles Street police station is added.

I put on jacket and tie and leave the fusty-smelling locker room. Half-way down a welcomingly warm corridor is a secluded phone box which I enter. Jacko goes on into an empty lounge to organise black coffee and brandies.

'I am sorry to disturb your day off,' Chand begins in a precise, polite tone, 'and thank you for getting things moving last night.'

When a police officer says 'Sorry' and 'Thanks' to a boss, he or she is after something. I say nothing.

She's making reasonable progress, she reports. She had already

40

informed Mr Mal's next of kin, the brother in Bombay. 'But I am worried.'

She hesitates. 'Mr Goodman seems to want it wrapped up quickly.'

And to attribute Mal's death to the dying driver and leave the rest to the coroner, I start to suspect.

No police chief will ever admit this but some forces financially categorise murders – prioritisation, they call it; a dreadful word.

Get a high profile killing – a child murder or someone famous, for instance – and they'll throw money at the investigating team because they know it will keep bouncing back into embarrassing headlines until it's solved.

In media (and, therefore, public interest) terms, an Asian living alone in the suburbs will quickly die the death.

Goodman is giving the inquiry no greater priority than a double-death domestic that solves itself and ends in an inquest conducted by a coroner at which the standards of proof are much lower than a crown court trial by jury.

From Goodman's point of view, it still counts as a homicide detected and, just as important, cheaply detected. That's what you get when you allow accountants to take over a public service.

'The motive put forward would be a hint of homosexuality that my hijra . . .' I break off. 'How is he this morning?'

'Still critical.'

I complete what I was saying, '. . . Is not in a position to deny, like Mr Mal?'

She says nothing, wisely not wanting to criticise Goodman.

I venture on. 'Or, maybe, robbery will be the motive.'

'We found no money in the house, certainly,' she replies guardedly.

'What about "hijra" on the calendar?'

'That was down against a day earlier this week, not yesterday.' She pauses. 'In any case, it is spelt differently.' She spells it. 'H-e-j-i-r-a.'

Close, I think. 'Is there a difference?'

'Oh, yes. The Muslim meaning translates as "departure". They date their calendar from it.'

Maybe it is close to an ignoramus like Goodman, but an

41

educated Asian would not be confused by it. 'Did Mal speak Urdu?'

'And Hindi and several other languages, according to his brother.'

'How are we getting on with my hijra?' I ask her. Why do I keep using 'my'? I ask myself.

'They're contacting all temples and drawing up a list of recent local weddings and birth celebrations at which he might have danced,' she replies.

Good thinking, I think. What's more, it's brave of her to come to me behind Goodman's back. If he finds out, she'll be straight into Community Relations, a shitty job.

A search of the control tapes had failed to locate any plain-clothes men or unmarked police cars dispatched to Mr Mal's home round noon yesterday, she continues.

'Any reports of bogus bobbies operating locally – you know, knocking on doors, conning and robbing old folk?'

'None.'

Mmmm, I can't think of anything else. She seems to have explored all current possibilities. 'What do you want me to do about it?' I ask bluntly.

'I have been assigned only a sergeant and a constable,' she answers indirectly. 'We have worked through most of the night.'

I say nothing, forcing her to go on. 'This is my first murder case as an inspector and . . .' She hesitates again. Then: 'I am consulting you for your thoughts.'

My first thought is that Goodman could be setting her up. Many senior officers, him among them (and me, too, in a way), don't know how to handle ethnic minorities. If she fouls up, he'll shrug and say, 'I'm not prejudiced and can prove it. I gave her every chance. She blew it.'

'Well,' I begin slowly, 'I can't submit my report on my hijra's crash yet to the Complaint's Authority, not without a name.' That 'my' again, I note.

'No, sir,' she says dully.

'And if there are no bogus bobbies in action and the Neighbourhood Watch man is right about that unexplained police visit, there might be a neglect of duty rap in it for someone for failure to log calls,' I go on, more or less to myself.

42

'Yes, sir,' she says, brightening a little.

'And I am weekend duty senior officer.'

It will get me out of donning uniform which I loathe and representing the Chief at various dog hangings like a church service or squiring visiting Cabinet ministers about.

And, of course, it will release me from this free lunch which, with my conscience nagging, will probably set off indigestion.

It's more than that, though. It's my bloody grandfather again. He was a policeman, too. Died suddenly soon after retirement.

He told me once about a theft he and his inspector had investigated up in the Peaks, his patch where I grew up. A petty job, some stolen farm tools that turned up in a second-hand store. A labourer with a few minor juvenile convictions was suspected, nothing ever proved.

Over a market day pint, his inspector revealed the man's record to his employer, a gentleman farmer, who promptly evicted him, his wife and kids from their tied cottage. 'I knew what the inspector was planning to do and I didn't speak up and stop him,' my grandad recalled sorrowfully.

Soon afterwards more missing tools turned up, traceable this time to the farm manager. 'The family had moved on, gone, and I couldn't tell him he was in the clear and say "Sorry".'

My grandad went to his grave (or, rather, his urn) still lamenting it. 'Always go into bat for the underdog,' I remember him saying.

This hijra is my underdog. Mine. What if I do nothing and Goodman's wrong? I'll never be able to say 'Sorry', now will I?

'Meet me at the scene in an hour,' I order.

Over brandy and coffee, I negotiate the loan of Jacko's ageing Cavalier for the rest of the day to save an eight-mile trip in the wrong direction to collect my own car from home. 'You'll easily get a lift from one of your old mates,' I plead.

'You know the deal,' he says, taking the ignition key off a fairly full ring and handing it over.

Since the car has no phone, I return to the kiosk in the corridor, call Em to tell her not to expect me home till mid-evening, where I'm going and why.

'Didn't I tell you at breakfast?' Her voice is some way away from the phone, addressing, I assume, Laura. 'Your father tells fibs.'

We both laugh.

6

Speed-reading through Mr Mal's antecedents, I stop at 'Parsi'. A literal, obviously. Should it be Paris? Slapdash, I think, irritated. She should cross-check her form-filling and she'd avoid errors like this.

Don't be so bloody hard, I chide myself. Look at her. I sneak a sideways glance. She's wearing the same dark suit as last night. Her thin lips are downturned. Her black hair has lost its gloss. Her deep brown eyes are dull, their lids unnaturally shiny. She's been up all night.

My eyes go back to the form and see that 'Parsi' is against 'Religion', not 'Place of Birth' which comes next and is given as: 'Bombay'.

Again I look across at Inspector Chand sitting in the passenger seat of this borrowed Cavalier parked only a few feet from where my Volvo stood last night. 'What's . . .' I look back at the form. 'Par . . .' I take a tentative stab. '. . . sigh, is it?'

'Parsee,' she corrects me.

'I was told by our Neighbourhood Watch friend that he was a Zoro . . .' I slow down, trying to get it right. '. . . astrian.'

'One and the same. The world's oldest religion.' She pauses. 'They are sometimes known as the Jews of the sub-continent.'

My, my. She, of all people, being racist? I ask myself, mildly shocked.

'They are talented and very hard-working,' she continues. 'They believe in attending to their material as well as spiritual needs.'

Now I'm fairly impressed. 'Did his brother tell you all of this?'

She shakes her head. She's just finished three years in Community Relations, she says, and I manage to hold off a commiserating 'Poor soul.'

44

She thought she ought to acquire a smattering of knowledge about religions other than her own.

Not wishing to pass up an opportunity which will never be bettered, I ask, 'Which is?'

'Hindu.'

Not Muslim then, I think, oddly relieved. Hindus never seem to be quite so strait-laced as Muslims. They don't have hard-faced ayatollas issuing fatwas and wanting to rule the world. To me, they are to Islamic public relations what those parson-MPs from Ulster are to Protestantism.

'It's a faith that may present us with a problem,' she says. 'His brother wants his body to be flown home so he can be fed to the vultures.'

My mouth must be hanging open in horror or disbelief or something, because she goes straight on, 'Their dead are laid out at a place called the Towers of Silence to be devoured by carrion-eaters. They are not in favour of burial and cremation.'

Well, I think slowly, hoping I'm not smiling, Mr Mal's a bit on the big side for the bird table and its sparrows in my back garden. 'We're going to have to tell his brother we can't release the body without the coroner's say-so and, in murder cases, that can take some time.'

'I will make that Her Majesty's Coroner,' she says brightly. 'He sounded very pro-British.'

I smile, not so much at her enthusiasm, but at another private thought. Once HM Coroner allows him out of the refrigerated morgue, there'll be plenty of defrosting time between here and Bombay, so the vultures will not get the sort of dicky stomach I once suffered after Christmas turkey that hadn't been out of the deep-freeze long enough. I wouldn't wish that even on a vulture.

On reflection, I think, still amusing myself, it's not much different from worms coming to eat thee up on Ilkley Moor.

I feel good, righteous almost, because I know I'm doing the right thing, coming back, being here. And, because I am feeling good, the merry little quips are back, too, but I'm keeping them to myself.

These days, I'm wary when working with women and ethnic minority officers I don't know. One joke that goes off at half-cock and you get slapped with a complaint of sexual or racial harassment and bang goes promotion, if not your career.

'His religion is one reason why I am not happy about taking everything at face value,' she continues. 'It is a very moral faith, hot on good, down on evil. It doesn't sit well with homosexual assignations.'

You could say that about Christians, priests included, and you wouldn't be right about them all, I think, head down, speed-reading on.

I've reached the bottom of the form. There are blanks against 'Previous Convictions' and 'Cause of Death' and I tap the latter with a finger.

'The pathologist's report only arrived as she was leaving the station to meet me,' she says, apologetically. Mr Mal had fruit for breakfast yesterday, but no lunch. Time of death had been narrowed to between 11 a.m. and 1 p.m.

'He has established that he was hit on the back of the head repeatedly . . .' She feels the back of her head. '. . . with a hard object with very short spikes.'

'Like a medieval cudgel, you mean?' I ask, startled.

'Something like that,' she replies, grimly.

Well, there aren't too many of them around, I think. 'Found a weapon yet?'

'No. He was not a collector of armoury.' She looks at me intently. 'Something else troubles me.' She starts to collect up her pink file from her knees. 'May I show you?' She opens her door and swings her long legs out.

I follow her over the red Tarmac, grateful for the fresh air. The clothes I wore under my golfing waterproofs are on wire coat-hangers in the back and are beginning to smell as ripe as overhung pheasant.

A uniformed policeman stands solitary guard at the heavy front door. He doesn't open it for her. Neither do I. She does it herself and goes straight up the polished stairs and into the small study where I found Mr Mal.

It's a ransacked mess, the work of Forensics, not any burglar. Desk drawers have been opened, shelves disturbed, a wire basket emptied.

I ask if there was anything on his answering machine. Only the messages to phone the shift inspector. Tapping out 1471 had disclosed that the final call came from the police station, she adds. From the timing – 17.55 – it was mine. She is still waiting for a print-out of incoming and outgoing calls.

She is looking at the desk. There are smears of silvery finger-print powder, dried blood and clean squares on the grained pine where the now-removed papers protected the surface from the bloody fall-out.

'See the small spread.' She gestures with both hands.

'The outer limits aren't that wide,' I concur.

'I know that you do not expect as much blood from a brain injury as a wound to the heart, but, surely, there should have been more than this?'

In the way she'd read up on religion in Community Relations, she's clearly mugged up on murder for CID and I see what she's driving at: were the death blows struck here or elsewhere? 'There was lots of blood in the crashed Mazda. I'll get the lab boys to recheck for a second type.'

We go back downstairs. Walking around the lounge for the first time I see that the furniture is western and modern, nothing cane and no scattered rugs; not exactly home from home. In a glass cabinet trays of expensive-looking silverware are on display.

A happy picture of Mr Mal and, I presume, his late wife hangs on a wall in a dark, ornate frame. Beneath, in a similar frame, is a script in a language I can't make out – a love poem, I'd like to think.

The place is cold because the central heating has been turned off. Recently, scenes-of-crime experts spent three days on a baffling killing. The executors of the victim's estate sent us the gas bill. Our accountants acted promptly to stop it ever happening again.

As we browse, she informs me she'd seen the cleaner who confirmed that Mr Mal sometimes had dollars about the study. For a month before a holiday in Florida, where a sister lived, she had been paid in them – 'at a very favourable rate'.

We go back upstairs and wander round the three bedrooms. Many of Mrs Mal's stylish clothes still hang in wardrobes, fifteen months after her death, too painful to give away, I suppose.

In the sparkling bathroom, I tell her what little I've learned about the sexual orientation of the dying driver.

Her mouth drops slightly. 'Goodness. Well.' A mystified shake of her head. 'I thought they were born that way.'

Her tiny smile is puzzled. 'I saw one once, dancing at a wedding when I was about ten, back home. She was very large and her voice too deep to be a ... well, lady-like. I asked my mother what was wrong with her. "Ask your father," she said. "Your mother will tell you when you're older," he said.'

I laugh. Like my grandparents when, at about the same age, I raised a question about sex change operations after an item on the BBC News had left me none the wiser.

We descend the polished steps again. Upstairs and down I've seen no signs of a break-in and say so.

'No,', she says. 'The killer either got in the same way as you did or had a key.'

'What about the home help?'

'She has got hers. I have seen it. She cleans up on Wednesdays. Her husband is in work, no record, no known criminal associates. She seems very trustworthy.'

Rule her out, she's telling me. She's already put in eighteen hours more work than I have on this job and I'm going to take her word for it. 'How about the police surgeon, Dr Service – how did he know him?'

Mr Mal was a trustee of Pillars of Faith, an inter-denomina- tional charity, she says, rattling off a whole list of religions supporting the aid effort, making it sound very ecumenical and cosmopolitan. Dr Service sometimes gave advice on what sort of medical supplies were needed at their destinations.

Mr Mal presented Pillars with a new white van nine months ago. 'A Mazda diesel, 2.2, costing more than thirteen and a half thousand pounds,' she adds expertly.

'He was fond of Japanese models,' I put in.

She shakes her head. 'The Parsi God is Mazda.'

A touching way to commemorate his late wife, I privately agree.

Every quarter, the Pillars truck is filled with medical supplies funded by the various congregations and goes off on its mercy missions, she briefs me.

The charity trust's accounts and the van's maintenance record were on the top of his wire basket. The constable on her small team, a former fraud squad man, had taken them and was trawling through them, along with other paperwork.

In the kitchen I open and shut doors and drawers, more out of habit than in the hope of finding anything that Forensics might have missed. They are filled with cutlery, dusters, instruction manuals for domestic equipment, the usual odds and ends, and packets of foodstuffs, some past their sell-by date, bought, no doubt, by his wife months ago.

On the breakfast bar is a bowl of fruit that will never be eaten now. On a wall, within arm's length of a bar stool, is a white clip-on phone.

It's a smart kitchen, the pale yellow wallpaper clean apart from faint darkening between the door to the hall and the silent central heating boiler tucked into a corner.

Between the door frame and a boxed-in down pipe is a strip of heat-soiled wall with a hook and, below it, a long oblong that's much cleaner than the yellow paper around it. I study it.

'Where his calendar hung,' she informs me. She returns to the breakfast bar and sorts through her pink file. From it she slides a photocopy which she hands to me.

February is printed below a picture of a cat so it is clearly an extract from his month by month wall calendar, a line for each day.

She points to Sunday, the 23rd. 'You see. Hejira. Not Hijra.'

I nod, eyes scanning up and down. Almost every other entry is in initials. Down for yesterday is: 'BUS – 11 a.m. and R at 6 Hills – 12.' Written down but crossed out against today's date is: 'DeM – 7.30 p.m.' Then: 'POF 7.30.'

Some entries are in pencil, some in pen. It's a bit like the last line in my office desk diary which I use for private purposes. Today's line reads: 'JJ, 8 a.m.' Next week has an entry for a retirement party where everyone will get pissed up, so: 'PU. 6 p.m.'

'We think we have worked out a bit of it,' she says over my shoulder. 'He was due to go to a symphony concert at De Montfort Hall with Dr Service. He phoned yesterday morning to cancel. "Something else has turned up," he said. We think he scored through DeM. POF for tonight is a Pillars of Faith function, perhaps.'

49

'Yesterday is the important day,' I say. 'Any ideas on the other two entries?'

She gives her head a tired shake.

I can't work it out either. You don't drive your car from home at ten thirty, the time the Neighbourhood Watch man saw him backing out, to catch an 11 a.m. bus. In my village there's a community ambulance that ferries around old folk. Everyone calls it the bus. Maybe he was going to see the vehicle he donated to Pillars of Faith in view of the fact that he'd dug out the van's maintenance record.

I hand it back and look at where the original calendar hung. The edges of the narrow, unsoiled oblong are irregular, I observe on closer inspection, like badly pressed trousers. I point it out. 'I reckon they always hung their calendars here. Did Forensics take any others?'

'Not that they have handed over.'

I return to the drawers, resume rummaging and from among the pile of makers' manuals withdraw last year's wall calendar.

We pull up two stools to the breakfast bar. I push aside the bowl filled with bananas, black grapes and oranges. I begin to flip through it.

Every month has a photo of a local scene on top of the page. Under a snow-whitened Bradgate Park, January is blank, but then, we work out, Mr Mal was still in Bombay, having bade farewell to his wife in the Towers of Silence.

He had a sparse programme over the next three months, a time when, according to the watchful neighbour, he was still in deep depression.

May, with a sparkling stream winding through Soar Valley, saw activity picking up. Several appointments are signified by initials and times only. 'Mazda – 5 a.m.' appears on a Sunday in the middle of the month.

'About the time he handed the new truck over to the charity,' Chand says.

On Wednesday every month POF appears which, we speculate, indicates regular meetings of the board of Pillars of Faith. 'Which means tonight's function, if you're right about it, is out of sync,' I say.

August has sweeps of golden corn ripening in fields in the Wolds. On a Sunday half-way down is 'AD – 5 a.m.'

'He was an early riser on occasions,' I comment.

He was busy by the autumn, lots of initials and times inked and pencilled in, only a few crossed out to denote cancellations. I turn to November.

Off the page, before I even notice the photo at the top of it, a one-line entry jumps out at me: 'Exodus – 5 a.m.'

As we retrace our steps off the red Tarmac on to the herringbone footpath towards our cars, Mr Norris waves from his leaded front window across the cul-de-sac. We take it as an invitation to call.

By the time we are going up his red Tarmac he has the front door open. He invites us in.

His house is in the same lay-out as Mr Mal's but furnished entirely differently; old furniture waxed in a polish with a smell that brings back boyhood memories, flowers in vases, lacy headrests on the maroon three-piece, a log fire burning in the black grate; cosy, cottagey, very English. On a half-moon mat in front of the fire lies a very old black and white collie which opens filmed-over eyes and shuts them again.

We sit side by side on a sofa, Mr Norris across the fireplace. His wife does not make an appearance, but I can hear her in the kitchen, slaving, no doubt, over a hot Aga.

'The caller just before noon . . .' Chand begins.

Norris nods. 'The detective.'

'We'd like to cross-check . . .'

'Can't you trace him?' he asks understandably.

'Could have been a Special Constable who's not on duty today,' I say evasively.

'Suppose so,' he says doubtfully. 'It was an old-type police car.'

He goes through it again, in far more detail than last night, now that he has had time to think it over.

It was just before noon. The car was an Escort, duck egg blue, with black and white chequerboard trimming under the windows.

Old-type police car? I think, puzzled. That type went out with *Z-cars.*

The driver was young, between twenty and twenty-five,

wearing a dark jerkin, 'like a pilot's.' He was tall, well built, hatless, short very fair hair, pale face. 'He definitely said he was CID. Mr Mal had told him to follow his red hatchback to Soar Valley, he said, but his own car had stalled in the driveway.'

On this occasion, Mr Norris hadn't seen Mr Mal driving away, but directed the man to the A46. 'He seemed to know the way, just wondered which route the car had taken because you can get there via the A6 too.'

Yes, he repeats, there was a passenger in the Escort parked in Mr Mal's driveway, but he didn't get much of a look at him because of the shrubs in the front garden, just the impression that he was bare-headed and dark.

'Not black.' He shoots Chand an uneasy look. 'Just dark, sort of sun-burn dark.'

Chand soothes him with an understanding smile. 'We will sort it out through the logs. Thank you so much.'

In my best by-the-way fashion, I ask if he is involved in Pillars of Faith, hoping he might shed some light on tonight's calendar entry.

'Just as a small contributor, not actively,' he says modestly. 'Sad, isn't it, them losing two stalwarts in the space of a few days?'

'Sorry?' says Chand, frowning.

'Mr Myles,' is all he adds.

Myles's suicide had made the *Mercury* so it's no surprise that Mr Norris knows of his death but they had made no mention of membership of Pillars of Faith.

'Did you know Mr Myles?' I ask.

'Only slightly.'

'Did Mr Mal?'

'Very well. They worked together on those aid missions I told you about last night. He was round to see Rav only on . . .' He stops to think. '. . . Monday morning.'

The morning of his death in the cell, I remind myself, excitement rising within.

'Saw him,' Mr Norris goes on. 'Waved when I was walking the dog. Such a shame to lose good men like them when there are so many wicked people in the world. A tragic coincidence.'

I'll go along with the first sentiment, but not with the last. Any detective worth his expense sheet (and mine are always long) believes in connections far more than coincidences.

7

In the courtyard at the police station, the space marked 'ACC' is empty which means Goodman is still out, freeloading at the golf club; good.

In the bay with 'Dr' stands a rust-coloured Rover, as old and as tatty as this borrowed Cavalier, which means Service is in; better still.

Chand has beaten me back and has parked her yellow VW in an area reserved for CID which is full. I nose into the ACC's slot.

Upstairs, I discover that Goodman hadn't even assigned her and her two-man team to neighbouring desks in the busy general CID office, let alone provided them with an incident room. So much for his logistical support, I privately fume.

I reclaim the first-floor office I used yesterday. A trio of cadets are detailed to carry in extra desks, a couple of computers, a trestle table and filing cabinet for exhibits and statements.

While they are moved in, I take the steps through a barred gate half-way down and enter the ground-floor cellblock in search of Dr Service. 'Just giving the once-over to a dope head arrested for shoplifting,' the burly, bespectacled custody sergeant informs me.

I lean an elbow on his long grey-topped counter and gaze idly about me, taking in the surgically clean smell. All is quiet. By midnight, it will be bedlam.

'Wrapped up the Myles inquiry?' asks the sergeant with feigned casualness.

'More or less,' I reply.

'First one we've ever lost.' He sighs deeply. 'It's a bugger, isn't it?

It's a bugger because we take inordinate precautions to ensure that not a hair is harmed on any prisoner's head. There's not a single step in the cellblock ('the custody suite', they call it these days), so no one can trip up and claim he was pushed. The tanks for drunks have bunks the height of a house brick from the tiled floors in case they roll off. Video cameras are bracketed to the low ceiling. Prisoners have their belts, braces and shoe laces removed. Yet Myles managed to end it.

'Don't worry about it,' I tell him – but I know that he will.

Eventually, a befuddled youth in torn denims is escorted through a blue door marked 'Medical Room'.

I tap on the door and walk in. Service, in a grey double-breasted suit, is standing, leaning forward, packing up his black briefcase on the examination table. It has a white sheet over a thick black mattress and looks extremely comfortable.

'Ah.' A darkening face tells me he's still not over-pleased to see me. 'Mr Goodman isn't here.'

'Should hope not,' I beam. 'I've just pinched his parking place.'

There's not a flicker of a smile. I'm going to give up trying to get through his guard and go straight in. 'I gather you were a pal of Mr Mal's.'

He looks down again, snapping the case shut. 'Are you still on that job?'

I snap back. 'Why shouldn't I be?'

His face becomes slightly flustered. 'No reason.' Actually, there is. He was present last night, outside Mal's house, when Goodman tried to jock me off the inquiry.

I don't want him shopping me to Good News and the distracting hassle that will flow from it. I'm going to have to cover my tracks. 'A suspect, the hijra in hospital, was being chased by one of our patrols when he crashed . . .'

A curt nod.

'. . . and a couple of bobbies, it seems, have failed to log a visit to Mal's house yesterday morning.'

Another nod, slower.

'Both are my department's remit. Right?'

'Quite a good friend, yes,' he finally answers. 'I'll miss him. Many people will.'

He doesn't ask me to sit in his consultation chair or sit himself, but he relaxes sufficiently to recount how he'd met Mr Mal and his wife at a musical appreciation society five years ago soon after settling in the city following fifteen years' service as a medical officer in the RAF.

'They were very kind.' He shrugs. 'You know, a stranger alone in a strange place. Invited me round for meals a few times. Lovely couple; she very cultured and caring, he charming and amusing, making fun of her religion and, indeed, mine, but never in a malicious way. And, of course, when he lost her, he carried on her good work.'

Drawing on his military experience, he used to advise Mrs Mal on what sort of medicines and vitamins would be of most benefit in her aid effort.

'Pillars doesn't go in for bulky stuff – blankets, warm clothing, tents and the like. They ferry light loads – phials, medicinal drugs, concentrated foodstuffs and so on. With volunteer crews, they have to get there and back in a week.'

'Have you ever been on any of these trips?' I ask, chattily.

'No. A couple from my church...' He names a saint so, presumably, he's either Catholic or Anglican. '... went a couple of years back, but, with this job...' He looks around the white-walled room. '... I can't manage the time off.'

'When did you last have social contact with Mr Mal?'

Two weeks ago last Wednesday, he answers, at a cheese and wine party at the university to raise funds for the charity. They'd arranged to go together to a symphony concert tonight. He confirms that Mal phoned him yesterday morning to cancel because something else had turned up.

To head off the next question, he adds, 'He didn't say what and I didn't ask.'

'Is there a Pillars of Faith function tonight?'

'Not that I've been invited to.' He frowns. 'They normally meet on Wednesdays.'

'Did you know Mr Mal was a friend of Abe Myles?'

A dumb headshake. 'Why?'

'So Myles didn't mention Mal in there?' I jerk my head in the general direction of cells down a corridor beyond the sergeant's counter.

'If he had...' Service's expression tenses. He's gone cold on me again. '... I would have mentioned it in my statement.'

In fact, Dr Service's testimony, taken the day after Myles died, didn't mention much at all. He'd been called out by the custody sergeant at the request of Inspector Chand who'd been worried about the solicitor's reference to Myles's illness and 'not being himself'.

He'd examined him, found him not unduly agitated, took the view that he'd got whatever had been troubling him off his chest in his earlier private talk with his solicitor. He'd given no hint that he was about to end his life. As a result, Dr Service had declared him fit to remain in custody without a special watch being kept on him.

I'd quizzed Dr Service fairly thoroughly because there have been a few previous complaints about him, minor matters, mainly from arrested addicts and their families who thought he should have administered heroin substitute more freely, and, of course, free on the NHS. He clearly resented my questioning at the time, and still does.

Speaking personally, I'm on his side. I mean, if I locked up, say, 'Jacko' Jackson and he ran out of cigarettes, would I send out for a packet of Bensons for him on the State? Give 'em cold turkey; a bit of military discipline, I say, but not, of course, publicly.

I've strayed some way from my department's remit and decide to get back within it. 'These plainclothes men who called at Mal's house yesterday...' The driver and his car are described in detail. 'Ever examined any officer like that?'

His look is vacant. 'Not that I recall without a name.'

'Might even be a Special Constable,' I suggest.

He shakes his head firmly. 'Sorry. No.' He gestures to a records cabinet in the far corner. 'With a name I could help, but, sorry.' He picks up his briefcase from the table, all but saying: 'If that's all.'

I thank him and walk out of the cellblock, wondering how long it will be before Good News Goodman lodges a complaint with the Chief that I'm trying to pinch his murder case as well as his parking slot.

In my borrowed and suddenly overcrowded office, I phone Forensics with a request for them to double-check the wrecked red hatchback for a second blood type.

56

Then I stand before the exhibits table, studying this year's calendar in its plastic bag. 'Uni – 8 p.m.' is next to Wednesday, the 12th. Dr Service's meeting with Mal for cheese and wine at the university checks out then, I accept.

Chand breaks off from setting up a keyboard in front of a blank screen. 'I have checked with the chairman of the charity's trustees. Tonight's meeting is not routine business. Mr Mal phoned him on Wednesday and requested a private chat, just the two of them. He was invited to the chairman's house.'

'To chat about what?'

'He declined to tell him over the phone.'

Must have been very private then, I muse, gazing down at the entry on the calendar. My eyes go up a line to yesterday. 'Anything on BUS yet?' I ask no one in particular.

No one answers.

'What do we make of "R at 6 Hills"?'

'Not sure,' says a fair-haired, thickset man in a local accent. He is sitting at a green metal desk with two phones that have been installed in my absence. 'There's a place called Six Hills down the A46 towards Nottingham.'

Since I drive through it regularly, the last time this lunchtime, I know it well: a scattered hamlet with a big roadside hotel surrounded by pleasant undulating countryside.

'Is there a street in the city called Hill or Hills?' I inquire.

'Another job for you,' says Inspector Chand to the local man.

He sighs, looking and sounding very tired.

Inspector Chand smiles as warmly as her exhausted features will allow. 'We call him Telephone Bill.'

'Why's that?' I ask, needing to get to know this team quickly, to encourage them to begin to enjoy the job. A happy worker will always go that extra mile for you. It's not modern man management, I know; old-fashioned, in fact, but it usually works for me.

'Because he's master of all directories,' she explains. 'We think he's got shares in British Telecom.'

Telephone Bill gives her a baleful look, accusing her of trying too hard. 'Your chris . . .' He stops, gives a younger man sitting opposite a sly glance. 'Birth celebrations.'

Bill must have guessed, as I did, that she's not a Christian and I suspect it was deliberate, to make her feel uncomfortable, a

57

foreigner. Could he be trouble? I ask myself. He's tired and ratty, so I'll give him the benefit of the doubt.

'No joy. No hijras. No dancers,' he continues. 'I'll start on weddings, shall I?'

She gives him a subdued 'Thank you.' She introduces the younger man as Dick Williams. 'Our wizard with figures,' she adds.

He's thirtyish, tall, dark and lean, more like an athlete than an accountant. An athlete who's just run a marathon, on second glance, because his eyes are red and his shoulders hunched.

I ask if anyone has eaten, get three brief headshakes and sit down, looking at Chand. 'What sort of sandwiches do you fancy?'

'Er . . .' She seems a trifle put out. 'Anything but beef, thank you.'

Bill smiles sourly, knowing, I suspect, she's avoiding the sacred cow of her religion. I look from him to Williams. 'Ham all round?'

He nods. Bill says, 'Beef, please.'

He is going to be trouble, I decide, dialling the shift inspector to dispatch a cadet to the canteen with the order.

I sit back in my chair and address Williams. 'What have we got so far?'

On a quick examination, he begins, eyes down on a bundle of loose papers, Mr Mal had been doing very well – six-figure profits for four years, a dip last year when he took time off either side of Christmas following the death of his wife.

Mal obtained orders from all over the world, filled most of them from foreign firms, which delivered direct to his clients.

He looks at Telephone Bill with an amused expression. 'He often dealt in telephone number figures, bigger than yours, but . . .' He looks back at me, face serious. '. . . when they settled down he ended up with a finder's and fixer's fee of around ten per cent which came in by bank credit, often via Switzerland.'

'Did he ever come a financial cropper?' I ask.

'Hardly. He lost out marginally, say, five per cent, on a few deals.' He shrugs. 'Written off as bad spec, I suppose, because he didn't do much debt chasing.'

'Could afford not to on those profits,' Telephone Bill grumbles.

'Any current debts outstanding?' I inquire.

'There's around £33,000 due in from a Bombay textile firm over new machinery supplied from Japan which hasn't turned up.'

'What about Pillars of Faith accounts?' asks Inspector Chand.

'Apple pie order at first glance.'

I sit back, recalling what the Neighbourhood Watch man said about Mal sometimes having dollars about the house. 'Was there a not-so-petty cash book in his study?'

Williams shakes his head.

'Nothing to indicate when the incoming was cash rather than cheque or in what currency?'

'No. Sorry.'

I nod. 'Well, you've covered croppers. What about financial coups?'

His head goes down again. 'His biggest in the last financial year was home-based – Wolds Investments. He loaned a quarter of a million and got back twenty-five thousand on top of his original stake inside six months.'

Bill whistles. 'That's twenty per cent. Wouldn't mind a piece of that.'

I turn to Chand. 'Do the initials WI appear anywhere on his calendar?'

'No.'

'It's run by a solicitor with an office at the other end of the street.' Williams flicks his head northwards. 'Name of Julian Perkins.'

'Heavens,' gasps Chand.

I know why she's surprised. So am I. More. I'm thrilled. Now we've got another connection.

Perkins is the solicitor who saw Abe Myles in his cell on the night he died.

8

Half-way down a misty Charles Street I stop at a newsagent's shop to buy the *Mercury*.

Mal's murder is the main article, relegating the aftermath of yesterday's motorway mayhem to a single column.

Running alongside the story is a photo of him in a smiling group of Pillars of Faith volunteers, from turbaned Sikhs to Sally Army girls in box hats.

They are standing in front of a long white van with sliding doors. On the side 'Pillars of Faith' is written in a circle.

Inside the circle is a picture of the Pantheon. I recognise its domed roof and stout columns from a long weekend trip with Em to Rome and recall our tour guide explaining it was built as a temple for all gods – a thoughtful symbol for a multi-faith charity, I acknowledge approvingly.

The caption reports that Mal was pictured as he handed over the key to the new van in May last year.

On the pavement, alongside a line of glass-enclosed shelters where throbbing exhaust pipes on idling yellow and red buses are turning fog into smog, I slow right down, head over the paper.

I read about the discovery of Mal's body (but not by whom), the shocked and laudatory quotes of neighbours (but not Neighbourhood Watch's Mr Norris) and fellow trustees of the charity.

There are much longer quotes from Good News Goodman which run on into an inside page. He speculates on robbery as the motive.

The last paragraph reads: 'Police are waiting to interview a man in hospital with serious head injuries.'

You should never knock a superior in front of a subordinate, so I groan only to myself to ensure that Constable Williams, at my side, doesn't hear.

All the same I'm raging inwardly. Any police chief who gives out a line like 'A man is helping with inquiries' needs to be absolutely sure he's solved the case – or he might never crack it.

It gives the impression that the mystery has been detected and witnesses don't come forward with further information. Even if it's later announced that the arrested suspect has been released, they think: No smoke without fire, all over bar the shouting. The tips dry up.

Every time an old miscarriage of justice is exposed, police chiefs and ministers trail around TV studios assuring viewers: 'Systems are in place to ensure that it can never happen again.'

Tell them often enough and people will believe that we no longer make mistakes. As I know only too well from working in this department, it can be a misguided belief.

I thumb on through the paper as we walk. Tucked away near the middle are two paragraphs reporting that the woman motorist from yesterday's crash on the A607 is still unidentified and critically ill.

Should have corrected my mistake over gender in a fresh press release, I rebuke myself. I find comfort in the thought that the error has avoided any linkage between the two cases.

At the far end of the street, just before a flower-filled roundabout, we enter the lobby of a tall white building.

'Perkins and Partners' are near to the top of a long list of occupants but, having called before, I don't really need to look. We enter a lift with glass and grained panelling on three sides. I press 11. On one mirror a notice informs us: 'These premises are electronically monitored by Secure World.' It's a swift, smooth ride.

Down a long corridor I tap on a grey door and walk in. A rather frumpy middle-aged woman sits behind a desk. Williams makes the introduction and our request to see Mr Perkins.

'I'll find out if he's in,' she says protectively, rising and walking into an inner office.

I gaze out of a wide window behind her vacated swivel stool. Wispy haze, like smoke from a giant bonfire, is slowly casting a grey cloak over the city.

I begin to fret. If it gets much thicker and this talk takes a long time, I may not be able to get home tonight.

'I was just about away,' says Julian Perkins, smiling, spreading his hands over his large desk, cleared of all paper, apart from the *Mercury*.

He's fiftyish, on the short side. His dark hair has receded. The bare patch left behind is tanned a walnut brown. An immaculately cut dark three-piece suit doesn't hide an overweight figure.

Politely Williams thanks the secretary who's shown us in. She closes the inner door.

To order, Williams gives his name and rank and adds, 'And I believe you already know Mr Todd from earlier in the week.'

He does, indeed. We spent almost an hour together in this warm, thickly carpeted office on Wednesday discussing Myles's death.

61

Perkins nods a greeting, but doesn't get out of his high-backed chair to offer a handshake.

Williams ploughs on. 'I am investigating the murder of Mr Mal.'

'Awful business.' Perkins sighs heavily. 'Very sad.' He spreads both hands to tell us to sit on two chrome-framed, black leather chairs by a cream-coloured wall, then drops one hand on the *Mercury*. 'Thought it was all over.'

'What do you mean?' asks Williams when he is seated.

'Haven't you got a suspect, the man in hospital?'

'We still need a motive,' says Williams guardedly.

Perkins pats the paper. 'Doesn't it say it was theft?'

Too good to miss this, so I come in earlier than planned. 'Of what? Money?'

'Are you on this case too?' he asks, acknowledging we have spoken before over Myles's death.

I nod at the paper. 'What it doesn't say there is that the suspect was involved in a police chase. That's my department.' Pause. 'Now.' Pause. 'We have reports from two sources that Mr Mal kept cash – dollars – about the house. Is that true?'

Instead of pleading the client confidentiality I was expecting, he says, 'Yes.'

'You see,' Williams comes back, earnestly, 'his accounts don't reveal which of his income is cash.'

Perkins's smile is slightly supercilious. 'They wouldn't, would they?'

To a financial incompetent like me he seems close to admitting false accounting. 'Why not?'

He gives me a pitying look. 'International trade, isn't it?'

This short silence should tell him that I haven't a clue what he means.

He leans back. 'To smooth the way.' Now he appears to be confessing to bribery by a client.

A fierce look on my face is intended to force him.

It works. 'Overseas, there are government officials, Customs, trade union wallahs who have to be squared to ensure an order reaches a client on time or the deal falls through.'

I'm going to call it what it is: 'How did he raise the cash to pay these bribes?'

He ponders, taps his chest. 'I'm Mr Mal.' He jolts his head

towards Williams. 'He's a client of mine in, say, India. He wants, say . . .' He smiles to himself. '. . . this deal is going to be greatly exaggerated, but, well, a million police whistles. He comes to me, knowing, because of my contacts, I can deliver at the right price. I phone around.'

He is looking directly at me. 'I discover you can produce them at the best price – a pound a whistle.'

He thinks. 'My commission is between . . .' He stops. '. . . for simplicity's sake, let's put it at ten per cent.'

He turns his head. 'I offer Mr Williams here whistles at £1.10 each. Now . . .'

He is clearly enjoying himself, displaying his expertise. He has a mellow fruity voice and it's no hardship to listen.

His amused eyes are still on Williams. '. . . "Right," you say, "it's a deal at £1.1 million. But send me a bill for only £900,000."'

He looks at me and reads my mind. '"Why?" you ask.' He returns to Williams. 'Because you will only pay import duty on the nine hundred thousand, not one point one million.'

I think I see. 'A tax fiddle?'

'Under-invoicing, it's called.'

'A tax fiddle,' I repeat, flatly.

'Only affecting . . .' He flicks his head at Williams. '. . . his country.' He sets his face, serious. 'Every penny UK side is fully accounted for, I promise you. There has never been any loss to our exchequer.'

I am going to keep up his pretence. 'How do you get your hands on the two hundred thou Mr Williams here owes you?'

Perkins backs off slightly. 'I don't want to give the impression that this is an everyday occurrence.'

'But it does happen occasionally,' I insist, 'so what about the two hundred thou?'

He begins to look worried. 'Well, it's never that much. It was just an inflated example.'

'However much, how?' I say patiently.

'Either via a foreign bank or, on rare occasions, in cash. Of course, half of it immediately becomes due to the manufacturer.'

I follow that, but ignore it. 'Let's stick to the cash. How does he get hold of that?'

'Some of it will remain abroad and be dispersed by trusted agents, oiling the wheels for future transactions. Sometimes it is

63

brought here by an equally trusted courier. In which case, it will eventually be shown in his account under incoming.'

'And was any cash due?'

Perkins pulls a face. 'Fifty thousand dollars.' He heads off another question. 'Always dollars; safest currency worldwide.'

'When was it due?'

'This week.'

A possible motive, at least, I think gratefully. 'Who was the courier?'

'Don't know and didn't ask. Never do. Maybe his brother in Bombay will know.'

It's a heavy hint and I pick up on it. 'Was his brother ever the courier?'

'Sometimes. Not, I believe, on this occasion.'

'Did the money arrive?'

He looks surprised. 'How would I know?'

'Well, did you see or speak to Mr Mal at any time, say, yesterday?' I ask.

'He wouldn't know my number.'

I pull my head back, quizzically.

Again he sees my unasked question. 'I was out of the office most of yesterday, at my new place.'

Fussily he tells us he is moving from a flat in Knighton, a rather posh suburb, to a cottage in a village near Bradgate Park, a beauty spot.

'Lovely country,' says Williams.

'Wonderful walks,' Perkins agrees.

He gets back on track. 'Tradesmen in and out all day. The phone was connected in the morning, a number which I haven't had time to give to everyone yet, Mr Mal included.'

Without prompting, he volunteers the information that at lunchtime he was supervising the installation of burglar alarms because he intends to hang some presumably valuable paintings at his new place.

For all his waffle he's only answered half the question and I pursue the other half. 'So you didn't speak to him on the phone either here or at your new home. Did you see him, perhaps, a personal visit to his house?'

He is shaking his head. 'Never been, actually. He always comes . . . came here for business discussions.'

Williams moves him on to Pillars of Faith. They have an honorary solicitor and auditor, he replies, so he knows little of their finances other than about the donation of the Mazda van on which tax relief was obtained under a charitable covenant.

'Tell me,' I say, 'are you a criminal or commercial solicitor?'

'Mainly company law and tax matters these days.' He had started out in a converted shop down the Golden Mile, a jack of all trades, he goes on, and had moved here when he took on a junior partner who handled most of the crime.

Casually crossing his legs, Williams says, 'The biggest single recent outgoing I can find in Mr Mal's accounts was a quarter of a million to your company, Wolds Investments.'

He laughs, a little uneasily. 'Hope you also found it was returned with agreed interest before the due date.'

'What was it all about?' Williams asks.

'A one-off.'

'Involving what?'

'Property.'

I come in again. 'Was Mr Mal able to get his hands on that kind of money?'

'Oh, yes, from accounts here and abroad. It was gilt-edge, good as gold, couldn't and didn't fail.' Perkins looks pleased with himself, too pleased, in my view, for someone who has lost two clients in four days.

I open up on a fresh front. 'If you are mainly a company specialist, why did you turn out to see Mr Abe Myles on Monday?'

'His son asked me to.'

'So the late Myles Senior wasn't your client?'

'His son engaged me after he took over and decided on a programme of major expansion, for help in raising development money.'

'But,' I point out, 'Abe Myles was being held on a criminal matter.'

'Well, yes, but the station is just a short walk away. I was merely assessing the situation. Had he been charged, I would have gracefully withdrawn and recommended my partner, a good courtroom advocate. He's away skiing at the moment.'

He gives me a suspicious look. 'I thought you were satisfied with the circumstances.'

In a tight corner, I'm inclined to fib. 'I am, but my supervisor at the Complaints Authority . . .' I drop the name of a titled Liberal to impress him. '. . . has asked . . .' I'm going to throw in a legal phrase here, to impress him even more. '. . . for further and better particulars.'

To explain my reappearance, I add, 'Since Constable Williams had to come to see you anyway, I tagged along. Hope you don't mind.'

A smiling headshake leaves me unsure whether he's seen through my lie or not.

'Just run through your chat in the cell again, will you?' I ask, pleasantly, 'unless, of course, there was anything confidential.'

He shrugs, unconcerned. 'There wasn't.' He sticks closely to what he'd said in his statement. He was working late. The phone rang. Peter Myles informed him that his father had been arrested after breaking the window of the back-street shop where the family business had been founded. 'The old man's confused,' the son said. 'Thinks the company's going bust . . .'

Perkins breaks off his account. 'It isn't, by the way. Quite the reverse.'

Then he gets back to the narrative. 'When I arrived at the station, your lady inspector allowed me to see him. By then he was calm, quiet. He told me it was a family matter, of no concern to me.'

I butt in. 'The police surgeon, Dr Dilip Service . . . Know him?'

He shakes his head, absently.

'He saw him soon after you and found him calm too. He got the impression that he'd talked through what was troubling him with you.'

Another headshake, more positive. 'He told me next to nothing. He said, "You're Peter's solicitor. Not mine. I will sort out my own salvation."' He put a pad of paper and a pencil on the bunk and advised Myles to write out his account of events in his own good time.

Perkins repeats how he saw Inspector Chand when he came out of the cell. She told him all Myles Senior had said to her was, 'It's family.'

He passed on the message to her that son Peter didn't want his father to be charged. She accepted there was no intent to steal from the window display, but there was still the question of the damage on which she was taking a second opinion.

He reported back to Peter that, if there was to be a charge, it would be relatively minor.

Within the hour, Inspector Chand phoned him to say that Myles Senior had been found dead, hanging. He broke the news to his son.

'He was very, very upset. He rather blamed himself. There had been cross words between them.' He looks away pensively. 'But, as I believe he's also told you, he has absolutely no reservations about the way his father was treated in custody or the conduct of any of your officers.'

'That's good of you,' I smile.

The question now is: Have I any reservations about the way they treated him? I don't think I'll ask it – not yet, anyway.

9

After the trip up and down Charles Street, on top of eighteen rugged holes of golf, my right leg isn't just stiff, but beginning to seize up at the knee: a recurring problem.

Williams walked back as slowly as me, apparently too exhausted to talk much.

In the office, Telephone Bill is yawning so theatrically his jaw is in danger of becoming dislocated. Just seeing and hearing him makes me feel tired enough for a long snooze on that comfortable bed in the medical room.

Only Inspector Chand seems to have any juice left. 'A good lead,' she enthuses. An Asian family had hired a hijra to dance at their daughter's wedding on Wednesday.

She gives me the name of a textile tycoon that begins with a Ven and goes on longer than a Sri Lankan cricketer's and an address near a village in the Wolds off the A46 close to Six Hills.

Bill finally swallows his yawn and seems to find it unpalatable. He gives her a bilious look.

'How about Hill or Hills Street?' I ask him sharply.

'Yeah,' he grunts. 'There's a Hill Street, but the name of the woman at number six doesn't begin with an R, she'd never heard of Mal and she hadn't a clue what I was talking about.'

Gingerly, I lower myself into my chair. 'Us on the parents of the bride,' I tell Chand. 'Separate cars, then straight home.'

I turn to the sergeant and constable. 'You two off before the fog comes down. Get plenty of sleep. It could be a hard weekend.'

They stand wearily, pack their papers in the filing cabinet and leave, Bill without a goodnight. I look at the door he slammed behind him. 'What's wrong with him?'

'Just tired, I think,' Chand says, picking up her notebook from the desk, about to stow it in a black leather shoulder bag.

I say nothing, suspecting it's more than that.

She gives her notebook a tiny flourish. 'Perhaps I should have told you in front of him that it was he who came up with this lead.'

Maybe she should have, I concur privately. Desk jockeys like a pat on the head when there's a boss about from HQ.

Reluctant to get up yet, I brief her on what Julian Perkins had said about Mr Mal's under-invoicing, passing on his suggestion that Mr Mal's brother in Bombay might know something about the courier with the cash.

She retrieves her notebook from her bag, looks up a page and taps out a long number. Soon she is talking almost musically in, I presume, Hindi, and making notes. It's a long time before the mushroom-coloured phone goes down and even then her hand rests on it.

Her cheeks are shadowing with excitement. 'Two of them travelled from Bombay on Tuesday for the wedding. They are due to return on Sunday. One is a former Bollywood star, now a politician, very well known over there. Gupta Shama. A good friend of Mr Mal's brother,

'It seems to me that he . . .' She pats the phone to tell me she is talking about Mal's brother. '. . . is in on the tax fiddle, collects the ready cash and brings it over sometimes. On this occasion, however, his friend was coming anyway for the wedding and for a film première.'

'When?' I ask.

'This Sunday, here in Leicester.'

Still around here then, I think, relieved. 'What about his travelling companion?'

'A street dancer who has played bit parts in two musical movies.' A beam breaks out on her face, completely lightening it. 'And, yes, a hijra.'

'What's his name?' I ask, feeling that familiar glow that always comes with making progress.

'He does not know his given name, only that, professionally, he is called . . .' It sounds a bit like Koosana and Chewtra and she spells it out, head over her book: 'Khazana fresh word Chutra.' Her cheeks go deeper brown in embarrassment. 'It means Treasure Bottom.'

I laugh so loudly that the pain in my knee fades. 'What was the one like you saw at the wedding back home?'

'Very strange, a figure of merriment. Everyone laughed. He was dressed as a woman, danced very energetically and sang off key in a deep voice that sounded like an old tractor ploughing a rocky field.'

Not true, then, that old joke about swimming in shark-infested waters and losing your balls turning you into a soprano, I think, smiling.

We exchange brief biogs. Back home is Simla. She had been educated at a private English-speaking school. She had married at eighteen, half her lifetime ago.

I feel I know her well enough to ask: 'Arranged?'

'Oh, yes. He was already here with his family. They came when he was three. His parents are old family friends, same caste, the Tailors. They brought him over for the introductions.'

Hurriedly, she goes on. 'I wasn't forced into it. I could have turned him down. I turned down others earlier.' Her face saddens. 'We are divorced now.'

Arranged marriages haven't worked in our royal family either, I remind myself.

He brought her to Leicester where he had a good job as a programmer with a computer company. Both are British nationals. She'd joined the police force at twenty-three. They had no children. 'I think that was part of the trouble. This job and babies don't work because of the shifts.'

69

Only if you're a woman, I realise with a touch of guilt.

Though I know her first name from the statement I took from her on Abe Myles, I ask it anyway.

'Primilia,' she says. 'Most people call me Prim.'

Not too prim for this juicy job, I hope.

Prim pulls up at black double gates in a high stone wall at the end of an uphill drive from the foggy A46 with visibility down to two hundred yards in places. Her head emerges out of the driver's window and she speaks into an intercom on a metal pole.

Slowly the gates swing back. Simultaneously a winding drive lights up like an airfield runway.

Her VW leads my borrowed Cavalier up it. Every twenty yards or so lamps concealed in border flower beds cast yellow merging half-moons over the black asphalt.

Getting closer is a floodlit entrance with white columns to a brick house big enough to be two barns. Probably once was, I think, unable to be sure in the grey-tinted blackness beyond.

We stop in front of two white doors. One opens before our car doors are shut.

'This way, please,' says a quite elderly woman when we reach her. We follow her through a foyer with black and white tiles. On each side of a wide staircase are statues with animal heads and human bodies, both female and extraordinarily busty.

We enter a room with drawn curtains, sage green from ceiling to thick carpet of pale gold. Mr and Mrs Ven-tongue-twister rise from a huge striped sofa to greet us. I resolve to call them 'Sir' and 'Ma'am'.

Sir has a long white shirt hanging outside dark grey flannels, very eastern. Ma'am is wearing a dark pink trouser suit, very western. Both are mid-forties. The subdued lighting and their white smiles make their faces look darker than they probably are.

Prim and I sit in matching chairs. There's no armoury about, a collection of cudgels, for instance; only a tiger skin hanging from one wall.

Ma'am smiles and courteously thanks the local help who closes the door on us; hardly a dismissal.

70

Taking her notebook from her shoulder bag, Prim expresses gratitude for their immediate response to her sergeant's phone query.

'I do hope nothing is amiss,' says Ma'am with a concerned expression.

'It is merely for elimination in a road traffic incident,' says Prim. 'We have to check on two of your wedding guests, I'm afraid.'

Their daughter was wed here at home after short legal formalities at a temple in the city on Wednesday, Ma'am begins. She gestures towards the green curtains. 'We had a marquee in the garden.' Among the guests, she confirms, was Gupta Shama.

'I have seen him,' says Prim, head down over notes she's making in the light of a reading lamp with a brass elephant as its base. 'Very handsome.'

For my benefit, the bride's mother adds, 'He has given up films now he is in politics, of course.'

No stranger as a career switch than Ronald Reagan becoming American president or Glenda Jackson in Parliament here, so I nod my understanding.

She looks at her husband. 'We came here with our parents from Uganda in the seventies, but our roots remain in India. We visit regularly and we have known Gupta for many years. He visits from time to time.'

'I support him,' says her husband, a touch imperially.

Financially, he means, like big business and the unions throw money around at election times here.

'Naturally we invited him and his wife to the wedding,' he goes on.

'Equally naturally we wanted our daughter to have traditional trimmings for the ceremony,' adds his wife.

'In what way?' asks Prim.

The reply is aimed at me. 'There was, of course, the matter of the dowry.' Customarily, she says, the bride's parents would agree on a price, often in gold, because it always improved its value in the long term.

Her daughter and fiancé had a more modern outlook. They had asked for, and got, a renovated and furnished flat in London where the groom worked as a barrister.

They would move in on their return from honeymoon on

somewhere called Ile Maurice. I must be giving her my blank look because she adds, 'Mauritius.'

'Also part of the wedding arrangement,' says her husband with a proud beam rather than a suffering sigh.

And when I took on Em, I took on her overdraft as well, I think, deeply envious.

'But, well . . .' His wife is doing most of the talking, in charge domestically. 'I wanted a little extra surprise. A pair of matching bracelets. And for a hijra to dance and present them along with a blessing.'

She gives me a quaint look. 'Does that sound silly to your ears?'

'Not at all,' I assure her. 'Brides here wear something old, something new, something borrowed, something blue.'

'Ah.' She seems delighted with me. 'Very propitious.'

Ma'am mentioned this planned surprise to their friend, Gupta Shama, in a letter enclosing his invitation. He phoned his acceptance, adding that he knew just the dancer for the job, agreed to hire him and bring the bracelets.

'What is the dancer's name?' asks Prim.

'Khazana,' says the wife, dropping the rude, adopted second name.

I don't show off by translating it as Treasure, just sit back, relaxing, trying to cross stiff right leg over left knee, but failing to get it off the thick carpet.

Prim begins to fire off some quick questions. 'When did they travel?'

'Tuesday, but in different classes, of course,' the bride's father replies.

'Has the wife of Mr Shama also come?'

A brief headshake, no explanation.

'How did they get from Heathrow to Leicester?'

'Hired car,' he says. 'A Saab.'

'Did Khazana deliver the gifts?'

'And gave a sterling performance,' she says. 'There was a substantial collection for him. Would you care to see the wedding video?'

Prim looks at me. Normally, holiday photos and wedding videos take me through the tedium threshold but my nod is very enthusiastic. This could be evidence on a plate.

72

She gets up and walks to a large carved mahogany cabinet in one corner. She opens twin doors on to a TV set with a video player beneath.

While she is finding the channel and fixing in a cassette, Prim grinds on. 'What about settlement of the price of the gifts and the dancer's air fare?'

'That will be taken care of,' says the father, a little flustered.

He's footing that bill, too; both fares, which is why he knew the class in which they'd travelled and about the hired car; perks for a politician in return for Parliamentary campaigns for bigger tax concessions at the Indian end of his business. It's no comfort to know that we are not the only country where MPs take cash for questions.

The bride's mother returns to her seat, carrying a remote control. The screen lights up with a segment of the groom. He has a rakish moustache and is wearing a white suit. He is arriving at the entrance we've just passed through in a horse-drawn landau. 'Traditionally, he should have ridden an elephant, but we couldn't hire one.'

Should have tried Twycross Zoo, I think acidly, a bit bored already.

Mercifully, she fast forwards, stopping here and there for longer views of a shy-looking bride in red.

She is sitting side by side with her new husband, both wearing golden headdresses, on chairs big enough to be thrones. Both are heavily bejewelled and garlanded.

Her mother freezes the shot and points to bracelets they are wearing. 'Our surprise present.' I study them closely and see she had neglected to mention they were handcrafted gold studded with gems.

She zips on through shots with lots of guests, the men turbanned in orange cloth, the bride's father among them, eating and noisily chatting at long tables under a white canvas.

Then she turns off the fast forward. The camera cuts to a sizeable band on a platform, but only a drummer and accordionist are playing. 'Here she is.'

She, I note, leaning forward, all attention now.

She ... He ... I'm going to have to sort this out ... The bride's mother is calling her 'she' which is good enough for me.

She begins to weave her way on coconut matting around tables

73

laden with mouth-watering sights – several whole roast piglets and turkeys and lots of colourful vegetables, salads and fruits.

There's a red rose in her long hair. A rather thick midriff is visible between plain turquoise top and flowing floral skirt. Ankle bells tinkle.

She dances in only approximate time to the drumbeat. Bare arms make a stab of snaking sensually. Her much-treasured bottom waggles. She flirts outrageously with several men in the audience, eyes rolling, working her strong jaw comically, kissing a few on their cheeks. Their faces fill with the faked enjoyment you see at strip shows on stag nights.

Ma'am pressed hold. 'There is much more, including her singing.'

'Don't,' groans her husband. 'P-l-e-a-s-e.'

I laugh. 'I think I've got the general idea.' I make a mental note to take the video with us when we go.

Ma'am gets up again and Prim immediately resumes her questioning. She asks for and notes down the names of the airline and the car rental firm. Then: 'What hotel did they stay in?'

'They are not in a hotel,' Sir answers. 'It is difficult for even a former star. He gets recognised and mobbed. His old films are still very popular on video. Hindi film fans are very enthusiastic.'

Prim smiles agreement. 'Where, then?'

He still doesn't give a direct answer. 'Unfortunately, we couldn't put them up here. We were brim-full with family – '

Returning from the TV set, his wife interrupts. 'And, with the reception going on till dawn, they would have got no sleep,' she says pleasurably.

'Both had things to do the following morning,' her husband resumes. 'We found a nice place for them near by, just three or four miles away, until the weekend.'

'Are they still there?' asks Prim urgently.

'Khazana, yes, as far as we know. He . . .'

He, I chaff inwardly. This is confusing.

'. . . said he had to see someone the morning after the wedding but mentioned no other plans.'

A worried look passes over his face. 'I have tried to phone him two or three times to take him to our showrooms but . . .'

Back on the sofa beside him, his wife interrupts again. 'The pick of our saris is part of the arrangement.'

74

'. . . no reply,' her husband finally gets to say.

'And Mr Shama?' asks Prim.

'He also had an early start yesterday. He was driving further north on business.'

'Alone?'

A guarded nod. 'They left here together about midnight. Gupta is dropping in again for Sunday lunch. They are going to a film show in the evening. They have seats on Monday's mid-morning flight home.'

As casually as I can I ask if they knew Mr Mal, but not casually enough. 'Is this about his murder?' asks Ma'am.

I spin a reply about a traffic incident, thus far unexplained, around the time of his death which has to be eliminated from the inquiry.

'Not Gupta's hired car?' she asks, still disturbed.

I shake my head. 'A Mazda hatchback.'

She seems satisfied. 'A terrible tragedy,' she says with a sorrowful expression. 'Such a waste. A good man.'

I lean forward expectantly. It's a bitter disappointment to hear that, though they knew of him through their mutual friend, Mr Shama, they had never met Mal.

They subscribed to the Pillars charity, via their temple, not directly. They knew no more about his murder than they had read.

The bride's father had never used him as a middleman in any spare parts deal. Mal was not a guest at the wedding and he had not been mentioned at the reception within their hearing; a total blank.

Somewhat dispirited, I look at the father of the bride. 'The house you rented for a few days . . .' He nods. 'Did you find it advertised in a paper?'

'No. No,' says his wife. 'Julian Perkins kindly loaned it.'

'Our solicitor,' her husband breaks in. 'You know him, I take it?'

'Slightly,' I say with a tinge of excitement that's anything but slight. 'Are you friends?'

'For many years.'

'Did he come to the wedding?'

'Of course, and his new lady.'

'And the reception?'

'For the meal, then they had to leave.'

I'm not going to push this; not yet. 'And he recommended a house for your guests?'

'Owns it, actually. It's available for sale or rent. Sadly, his marriage has broken down.'

Politely, Prim requests the address.

Soar View, Barrow-on-Soar, he says.

'Upon-Soar, dear,' His wife corrects him with a playful nudge. 'It says so on the village sign. Get it right. Barrow-upon-Soar.'

My spirits soar as I picture Mr Mal's wall calendar and the date yesterday at 11 a.m.: BUS.

10

The roadside sign for 'Barrow-upon-Soar' comes into ghostly view after a short but slow journey along winding country lanes, downhill all the way.

The nearer to the river we get, the thicker becomes the fog that's beginning to freeze.

On the way from Leicester, the Cavalier's heating didn't work so, after stepping out of the bride's house, I'd put on my raincoat and floppy hat.

Prim, who took the directions to Soar View, has led me round two roundabouts at a crawl and just halted at traffic lights on red. I can make out a pub to my right and a triangular sign on the left which warns the road is liable to flooding.

Must be at the river, I think – a guess that's confirmed when we move off and over a hump-backed bridge with single-line traffic.

I trail her VW left and right down even larger lanes until she pulls up at a white gate in a thick hedge. She gets out, opens it, and I drive in. She follows me up a dark driveway.

No lights shine through any window at Soar View. I get out, knowing I am wasting my time. My shoes scrunch over deep pea gravel, heavy going with this leg. Drops drip on my hat as I step up to a porch arched with honeysuckle.

I ring the bell. Silence. Prim joins me and hammers on the brass knocker, then tries the door. Silence.

We step back on to the pea gravel. All I can make out in the headlights from our two parked cars is a square and solid place, white double doors in the porch, no *Mercury* in the letterbox, two white-framed windows on the ground floor, four above, all with curtains open.

There's a sizeable front garden at our backs alongside the driveway where our cars stand bumper to bumper.

Across her shoulder, Prim says, 'If house guests are staying, there should be a housekeeper, not necessarily living in; back in the village, perhaps?'

My spirits have sunk again. 'I'll hunt her out on my way in first thing in the morning.'

'Not now?' She seems very agitated, presumably frustrated by sudden failure after so much progress today.

'If one guest is up north on business and the other is in intensive care, there'll hardly be anyone in we want to talk to, will there?'

Now she looks disappointed. 'It is so remote. If Mr Shama has taken the hired car, how has Treasure . . .'

She, too, has coyly shortened his professional name, I observe.

'. . . been getting around?' More or less to herself, she adds, 'Would a street dancer from Bombay know how to drive at all?'

Not very well, according to motorists who witnessed his efforts on the A607 yesterday lunchtime, I have to agree.

'In his circle, I would have thought, cars are an unheard-of luxury,' she remarks.

Beginning to lose interest and to feel hungry, I ventured that he may have earned above the average for a street dancer as a bit player in Bollywood, so maybe he bought and learned on an old banger back home.

Prim, so enthusiastic she's becoming wearing, raises Mal's calendar entry for yesterday. 'Could it have meant a meeting at this place?'

She spotted the possibility too, I'm pleased to note.

Treasure Bottom arrived on Tuesday, was busy at the wedding on Wednesday to which Mal wasn't invited, so, yes, the hand-over of the money could have been here at BUS.

What am I doing, I ask myself with sudden urgency, standing here on one good leg in the fog in the middle of nowhere on a day off, pondering this? 'Come on. Let's go home.'

'But – '

'Home,' I repeated sternly. 'Sleep for you. You need it. I'll call back tomorrow on my way in and dig out the housekeeper if there's still no reply.'

She is making no move to go to her car which is blocking my way out.

'Tomorrow, first thing, you organise fingerprints at the hospital from the patient,' I instruct. 'Fax them to Bombay with the stage name and ask them if they can come up with a proper name and full address of next of kin.'

'Anything else?' After twenty-four non-stop hours, she still seems a glutton for work.

'Get your two boys hammering the phone to trace this Gupta Shama up north and find out if there's any reports of the rental car being either damaged or missing or in any accident.'

A street dancer the Indian government might not miss, but an MP dead or dying and me knowing nothing about it would create a diplomatic incident I can do without.

'I'll be in about ten,' I say, crunching a couple of steps towards the Cavalier.

She turns away, saying she intends to take the A6 home and recommends me to do the same in these conditions.

'The A46 is quicker for me,' I reply. 'I know the way back there.'

At the cars, she says, 'Goodnight, sir.' I nod, open the door and climb in.

She starts up and backs down the driveway. I belt up and start up and follow at a reasonable distance. At the exit, she reverses with left hand down. With a flash of her lights she drives slowly away.

I back out in the opposite way. Remembering the country code to shut what you've opened, I stop, but don't switch off the engine or lights, unbelt, get out and take a few noisy steps back down the driveway.

As I'm pulling the five-bar gate back into its gap in the hedge, I notice what I missed on arrival – an estate agent's placard on a wooden pole advertising the property for sale or to let. 'Viewing by appointment only,' it stipulates.

Beneath it is a much smaller blue sign edged in black and white check which says, 'Patrolled by C&D Security.'

They won't be exactly overworked around here tonight, I think.

That Prim Chand is quick and keen, I think, leaning over the steering wheel, face as close as possible to the inside of the windscreen on which a wiper is gratingly scraping.

I'm crawling in third gear, lights dipped to prevent full beam reflecting back out of the fog which thickens and thins in swirling patches.

Good point she raised about Treasure Bottom's transport – or lack of it, I muse on.

Yes, the hand-over of the dollars could have taken place here; fits with the calendar entry. And, afterwards, Mal could have given transportless Treasure Bottom a lift into the city, dropping in at his place on the way.

But would Mal, wealthy and tax-wise, trust a street dancer to bring in fifty thousand dollars in cash? I mean, what was Prim's phrase for them – figures of merriment?

Perhaps Shama was the courier. He knows the Mal brothers. Makes more sense, so I'll polish it.

A clearer road ahead now and I slip into fourth gear, only twenty miles an hour.

Treasure Bottom was just the bagman who carried the money through Customs at both ends. If stopped, Shama wouldn't have had to answer embarrassing questions. His good name back home would be protected.

Could be, I agree with myself. A street dancer is dispensable. I'll buy the fact that Shama knew of Treasure Bottom from their Bollywood days and engaged him on behalf of the bride's parents. But why travel with him and stay together out here? Treasure Bottom is a homosexual transvestite; a sort of court jester.

I think of an international con man I once helped to investigate. He made millions from a pyramid-selling fraud in cosmetics, so much he could afford his own jet. He used to fly from capital to capital with two dwarfs on his staff – 'to let the underprivileged see the world,' he greasily explained.

My cynical CID chief thought he was merely abiding by the old German ringmaster's dictum: 'When short of laughs, kick the midget.'

I smile to myself, then switch it off as a grey shroud looms. Concentrate, you berk.

I slow down to negotiate a tree-lined bend. From a side road a car emerges behind me, headlights dipped, and I don't feel quite so lonely.

Wish you wouldn't do this, I rebuke myself; get so lost in such deep thought when driving.

Sometimes when I'm heading home my mind wanders so far that I can't remember which villages I've gone through and I have to look about me for landmarks to check my whereabouts. And that's in daylight on a familiar road in my own car, not in a strange vehicle and country lanes in fog.

I concentrate, see a sign for 'Village Centre'. Right road. Good. Where was I?

Perhaps Shama contacted Mal on arrival and told him to come here to collect the cash yesterday. And he left the money with Treasure Bottom and headed off north to keep the transaction at arm's length if questions were raised by the tax authorities.

And, I theorise on, when Treasure Bottom finally realised how much he'd been conned into carrying he helped himself to it, killing Mal in the process, and fatally injuring himself in the getaway. In which case, where is the money, if not at Mr Mal's home or in his wrecked car?

I can't be bothered to answer. My job is to identify a driver dying as a result of a road crash involving a police pursuit, report to the Complaints Authority and notify the hospital of next of kin. I've got a name to start on, a stage name anyway. Forget the rest.

Can't forget though, can you? It's fascinating. You're hooked by the basic question: Are Abe Myles and Ravid Mal's deaths linked?

Not by murder, that's for sure. Abe's was suicide. The pathologist says so. The evidence is all that way. He was lonely, had fallen out with his only son and was ill with what the post-mortem confirmed was prostate cancer. And he left a one-word suicide note. Exodus.

There's a link with that on Mal's calendar for openers.

What others?

Pillars of Faith, certainly.

And?

Dr Service saw Myles in the cells, knew Mal well, but thus far, has no connection with Treasure Bottom.

A green circle in a silvery halo shines ahead. The bridge lights are on go. I change down a gear on a curve that approaches the river.

And?

Well, Perkins saw Myles in the cells, represents his son and Mal, and is linked to Treasure Bottom in so far as he gave him a roof over his head during his stay.

So tomorrow, concentrate on . . .

Suddenly I seem to be in dense low cloud and something is flying out of it towards me.

Concentrate. What is it? Two yellowish lamps high above road level.

Christ, a heavy goods vehicle shooting the lights and it's going to hit me.

I pull the wheel down, sharply and to the left. There's just a blur of blue, car from the size of it, not a HGV, flashing by to my right.

Headlights flash behind me.

The top of my head hits the roof as the car mounts a grass verge. Twigs lash the windscreen on my side. My empty stomach heaves as I'm bounced across rough ground towards something that steams white.

All of me is tipped forward against the steering wheel as the car bonnet dives forward with an angry sizzle. Suddenly, the car stops with a jerk that shudders through me.

My mind is in pea-soup fog; can't think. Get out, an inner voice screams. You're in the river. Out. Don't let the pressure equalise on the outside. I punch the belt free with one hand and open the door with the other.

I lower my bad leg into freezing cold that strikes up to the knee and on through my body, followed and being overtaken by a surge of panic. I try to pull my leg back. It's stuck, won't shift. I put both hands under my knee and tug. Pain pierces my brain. My foot is freed with a strange sucking sound. I cup my knee and look at my shoe and trouser leg caked in thick slime.

Not the river. You've ended up in the floodplain. A field. Sweet mercy.

I turn off the protesting engine and sit with the door wide open, trying to calm myself. The car behind will have seen you run off the road. He'll call out from the bridge. He'll get help.

I sit for what seems a long time. No call, no help comes.

Sighing, I lower my shoe into the soggy ground. My left follows. I feel my way to the back of the car. I can just make out deep tyre tracks in lumpy grass. Stooping, elbows out to keep my balance, I pick my way between them. Knees up like a guardsman about-turning, I'm wading in what feels like glue, the suction so great that the heel comes off one shoe.

The further I get from the car the easier the going until I reach the verge. I can see now that I've gone through an opened gate and only clipped the roadside hedge.

I walk beside the high wall over the hump-backed bridge towards the pub by the traffic lights.

Water splashes below me as if wings are flapping on it and I wonder if I've disturbed some ducks.

Duck egg blue, I tell myself. That car was duck egg blue.

Em is surprised to see me in my baggy blue golf-cum-gardening trousers and white shoes when I finally get home. Her face registers mounting horror when I explain why.

The landlord at the riverside pub let me use his domestic quarters to phone Charles Street. He put on wellington boots and went off to retrieve my golf gear from the car. I changed shoes, socks and trousers. To settle my nerves, he offered a brandy which I declined.

Just as well, because the patrol car crew gave me a breath test when they turned up. Bagging the head of the Complaints Department would have resulted in free booze for weeks in the social club. Miffed with a negative result, they gave me a silent but reasonably swift ride home. I got my own back outside the house. 'Sorry, but I won't ask you in for a drink while you're on duty, boys.'

Em runs a hot bath while I strip off. Completely naked, I sneak into Laura's room. She's sound asleep.

Oh, God, I think. My hat. Your present. I've lost it. Think. I

82

wasn't wearing it in the police car or the pub. The car. It must have been knocked off when my head hit the roof. 'I'll find it tomorrow,' I silently promise her.

I've stayed so long, just looking down on her in her cot, that Em pops her head round the door. 'Moussaka in fifteen minutes,' she announces in a whisper.

Thought I might have got away with that, but, twenty-four hours behind schedule, it's caught up with me.

The slime on my feet and shins is soaking away, but not the delayed shock that makes me shiver. Somebody was trying to kill you. And why didn't that car behind stop to help?

Em comes back in, carrying the white walk-about phone from the kitchen. 'Jacko,' she says.

I sit up in the foam and put it to my ear. 'I was just about – '

I stop to listen to a rendition of 'To the victor the spoils'. He starts to talk normally. 'You'll never guess.'

'Neither will – '

He's not listening. 'Tenth place and last prize . . .'

He's talking about this morning's golf which seems so long ago I'd almost forgotten we played.

'. . . a mini tape recorder for both of us. Just the job for you to use when you're telling me your tales, eh?'

He'll bring it round tomorrow night when he and his wife are coming to dinner. 'Pipped the Chief and Good News Goodman by one point,' he goes on happily. 'That wasn't very politic of you, now was it?'

Finally I get in several consecutive sentences to tell all about his car and how it happened, concluding, 'The recovery team are pulling it out in the morning.'

'Is it a write-off?' he asks apprehensively.

'Can't tell yet.'

'Hope so,' he sighs. He'd been thinking of trading it in for months. A generous pay-out on police insurance would ease the financial pain. Meantime, he'd borrow his wife's. He wasn't planning to go out much for several weeks, because a new book was welling within and was about to burst forth.

'Soon, of course, I'll have another plot to work on, won't I?'

11

The woman who opened both inner and outer porch doors of Soar View wears a yellow plastic apron over a late middle-age spread and a very dour expression.

'Ah, you're in,' I say, forcing a bright smile, about the only brightness around on another of those grey mornings that make you wish you were *en route* to Lanzarote, not Leicester.

She just holds off saying, 'Obviously.'

'I called last night,' I inform her.

Now she does state the obvious, somewhat testily. 'I wasn't here.'

I produce my card. 'It's your guests I'd like to see.'

She barely looks at it. 'They weren't in either, still aren't.'

I'm about to ask a silly question because my Volvo is the only vehicle parked on the pea gravel and the open-fronted garage next to the dark, rambling house is empty. 'Aren't they back?'

'No.'

'When are they expected?'

'Don't know.' A palm of one pink rubber-gloved hand is behind the outer door, about to close it. 'Try tomorrow afternoon.'

This, I realise, is a woman who, when interrupted in her chores, would uncheerfully slam any door in the face of all gypsies selling clothes pegs and take her chance on the curses.

'Look.' I switch my face to serious. 'This is an urgent police matter and I do need to speak to them. Mind if I come in for a moment?'

Gently, I push back the door and take a painful step up into a cold tiled porch to be met by the fusty smell of browned, dormant geraniums that hang in tied bunches from hooks on an empty ledge.

Beneath the shelf is a rack of assorted walking-sticks. So stiff and sore is my leg this morning that I'm tempted to request the loan of one to lean on.

She doesn't resist my semi-forced entry, but doesn't take her hand off the door either. 'Can't help you.'

'Try,' I say, mildly threateningly.

She is my height – about five-ten – and not giving an inch, standing eye to eye, toe to toe.

'When did they arrive?' I go on.

She is holding my look as well as the door. 'Tuesday night.' I try to outstare her. 'I had a meal ready for them,' she goes on. 'Anything but beef, I was told.'

'Who by?'

'Mr Perkins, the owner. They are friends of a friend.' Her watchful eyes break away as she moves to her right, blocking the opened inner door to the hallway. So far, no further, she is telling me, as dogged as a guard dog.

I persist. 'Were you given their names?'

'Mr Shama. He's an MP, you know.' There's quiet pride in her face and tone, honoured to have served him. 'And a ... er ... lady with an Asian name I didn't quite catch.'

'Did you see them again after Tuesday dinner?'

'Wednesday for breakfast.' At last she volunteers something. 'They didn't want much because they were going to a big wedding. That's why they were over here. They're from India.'

In reply to chatty questions, she opens up a bit more. She doesn't live in. She bikes to and fro from her home down in the village.

On Wednesday, she tidied up after they had left together in Mr Shama's hired car – 'a big silver one'. Then she went home. She didn't return that day as no further meals had been ordered.

She saw them again when she served Thursday breakfast, but they didn't eat much. 'Got home at gone midnight, they said. Had a good time.' After breakfast, Mr Shama told her he was driving further north, but didn't say exactly where or why.

'From what I could make out, the lady ...' She pulls a face that's slightly disdainful. '... had something to do at lunchtime, but wasn't altogether sure of her movements after that.'

They were still here when she left about ten. 'I promised I'd pop back in the evening to rustle up something for her if required.'

Her guard is coming down. 'She didn't come back. I haven't

85

seen her since. I presume she's gone off with Mr Shama without telling me.'

She shakes her head huffily. 'They'll not be back here until tomorrow, so Mr Shama said. So, you see, I can't help you.'

'Well, thanks for trying.' I smile ingratiatingly. 'Did anyone else call or see them during those two days here?'

'Only my husband and then only briefly in the kitchen.' Two mornings a week he works as the gardener, she explains. They cycled here together on Thursday morning.

'He had a bonfire in the back all laid and ready to go . . .' Her head jolts back towards the inner door to the hall, kitchen and, I assume, a garden at the rear. '. . . but it was far too wet to start, so he left it till Monday and pottered about in the greenhouse.'

She thinks. 'The guard from C&D could have, I suppose.' That's a security firm engaged by the agents to do occasional spot checks, she explains.

'How did you find Mr Shama?' I inquire casually.

'Charming.' She smiles for the first time. 'Very courteous.'

'And his companion?'

She says nothing, face set.

'Not so charming?' I offer.

'It's not that.'

'What is it then?'

Her guard is up again. 'It's not my place to say.'

Were they sleeping together? I ask myself. Is there a homosexual triangle behind this? 'Do they have separate rooms?'

She looks quite shocked. 'Of course.'

'And slept in them?'

Her hackles come up. 'Now look here.'

I put on my pleading face. 'May I see them?'

'Certainly not, not without permission.'

'I'm not snooping, just looking for documents to help me identify someone in hospital.'

'One of my guests?'

I tell her the truth. 'Not absolutely sure yet.'

She thinks for only a second or so. 'No.' Firmly. 'Not unless you have a warrant or an order or whatever you need. Sorry. Everybody must get permission from the agents first before they look around.' She points down the drive to the gate. 'It says so on the board. Ring their number.'

'I'm here on police business, not with a view to purchase or rent.'

She ignores me. 'Tell them to ring here and I'll let you in if it's all right with them.'

I keep trying. 'They'll be closed at the weekend and this is urgent, can't wait till Monday, life or death.'

She's unmoved. 'Try the owners then.' Her face fills with regret. 'Well, Mr Perkins anyway.' A slight, sad shrug. 'They've gone their separate ways, I'm afraid. She's taken the children to her parents in the Lakes, but he's still living locally.'

I ask for his number. She doesn't know it, just the name of a village near Bradgate Park into which he's moving this weekend. She pauses to think again. 'His office will be closed. Try the security firm then.' She gives me an address off Melton Road.

'Will they be round soon?' I ask.

She says nothing.

'It might save me trailing all the way into town and back again.'

She shrugs. 'Hard to say. They're supposed to do checks in the morning and in the evening, but I've only seen them three or four times. They don't stop long.'

I step back out of the porch. 'Just in case I pass one of their patrols, what sort of vehicles do they use?'

'Pale blue with black and white squares. You can't miss 'em.'

Only just managed it last night, I think, bitterly.

'You were bloody lucky,' says the boilersuited head of the recovery team.

Not half, I agree, leaning on a wall of granite blocks looking down from the hump-backed bridge.

I'd travelled fifty yards or more into the field before the swampy land had stopped me just short of a hedge. Beyond the hedge is a path and then the river, forty yards wide and flowing fast through three arches below me.

A towing wagon is parked in the open gateway I unknowingly steered through. A thick wire rope runs from it to the Cavalier whose wheels have half vanished in a green bog.

'Is there a floppy hat inside?' I ask.

He gives me a nonplussed look. When I explain its sentimental value, he laughs. 'I'll take a look.'

He strides in wellington boots off the bridge, I follow slowly, stopping here and there, studying the brick blocks. Near the southern end I find what I'm looking for.

I walk back over the bridge to my Volvo which I'd left safely off the road on land between moorings for houseboats and the white-walled pub, appropriately called the Riverside. On the flat roof of the bay-windowed entrance to the pub sits a blue rowing boat. That warning sign wasn't kidding, I think, amusing myself, happy in my work. They do get flooding here.

I head back across the bridge with a plastic bag and my Swiss army knife from the glove compartment. Crouching, I scrape what I'm sure are fragments of light blue paint from the wall into the bag, not stopping in the delicate task when I hear heavy footsteps approaching.

The job done, I look round and into my olive green hat which the recovery chief is holding upside down and open. I pop the plastic bag inside and say, 'Thanks.'

Maybe it was excitement over what I'd heard about C&D Security at Soar View or found at the bridge, or maybe Em overdid the onions and garlic in last night's moussaka, but somewhere short of Leicester I was taken, well, short; very short, underwear-threatening short.

Driving on the dual carriageway opposite the spot where Treasure Bottom crashed, I must have touched his sort of speed.

The only relief I felt was that I was behind the wheel of my own car again, knew its capabilities as I put my foot down.

No police patrols were about to spot me take a chance on two amber lights and the traffic on Belgrave Road was thankfully free of its usual weekday jams.

I meant to take a peek at the posters outside Bollywood cinema to cross-check what the bride's family said about the film première Mr Shama is due to attend tomorrow night, but kept my eyes in front, grimly determined.

Had I been concentrating as hard last night, Jacko's car would not be parked on the floodplain.

Sweating, I made it to Charles Street and the station. I pulled into the ACC's empty slot and, desperate by now, headed straight for the ground-floor loo.

Phew. Close.

Now I've rezipped and rebelted my fawn suit trousers and am unhooking the jacket from the peg behind the cubicle door.

The corridor door swings back with a soft thud against its rubber stopper. '... and then she lumbers me ...' The door returns loudly to its frame. '... with this crock of shit.'

It's Telephone Bill, sounding disenchanted. 'Bloody hell. Worked night and day, dug up the lead.' The footsteps stop – on reaching the urinal, I assume. 'And she grabs all the glory and swans off with that smart-arsed sod.'

I know he's talking about me. The Weekend Duty Senior Officer used to be known as Senior Officer on Duty and everyone called him Sod. So they changed the title, but everyone still calls us Sods.

'She speaks the lingo.' A second voice, Williams, trying reason.

'Bollocks,' snaps Bill. 'On the blower the bride's mum spoke better English than she does. She was just buttering up to that bastard from HQ, the black bitch.'

I put on my jacket as he complains bitterly about racial and sexual discrimination, mainly against ambitious white male sergeants. I pull back the lock and step out.

Williams shoots a startled glance over his shoulder as I walk behind them to the hand basins. I nod and say, 'Morning.'

All has gone silent at the urinals, even the splashing of running water on stainless steel. In the mirror above the basin, I see Telephone Bill remain in position. His shoulders have sagged; not the only part of his anatomy, I'll wager.

Finally, Williams turns and walks over the grey tiles towards me, zipping up. He takes the next basin. We grumble amiably about the weather. Both of us are taking longer than a hand rinse should, so I say, 'See you upstairs.'

He turns to the drier, briefly holds his hands under the warm air and departs, firing an anxious glance at Telephone Bill's back as he does so.

Only when the door springs shut does Bill step away and walk up behind me, very slowly. As he reaches the basin Williams vacated I turn to the drier and punch it on.

89

'Listen,' I begin over the drone. 'I have no quarrel with you calling male bosses bastards. Biologically, in my case, it's true.'

He runs the water, staring into it. 'And I've no complaint about you calling female bosses bitches.' I don't tell him there's a woman assistant chief I respect and admire, but that doesn't stop me thinking of her as (if not calling her) a bitch when we clash.

I raise my voice. 'But never ever a black bastard or a black bitch. Got that?'

His head is hanging as if he's about to sluice his face, but he doesn't. Nor does he reply.

'Why did you call her a black bitch and not me a white bastard?' I demand.

'Don't know, sir,' he mumbles.

'Tell me, do you know, really know, any black people?'

'On the streets . . .' His hands come out of the water and his head comes up defiantly. '. . . as a beat officer my best mate was Afro-Caribbean.'

One better than me, then, I think, feeling a humbug. I've never got that close to any officer other than white.

He walks towards me. 'We pulled each other out of the shit many times. I'd have died for him.'

I step to one side to let him use the drier. 'And how many others?'

He just rubs his hands together, saying nothing.

No more, I realise with relief. 'So the one you know really well you'd die for. What does that tell you about yourself?'

'Don't know, sir,' he repeats.

'Well, you're a detective. You work it out.'

Wheeling away from him, I wonder if I've been hard enough. Should I have told him, 'I've got your number and will be watching you'? Should I have used the word 'advice'? In disciplinary terms, it's close to an official reprimand.

I pull the door open and turn back. 'A word of advice.' I nod at the cubicle doors, all open. 'If you want to make inspector, always check the traps before you sound off to your mates, black or white.'

*

Sitting at her desk, a refreshed-looking Prim, in a crisp pale yellow suit, waves a blue sheet of paper at me when I walk into the incident room.

I wonder for an embarrassed moment if she knows where I've just been. One day working together doesn't make us close enough for lavatorial jokes. Then I see that it's the standard report form from Forensics.

So keen is she to get on with the job that she doesn't greet me with a good morning. 'Two different blood groups in the wrecked car. One's Mal's. The other is the same type as Treasure's.'

Her gaze goes behind me to Telephone Bill who is following me in. 'He's got a sample from the hospital and we've asked for a DNA check. He's also got the fingerprints.'

I turn to him. 'How is he?'

'Still critical,' Bill mumbles, not looking at me, as he sits down. 'Just a matter of time, they say.'

'This . . .' She flicks the form. '. . . means we're not even sure of the scene of the murder yet.'

I brief them on my call at Soar View. Mr Mal could have been attacked there or in the red hatchback or at his own home, we all agree.

Prim gets up from her desk and walks to the exhibits table, picking up the current and last year's wall calendars. She talks as she walks back. 'It also means that Mal's entry for . . .'

She stops both to sit and to find what she's seeking.

'. . .last Sunday, "Hejira" . . .' She looks up. '. . . can't be a reference to Treasure.'

She's right. Treasure only arrived here on Tuesday.

'What does it mean then?' asks Williams with a baffled expression.

For his and Bill's benefit, she repeats the Muslim meaning – departure. 'It was the term they gave for their exit from Mecca to Medina,' she adds knowledgeably.

'Exit?' queries Bill. 'Doesn't Exodus mean the same thing?' Losing confidence in his question, he adds, 'More or less?'

'Why, yes,' says Prim, thoughtfully. 'The departure of the Israelites.'

All three look at me, awaiting wise words from the top. I have

91

none, not a clue what to read into it, except that it's intriguing. I have to say something. 'You two do an analysis of both calendars.' I yank my head towards one of the two computers. 'Feed in all the initials and details. See if we get a pattern.'

Prim nods and offers towards me a fax she's prepared on Treasure for the police in Bombay.

I wave it away, hoping to tell her I trust her. 'Ask them if there's any dirt on Mr Shama too,' I add.

Williams asks, 'What now?'

Since he knows the walks around Bradgate Park, I reply, he's with me tracking down Julian Perkins at his new place to get permission to search his old, Soar View.

I enquire how the query on Shama's rented car is coming along. 'No time yet,' says Prim. I add background on Perkins and C&D Security to their jobs to do.

Bill looks downcast. I tell them about last night on the humpbacked bridge and show them what I found there this morning. 'It's a lot of ringing round on a Saturday when people aren't easy to contact, I know,' I half apologise.

It's what's known in my trade as wallpaper investigating – cover everything – and to prove I'm not about to delegate all the phone bashing I pick up an extension.

'No trouble, is there?' asks the patrolman, understandably nervous when his wife puts him on.

'No. No.' My reassuring tone. 'And I'm sorry to trouble you on a well-deserved weekend off.'

I take him back to Thursday around noon when he was parked up in a pub forecourt on the A607. 'On standby,' I say, not reminding him he was actually taking a break for a quick smoke.

'You see the red hatchback go by, being driven erratically and far too fast for the conditions,' I recap. 'You follow. Did you tailgate him?'

'Never that close, no.'

'Why?'

'We had to wait to get into the traffic. There were two or three vehicles between us and it.'

He goes on to explain that once Control told them the speeding car had not been reported stolen and was heading straight towards a faster patrol on the outer ring road he didn't put his foot right down.

I return him to the very start of the pursuit. 'Did you recognise or do you remember any of the vehicles in the passing traffic which got between you and the hatchback?'

He is silent for a while, no doubt picturing what ended as a scene of horror for him. 'Only a C&D patrol.'

'Who are they?' I ask as calmly as I can.

'C&D?' He sounds surprised at my ignorance. 'They've operated around here for years.'

I tell him I don't live round here. 'What do they do?'

'Security. Specialists in the jewellery trade – or were. Used to be really big.'

'But not now?'

'There's lots more competition these days.'

'Why do you particularly remember it?'

'It was going very slowly, unusual for them . . .'

I'll second that, I think acidly.

'. . . as though he was looking around, for someone or something. I dropped in behind him, had to give him a blast to get round.'

'He?' I double-check. 'Just the driver, no passenger.'

'Correct.' He didn't know the driver by sight because there was such a high turnover of staff. I ask for a description. 'Bareheaded, fair, wearing a dark top, as I remember.'

Ties in with what the Neighbourhood Watch man said, I recall. 'Who owns C&D?'

'An ex-prison officer, name of Sutton.'

'Do you know him?'

'He used to pick up prisoners from the cellblock and transport them to the jail. Haven't seen him for some time. Has a place off Melton Road. Only runs a small staff and fleet these days.'

'What sort of vehicles do they use?'

'Escorts. Fairly clapped-out now. Pale blue with black and white trimmings. You still see them about.'

Don't you just, I think, delighted.

12

The young woman who opens the white door of Julian Perkins's new place wears red jeans so tight that some of her lower half seems to have been squeezed upwards, like a tube of toothpaste, into a white sweater that bulges; tasty.

Her hair is bunched up under a silk striped scarf. There's no make-up on a face that's attractive in a slightly worn way.

I introduce Williams and myself and ask to see Mr Perkins.

She gives me a Colgate smile, completely unconcerned, says, 'Come in,' and opens the door wider to let us pass, then shuts it.

In the narrow street outside, a black BMW stands in front of this long, low, brilliant white stucco house with a newly installed 'Secure World' burglar alarm under the eaves of a newly thatched roof.

It had not been hard to find, even without the full address, after a short drive up the A6.

Soundless, in black moccasins, she leads us through a hall with more white walls. 'Two gentlemen from the constabulary, darling,' she calls ahead in an accent that's neutral and a touch nasal; sexy.

Concentrate, I order myself. I make two deductions. She's half his age and is the cause of the break-up of the Perkins marriage.

In a room that's beamed, irregularly shaped and cluttered with partially filled tea chests stands Perkins, holding a framed painting in both hands in front of him, looking over his shoulder at us. 'In. Come in. Please.' His whole demeanour is welcoming and I gain the impression that both are not unused to unexpected police callers.

'Sorry to bother you,' I say, standing still, glancing about me, 'when you're in the middle of moving.'

A tired sigh. 'What a rave.' Then a smile. 'Not at all.' He looks down at a landscape painting. 'Come in. Come in.'

He takes a few paces in front of a black fireplace laid with unlit logs and crouches as he carefully leans the frame against an unoccupied wall.

He brings himself upright and turns. 'Sit down. Sit down.' Both arms go to the horizontal to gesture towards two low-backed chairs on either side of the fireplace.

His thick, fawn sweater has brown leather patches at the elbows. His brown cords are fashionably loose-fitting and hide some of his bulk. 'Sorry about the mess.'

Williams and I sit. Perkins looks down at me, expectantly.

'We've come to ask your permission to enter and search Soar View,' I begin.

He frowns fiercely. 'Why?' Some of his healthy tan and all of his bonhomie have gone.

'You'd better sit down.' I nod towards the leaded street window beneath which is a couch covered in the same expensive floral fabric as the chairs. 'This may come as a shock.'

He picks his way in white trainers across a thick, golden carpet and lowers himself against one arm of the couch. The woman takes the other cushion, looking very concerned now, as if her new world is about to collapse.

'Well.' I lounge back in my chair. 'It's in connection with the murder of your client, Mr Mal.'

His mouth opens slightly. She holds her breath; a breathtaking sight.

I go on, 'We have reason to believe that a suspect in the inquiry stayed there.'

'Impossible,' he rushes out. 'The only two people who have stayed are both guests of Mr Ven . . .' Expertly, he reels off the tongue-twisting name of the bride's family. '. . . at his daughter's wedding. One is a highly-placed politician. The other is a professional entertainer.' He glares at me.

'He's the person we're waiting to interview in hospital,' I say.

The shock on both their faces seems genuine enough. 'Really?' gasps the woman.

Williams gets out his notebook and rests it on his knee. 'Tell us, please, how you got to know him.'

'Well, I, er . . .' Perkins hesitates, bothered. 'I don't actually know him, as such.'

He'd been a legal adviser of the bride's father for years, helping his expansion from humble beginnings, making it sound suspiciously like the business started out as a sweat shop, as, indeed, many did.

As he talks, the woman, no more than twenty-five, visibly relaxes. When he says, 'I saw their daughter grow up,' she pulls her legs beneath her on the sofa and places an affectionate hand on his shoulder as if to say: There, there, dear. I know I'm only her age, but don't worry about the age gap.

She's supportive and gorgeous, but I don't envy him. Fancy going through this courtship display again at his age, having to have it off when you're knackered because you think it's expected of you; not knowing if it's OK with her to scratch or fart; ghastly.

'When her father asked if he could borrow my old house for his MP friend and the entertainer, I was happy to oblige,' Perkins continues, composed again.

'And . . .' I try to twinkle. '. . . while making those arrangements, you instructed your housekeeper not to serve them beef.'

An enlightened smile. 'You've already been, then?'

I nod.

'And encountered the old battleaxe?'

Another nod as the young woman giggles. Her blue eyes have their sparkle back.

His smile is very broad now. 'And she wouldn't let you in?'

'Not without your permission.' I lean forward. 'I don't want to pry, just see if there's any documents to help in identification. We haven't got a name, not a proper name, for him yet. Have you been to the house during their stay?'

He shakes his head.

'But you met them at the wedding?'

'Had a long chat with Gupta and saw him, er, her . . . mmmm . . . dance, but we weren't introduced.'

The woman gives out a merry laugh. 'Never seen anything like it before, have we, Jules?'

He flashed me a shy glance to say he's embarrassed by her use of his shortened name.

'I couldn't work it out,' she chuckles on. 'I asked one Indian chap, "Is that a man or woman?" He said, "They're a sort of third sex." I never got to the bottom of it.' Her laugh becomes schoolgirl-ish and she puts a hand to her mouth which doesn't immediately cut off what's a delightfully dirty laugh. Smiling indulgently, Perkins reaches out with his hand and nips her knee, very gently.

I resume, 'Our problem is that Mr Shama is away until tomorrow and the other guest, we think, I put it no higher than that, is the person in hospital. We need to contact his family urgently.'

'Well, of course. I'll phone the old dragon. Call me with any further problems.' He dictates his new number to Williams, adding, 'It's ex-D,' meaning: Keep it to yourself. Then he appears to have a second thought. 'You will be discreet, won't you, bearing in mind Gupta's position back home?'

I give him my word.

'Well . . .' He cups both knees with his hands, about to stand.

'There's one other thing.' I need a preamble while I select my words carefully. 'This lead has only just come in and it's early days on this particular line of enquiry, but it appears a driver with C&D Security may have witnessed movements of a vehicle we're anxious to trace.'

He sits back again.

'I noticed at Soar View that they patrol your property. I've never come across them before.'

'Been around for years,' he says.

'I'm from out of town,' I reply. 'Can you help with their background?'

The woman unwraps her legs. 'Coffee?' she asks. All three of us say, 'Please.'

Belatedly Perkins introduces us. 'Marilyn, by the way.' We exchange smiles. She gets up and walks, loose-limbed, across the carpet and out of the room, not as interested, I presume, in security as transvestites.

Perkins says nothing, just watches her departure, miles away, impossible to guess where.

'Unless . . .' I pause until his attention comes back. '. . . they are clients in which case . . .'

'Oh, no, no, no.' He's back. 'Well.' Gone again. 'We've appeared for a couple of their drivers on motoring offences. Routine stuff. Guilty plea and mitigation. And occasionally he picks my brains over a lunchtime pint.'

He names a local, the Melton Hotel, which both frequent.

Williams breaks in. 'That's a mile or so from your office.'

'Yes, but my old office was near by. I still like to use it occasionally, see old chums. But he's not a client. Quite the reverse. I'm a client of his, I suppose. I can tell you nothing that you wouldn't glean in the pub.'

Williams is still confused. 'Who are we talking about, sir?' – an understandable question since, unlike me, he's not talked to the pursuing patrolman.

The boss, called Gerry Sutton, a forcibly retired prison officer, Perkins answers.

'Can't miss him if you pop into the pub. Disfigured face and a lazy bloodshot eye, the result of being hit by a heavy table in a jail riot, apparently. Still got a steel plate in his forehead. Got finished on health grounds with a pay-off.'

'Did you handle that for him?' I ask.

He shakes his head. 'Didn't know him then. His union, I presume.' He looks at me intently. 'He's no cowboy or anything. Never in trouble. Hired good men, retired bobbies and ex-servicemen and the like. He's just had a few bad breaks, that's all.'

'Such as?'

He goes back some way. 'About, oh, four or five years ago he bought the Leicester end of C&D, ill-advisedly, in my view. Founded by a retired superintendent from Scotland Yard's Robbery Squad and started out as C 'n' D – a play on Cash on Delivery with a bit of Rock 'n' Roll thrown in.'

I smile, thinking: He undersells himself. He has a nice way with words and would make a likeable courtroom advocate.

'Branches in Hatton Garden, Birmingham Jewellery Quarter and eventually here when the Golden Mile first took off. Lots of couriers. Good idea at the time with so many gems and so much ready money on the move.

'But then plastic increasingly took over from cash transactions and big multinationals moved into the security field and small outfits like his got squeezed. He's had to layoff, cut down the payroll, hire casuals.'

'You said you were a client of his,' I reminded him.

'Just an insignificant one. I suggested to the estate agent that he hired him to keep an eye on Soar View while it's empty. And yesterday there was a bit of guard duty when we moved those.' He flicks his head towards the painting.

'That's thoughtful,' I creep.

'Not really. He had the contract for the whole of our office block, a good one, but lost it to Secure World. They've got all the high tech equipment he can't afford. It just pushes a bit of work his way, that's all.'

Williams asks for a description of the guard who escorted the paintings.

'Dark, swarthy, about fifty,' Perkins answers. He looks at me. 'The driver you want?'

I pull a non-committal face. 'Has Sutton lost many more contracts?'

'It's no secret, because Secure World signs are up all over the place . . .' He is answering in a roundabout fashion, mind straying again. '. . . and since you know the family, Myles, for instance. He was courier for the old man for years, but when Peter took over and moved into bigger workshops, that contract went, too. Like Fort Knox, his new depot.'

A connection. Another connection, my heart sings. 'You know, it astonishes me . . .' I stop when Marilyn returns, carrying four stacked bone china cups and saucers in her hands. She offers them round, apologising for having no tables, leaves and returns at once with a silver pot of coffee. She pours into the cups which sit in their saucers perched on our knees.

Perkins sips. 'You were saying?'

I begin again, a slow build-up. 'Just that it astonishes me how the same names keep cropping up.'

'Oh, it's like a big village, the Golden Mile. Everyone knows everyone.'

I slip in the first of three quick questions. 'Does C&D work for your friend, Mr Ven . . .' I give up. 'The bride's father?'

'He has his own permanent staff on security.'

'Or Mr Mal?'

'No.' There's a hint of uncertainty in his answer. 'No such transaction has ever shown up in his accounts.'

'Or Pillars of Faith?'

'Wouldn't know. Doubt it.'

Marilyn resumes her seat and picks up on the previous topic, burbling happily about the friendliness of shopkeepers around Belgrave Road and Melton Road and their value-for-money goods. She seems to know the district well, making me wonder if this all started as an office romance; always dangerous liaisons which I avoid – now that I'm happily married, that is.

99

Perkins chimes in: 'Great entrepreneurial spirit. That's why I stick to commerce in the main. Everyone works too hard to commit too much crime.'

Good job I'm sipping coffee or I might have responded with a sarcastic 'Really!'

The housekeeper has both porch doors open when my Volvo crunches to a halt on the gravel driveway at Soar View. She gives me a wintry smile and Williams a curt nod when I introduce him.

As she ushers us in, I ask if C&D Security have made their routine visit and hear that she hasn't seen them yet.

The hallway is dark and gloomy, ideal for a collection of medieval weaponry, like cudgels, but only hooks are attached to the walls. Beneath them are dust-free squares on maroon flock paper where paintings have been removed.

She leads us up a set of creaking stairs and on to a large landing with a brown carpet and five pine doors, all shut.

She motions to a room which, if my geography is correct, overlooks the front garden. 'Mr Shama's, but Mr Perkins says you won't want to look in there, will you?'

'No,' I lie.

She moves to a door opposite and pushes. 'This is the one you want.' Perkins has given her strict instructions, I detect.

We follow her into a smallish room with furniture that's almost antique. A high double bed is neatly made up.

I head straight for a shiny chest of drawers, pull open the top one and look down on several wads of dollars.

She peers over my shoulder and displays no reaction. I guess she's peeked in before.

Instead of elation at a significant find, I feel oddly deflated.

Oh, Treasure, I brood. You've let Prim and me down. You murdered Mal and stole his cash. Good News Goodman was right all along. I've wasted two whole days on you.

I pull out a notebook. 'I'm going to have to do a complete inventory. I'll give you a receipt for anything we take.'

The housekeeper's face fills with annoyance. 'Will it take long, 'cos I've got to put my husband's meal on?'

'Some considerable time to go right through the house,' I say

100

with a grave face. 'Sorry.' I look beyond her at Williams. 'Shall we speed things by splitting up?'

'Could do,' he says, feigning indifference.

I turn back to the housekeeper. 'Can you show him downstairs, particularly the kitchen, garage and garden?'

'If you like,' she says, suddenly agreeable.

They depart. I open more drawers, see folded shawls, balled white socks, white bras and rather large cotton briefs I don't think I'll rifle through.

Faint voices rise from immediately below and I make heavy work – not difficult with one aching leg – of crossing the bronze carpet to a wardrobe. On coathangers are half a dozen colourful saris, skirts, petticoats and blouses. On the floor are two pairs of soft shoes. A cardboard suitcase is empty.

Downstairs, a door beneath my feet opens to either the garage or garden. As swiftly as I can, I cross the landing and try Shama's door. It opens on to a bigger room with more modern furniture – bed with pink padded headboard, fitted light brown wardrobes and matching chest of drawers.

A quick but fairly thorough search locates two suits cut from expensive cloth with a sheen, a pair of black leather shoes, men's underwear and socks, but no passport, no dollars, no sex aids, nothing of interest at all; shit.

I return to Treasure's room and make the back window my first port of call. Williams and the housekeeper are at the far end of a long garden that looks very dank, even though the mist has risen and there are bits of blue in the sky.

They have obviously walked down a winding ash path, past a greenhouse and dilapidated shed with a rusty, overflowing water butt. A patch of black earth that's been rough dug contains nothing but a six-foot-high bonfire on top of which is a browned Christmas tree.

She is standing, looking up at me. I give her a brief thumbs-up. Williams is crouching, peering inside the piled-up branches and broken boxes that tumble down the sides of the bonfire.

I go back to the top drawer and transfer the dollars to the primrose-coloured bed cover. No sterling from the whip round among wedding guests for that sterling performance, I note.

I search every drawer again, rifling through everything this time, failing to find a single Bank of England note or passport.

Strange that, I muse. Stranger still that Treasure had the loot here and not in the crashed car. Why go to Mal's house if the money was already in this drawer? It makes no sense.

On the bedside cabinet stand three miniature brass animals – religious images, I suppose. Behind them is a framed coloured photo of eight people sitting on a dusty stone step in front of a brown plank door.

I pull open the cabinet drawer. A handful of small change is among a twisted jumble of cheap jewellery. A plastic toilet bag contains lipstick, eyebrow pluckers, nail scissors and a small bottle of pungent scent; no sex aids again.

I pick up the photo and study it. Four of the figures are white-haired and wizened with age. All but one are in long, white, female attire. The odd one out is young, black hair swept back. She wears a vivid green sari. She looks remarkably like the dancer in the wedding video.

Any place or date written on the back? I wonder. It's a cheap frame with four soft metal clips I prise open with a thumbnail.

No caption, as it turns out, but there are three English ten pound notes and a passport with a plastic cover that's dark blue, almost black. On the cover is 'Republic of India' and three golden lions.

Inside I read:

Name:	Khazana Chowde
Date of Birth:	23rd March 1968
Place:	Poona
Sex:	Female
Profession:	Entertainer
Marks:	None

Well, I could think of one, I muse sadly.

The mid-brown, smiling face in the photo is too square-jawed to be pretty, but somehow it seems full of joyful anticipation.

There's a strong resemblance to the dancer on the video. I turn the picture over and compare the passport portrait with it; a good likeness, too.

I should be pleased. I'm not. I'm puzzled. She'd hidden her passport and thirty quid, yet kept thousands of dollars in a place where the housekeeper and anyone else could easily see it. And where's the rest of her collection from the wedding reception?

Silently I address the passport photo: Know what I think, Treasure? Someone is setting you up.

Driving away, I hear out Williams who sits in the passenger seat with the cash, photos and passport in a briefcase across his knees. No bloodstains in the kitchen or garage, he reports. No likely murder weapon in the shed or greenhouse.

No dismembered bits and pieces of Gupta Shama, MP, in the bonfire, awaiting the sort of disposal that was the fate of grieving widows in India. 'Something like sati, it's called,' he adds, displaying more knowledge than me.

So, I think, Mal wasn't murdered here. Then where? At his home? Or was he fatally attacked in the car, then dumped and left to die there?

In the incident room the atmosphere is as gloomy as the hallway at Soar View.

No trace on Gupta Shama, Bill reports. The hire car firm had received no panic calls. Nothing on 'R at 6 Hills' either. The hotel at Six Hills on the A46 knew of no Mr Mal and no one had been in on Thursday asking for a portly, silver-haired Indian.

Prim turns away from her screen. She had logged all the diary dates into the computer, but no pattern had emerged.

Bombay police regret that the film company which twice employed Treasure had him on the payroll under his stage name, so they're no further forward.

Perkins, she goes on, is highly rated in his profession. True, he's in the middle of another expensive divorce (he'd been married before) but she doubts if the missing fifty thousand dollars would help him much.

Williams puts his case on my desk alongside a couple of cheese and salad sandwiches on a canteen plate. 'Deeeer . . .' With a bad imitation of a drum roll he opens the lid with a flourish. '. . . dum.'

Bill gapes. Prim gasps.

Grudgingly, she volunteers to get back to Bombay with details from the passport. Her face has clouded with sorrow, thinking, no doubt, the first thought that came to me when I saw the dollars in the top drawer.

My disappointment, however, has lifted with the fog.

13

No one chatting on the red benches in the bar or drinking at round tables in the TV lounge at the Melton Hotel is remotely ugly enough to qualify as Gerry Sutton, the regular Perkins described this morning.

Williams and I don't stop to wash down our canteen sandwiches with swift half-pints. We walk out again into a narrow bay-windowed street to my car. I drive slowly behind a push bike. The street is so choked with cars parked on each side that overtaking is impossible.

Half-way down stands an unoccupied blue Escort with a black and white check strip beneath the windows.

There are spaces in front and behind it because three orange and white 'No Parking' bollards have been placed on the kerbside to deter other motorists.

It is parked directly outside a shop-sized window with a corroding grille. Above it, in black capitals on a pale blue board, both colours peeling, is C & D SECURITY. A radio mast is fixed to a rooftop chimney.

I drive beyond the Escort, and, with nothing coming up behind, stop and study its offside. It's as old as Jacko's Cavalier and in a worse state (at the start of yesterday anyway); lots of dents and scratches. There's a microphone on the dashboard and a swept-back aerial on the roof.

I reverse with great care into the space behind, get out, lock up and walk along the driver's side of the Escort. None of the scratches look new. Pity.

Williams has a hand on the handle of the shop door and pushes it open as I stroll over the pavement. He lets me go in first.

Inside is like one of those twenty-four hour taxi offices I used

104

to stumble upon around dawn after wild nights out in my bachelor days. They always look as if they are never cleaned.

A bare bulb hangs from the nicotine-stained ceiling. It's on because the grille and the grimy glass in the window exclude most of the ever-improving natural light.

To the right is a sofa so old that foam stuffing is escaping from both arms. Its sagging cushions are oily black.

Behind a counter, a heavily made-up brunette sits at a big desk that's ancient without being antique. On one corner of the desk is a bog standard transmitter and receiver – just a small black box with what could be mistaken for a car radio on top. A coiled lead runs from it to a mike on a stand in front of her. Papers are strewn about the rest of the surface.

She's not working on them or transmitting or receiving. She's looking at us.

'Mr Sutton about?' I enquire with my pleasant smile from the door.

She shakes her head, dumbly.

Crossing lino that's cracked and holed here and there, I tell her who we are, fish for my warrant card and slap it on the counter. 'When will he be in?'

Closer to, she appears to be no more than of school age. 'Dunno,' she says, distinctly unimpressed by my credentials. Nor, she adds indolently, does she know where he is.

We're both going to have to try harder. 'We're on a very serious mission, a major inquiry.' I add an edge to my tone. 'We have to check on the movements of a couple of your patrols whose drivers may have vital information.'

She lounges back in her swivel chair. 'You'll have to ask the gaffer.'

'It's important.' I nod at the mike. 'Can't you raise him on that?'

'Out of range.' She motions to the sofa. 'You can wait, if you like.'

'It's urgent.'

A casual shrug. 'Can't help.'

I'm beginning to doubt if she's ever been to school; charm school certainly. I've tried words like urgent and vital and am not getting through to her. Threats now.

'Yes, you can,' I say, very quietly. 'Otherwise, I'll have some traffic cops come round here and remove those illegally placed "No Waiting" bollards outside and then your boss will have to take pot luck on finding a parking place like every other motorist in this street.'

Now she's taking notice. 'What do you want anyway?'

A smiling nod is designed to tell her: That's better. 'Two days ago, Thursday. Did you have an escort assignment about lunchtime at the home of a Mr Julian Perkins?' I give her his new address.

Po-faced, she hunts among her papers, untidying them all the more, before extracting a brown hard-backed book, the size of my page-a-day desk diary at the office. She begins to thumb through, deliberately taking her time.

Standing above her I have a sneak view of several blank pages flicking by. What entries do appear would hardly have filled Mr Mal's line-a-day calendar.

Julian Perkins was right, I think. C&D has the financial skids under it.

Finally, she repeats Perkins's name, stumbles over the address and adds, 'Eleven to three.' Frowning, she reads on, 'Ferrying some stuff from a place called Soar View.' I ask for and am given the name of the guard who'd been assigned the duty: Tommy Keyworth.

I trot out Perkins's description of his escort. 'Dark, swarthy, about fifty?'

'That's him.' She snaps the book shut.

I smile down on her. 'Same day, about the same time. Escort duty for a Mr Mal.' I give his address.

She sighs, reopens the book, refinds the page, studies it and says, 'No.'

'Thank you,' I say, politely. 'Ask Mr Sutton to call me at Charles Street police station when he's back in range, will you, please.'

Outside, another battered Escort is backing into the one gap remaining in front of the shop window.

It's a tight manoeuvre on which the driver has to concentrate, looking over his left shoulder, ignoring us on the pavement, giving me time to study his crew-cut blond hair, my colour, and broad shoulders beneath a black bomber jacket.

I wait till he turns off the engine, then shuffle sideways through a gap of about a foot between the two cars and a few more steps to the driver's door. A fresh scar runs along it.

The driver looks round and up. Our eyes meet, lock on to each other's. It's like one of those sightings across crowded rooms they turn into love songs, except that here and now there's only fear and hate at first glance.

He knows and I know. This is it.

His blue eyes break away and go to the windscreen, see no escape and return to me. I open the door for him. 'Step out, please, sir.'

He sits very still. 'What's the trouble, mate?' he says at barely above a mumble.

I stiffen my tone. 'Out, please.'

He's muttering unintelligibly as he emerges very awkwardly, on the big side for a smallish car.

By the time I've gone through the necessary introductions, his black boots are firmly on the street surface. He is towering five or so inches above me. I have to lift my chin to say, 'I'm arresting you and taking you to the police station.'

His eyes fill with alarm. 'What for?'

As I hand my car keys to Williams, the formal caution is recited.

'What for?' he repeats, raising his voice.

Good question, I think, taking his arm, feeling hard muscles under his leather sleeve. Murder of Mal on or about Thursday lunchtime? Attempted murder of me last night? Play safe, an inner voice pipes. 'Impersonating a police officer.'

'What?' He could not have looked more aghast if I had accused him of the murder. 'When? Where?'

I grip his arm tighter and propel him towards my car. Williams is opening a rear door. 'Let's save it for the station, shall we?'

Unresisting, he falls into step, yanking his head towards the shop. 'Let me tell the gaffer.'

'He's not in.'

'Leave a message then.'

'Already left one with your charming receptionist to tell him to come round.'

107

He's looking frantically about him, close to panicking. 'I'm on sodding duty,' he shouts. 'I have to let them know. It's only right.'

'Inside,' I say softly, guiding him to the opened door.

I'm half expecting a rough-house and I'm pleased to have the athletic Williams with me.

Surprisingly obedient, my prisoner lowers himself into a sitting position on the rear seat, but keeps his legs outside, boots on the pavement. Suddenly, he leaps upright. 'I'm not fucking having this.'

Williams takes a quick step towards him. They eye each other up. Here it comes, I think; a roll in the gutter.

'I'm expected,' the prisoner shouts, louder this time.

I try to pacify him. 'Maybe you'll be released once we've sorted out a few things.' Some hope, I add privately.

With a groan that's resigned, if not defeated, he turns, stoops and gets into the back, Williams following.

I sit in the passenger seat, door open, resting for a moment, deciding: No way I'm going to drive this blond Adonis to the station on my own while Williams follows in the impounded Escort. I unclip the phone and call the incident room extension.

The door of the shop opens and a short, stoutish, black-haired, middle-aged man approaches cautiously across the pavement towards us. He, too, is wearing a dark bomber jacket, a workmate, I guess. 'What's up, Nick?'

'Piss off,' hisses Williams from behind me.

'Tell the gaffer I've been nicked,' says Nick, sitting next to Williams.

'What for?' asks his startled workmate.

'Inspector Chand,' says a female voice into the earpiece. I tell Prim to hang on and hold the handset away from my ear. 'What's your name, mate?'

Nick talks over me. 'For something I didn't do.'

'Shut it,' snaps Williams from his corner.

The workmate looks from me to him and back again, unsure who's being addressed or who to address.

I step out of the car, still holding the phone to my ear, and speak to him across the roof. 'What's your name?

'Tom Keyworth.'

'Did you do an escort job last Thursday?'

108

'Why?'

'Yes or no?' I nod down at the roof. 'Unless you want to join him.'

'Yer.'

Nick interrupts. 'Tell him to get round and sort it out – and quickly.'

'Where?' I ask Tom.

'Done nothing wrong, me,' he protests.

'Where?' I repeat.

'Or failing that get me pills round.' Rather dramatically, Nick rubs his stomach. 'Them gut pills.'

Tom's head is going between the back and me as if following a ping-pong game.

'Where?' I repeat.

'Got that, Tom?' demands Nick. 'Get me out or me gut will give out.'

Tom answers both of us together. 'Yer.' Then he gives me both Perkins's old and new addresses and the times of his duty. 'There's no complaint, is there?'

'No. Thanks.' Mouth to phone, I complete my orders to Prim, then thumb the phone's off button.

'Right.' I yank my head towards Nick's car. 'That will be collected by a police recovery truck very shortly and taken to our pound. If it's moved one inch, touched even, you will be joining your mate in the cells. Got that?'

'Yer.'

'Got that?' echoes Nick from the back as I climb behind the wheel.

'Yer,' says Tom, confused and frightened.

In the back of the Volvo, half round a block of one-way side streets that lead to the main road, Nick says in a flat, local accent, 'Don't know what all this is about but I'm saying nothin' till I've seen me gaffer, got that?'

He's as good as his word travelling down Melton and Belgrave Roads and Charles Street, into the station courtyard where again I commandeer the ACC's slot, and walking through double blue doors into the custody suite.

Only when he's emptied his pockets and I've fingered through his wallet to his driving licence do I put a full name to him: Nicholas Hewitt. The licence is valid. He's carrying more than a hundred pounds in tenners.

I leave Williams to complete the formalities and slowly climb the steps to the incident room. 'The car's being fetched and Forensics alerted,' Prim reports.

We sit around, drinking tea, updating each other, me with a lot more to tell than them. Prim is detailed to arrange an identity parade, Williams to fetch Mr Norris, the Neighbourhood Watch man, to establish if he can pick out Hewitt as the CID caller at Mal's home and the pursuit patrolman to see if he recognises the dawdling driver.

Rising again, my bad leg protesting, I tell Bill, 'You with me at Hewitt's place.'

'Where's that?' he asks.

I read out the address from the driving licence.

'Oh, dear,' says Prim, tensing. 'That is the estate where Mr Mal's cleaner lives.'

She's wondering if she made a mistake ruling her out so quickly. So, frankly, am I.

Going down the stairs, I decide to give my accelerator and brake foot a treat, leave my car where it is and ride in Bill's. 'Flam your mileage up a bit,' I tell him, trying to cheer him up.

In the courtyard Bill blinks at his first sight of daylight this shift and I do a double take as a duck egg blue Escort with black and white trimmings drives slowly through high blue gates operated automatically from the control room.

Thought I'd told that Tommy Keyworth not to let anyone touch it, I think angrily. Thought Prim had organised its immediate collection. She knows how important the forensic examination is. I'm going off her, rapidly.

My blood pressure drops when I note it is not the car Hewitt was driving. Behind the wheel is a man I've never seen before but immediately know: Gerald Sutton in the standard uniform of C&D Security.

He parks in a bay leading to the cellblock within white lines which have 'Custody Vehs Only' painted inside them. Must

110

know the spot from his days on the collecting run from HM Prison, I surmise.

He gets out, doesn't lock up and strides purposefully towards the door we've just walked through. The closer he gets the more obvious becomes his facial disfigurement.

His head seems too big for a body that's wide-shouldered and lithe with just the beginning of a boozer's belly.

It's difficult to put an age to him because of his face. His forehead is so protruding that it seems to have a double depth of bone. His right cheek puffs out as if a wad of cotton wool has been stuffed that side of his mouth. The eye above is bloodshot with the lower lid curled under. He looks like a bloodhound that has just run face first into something hard.

Bill at my side, I wait till he reaches us. 'Mr Sutton?'

He comes out of some sort of daze. A frown corrugates a cowhide brow.

I introduce myself. 'You may want to see me.'

He scowls, an unnerving sight. 'I want to see Nick Hewitt, an employee of mine.'

I shake my head. 'Not possible. Not yet. Sorry.'

'Why?' he grunts.

'Come on.' I nod over his shoulder towards his car. 'You were in the prison service. You know the formalities that have to be gone through booking someone into custody. They take time.'

I'm not going to tell him that more time will be taken up organising an ID parade. I don't want him beating us to Mr Norris and putting the frighteners on him. This face at any door would seal most lips.

'What's he supposed to have done?'

'Not at liberty to say just yet.'

'Is it serious?'

Dumb question, that. Does he think a chief super would be here on a Saturday on a minor matter? I summon up a smile. 'Later, perhaps.'

'You bloody well left a message at the office for me to come round.' With his voice raised, he has a noticeable southern accent.

'Things have moved on since then.'

111

'You asked me to come. Here I am. Why can't I see him now? He's entitled to a visitor.'

He's not, actually. It's a privilege that I'm not going to grant. Nor am I going to correct Sutton. 'He's entitled to a solicitor when we formally interview him, but we're not at that stage yet.'

'Once you've questioned him, can I bail him?'

'Perhaps. Do you want to give us the name of your firm's lawyer so we can call him in later?'

I'm expecting Julian Perkins's details, fishing for a link. Disappointingly, he doesn't bite. 'Does his family know?'

I'm not going to tell him we're just on our way round. 'That's being attended to.'

'I can't understand any of this.' Some of the aggression drains from him. 'He's a good lad, you know.'

I'll try a preliminary probe. 'How long have you known him?'

He goes silent.

I persist. 'How long has he worked for you?'

'A week. He came out of the army with an exemplary record. Ex-MP.'

He means Military Policeman, I realise, not the sort of MP Gupta Shama is in India.

'What sort of work is he engaged on?'

'The usual security stuff,' he replies vaguely.

He got my message to come to the station so he's spoken to his receptionist. He must know from the questions I asked her that Hewitt's arrest centres round Mr Mal's home over Thursday lunchtime. Yet he is offering me nothing about it. I'm not ready to ask yet about the absence of the assignment from his records.

I sense I am wasting my time and he seems to accept the deadlock. 'So I can't see him?'

I'm going to have to talk to him again. He could turn out to be important. If Norris, the neighbour, eyeballs Hewitt, Sutton could testify to the fact that he'd no official business, no reason for being at Mal's house. I'm going to keep him sweet. 'We'll have a longer chat later.'

'And you won't tell me what it's about?'

'Later, I promise.' I'm still buttering him up. 'Depending on progress, the question of bail might arise and I'll contact you immediately.'

He lowers and turns his head slightly and gives me a strange sidelong look with his bad eye. 'You're making a big mistake, you know,' he says coldly.

Always a possibility in this job, I concede, but I don't tell him that either. 'Later' is all I say as we turn away from each other.

14

Travelling through some outlying housing estates which replaced slums demolished in the fifties is like leaving an oasis for the desert, I've often thought.

Road after road has proudly tended front gardens, box evergreen hedges and tiny emerald green lawns, clean windows and paintwork, polished cars in the driveway.

Then you turn a corner and see front gardens of caked mud, windows that seem to have been hit by sandstorms and caravans of clapped-out vehicles. The smell is something akin to camel shit.

Town halls claim that they don't have sink cul-de-sacs or sin bin ghettos for bad tenants, so, giving everyone the benefit of any doubt, the avenue where Nick Hewitt lives must have grown organically.

Two houses are boarded up, obscene graffiti misspelt on streaked stucco. Broken furniture is piled in one front garden. Sump oil meanders along another. One upstairs window has an irregular rust-coloured semicircle beneath the sill as if its tenants have sat there and shat from it – hence the phrase 'bum out the window', I suppose.

It's the sort of street where you expect to get chip pan fires on Christmas Day.

Bill is driving very slowly, just as well because a blond boy, thinly dressed and thin, no more than five, dashes from behind a stationary banger in pursuit of a mangy mongrel pup. He is swearing foully, waving a stick which he appears to have ripped from a kerbside tree, already condemned to a lingering death from vandalism.

Christ, this is a shit-hole, I brood, depressed.

Bill stops. We get out. He locks up and wisely tries all doors.

Across a patchwork footpath two cars and a van are parked on crumbling concrete in what passes for a driveway. The boot of the last in line butts out into the footpath and would normally block the gateway, except that there's no gate, no gateposts and not much of a front hedge.

We step over mud, walk beyond two vehicles to a third before a flat-roofed garage that has no door and is stacked from floor to ceiling with spare motor parts and, half-hidden from passing view, a word processor with a busted screen.

A burly man in grimy overalls is leaning forward over a wing. He doesn't hear our approach because he's operating a whining drill as he tries to smooth away some botched plastic padding.

I tap his shoulder, but he yanks it angrily without looking round.

For something to do, I gaze back down the line. This particular caravan of vehicles is resting because it's incapable of movement. One is on blocks, one has no engine, one has no front seats. None has a current road fund disc. Jacko's Cavalier would be much prized here, even in its present state.

It's obvious he's running a repair business without planning permission and not paying tax on his earnings while drawing the dole.

Neighbours won't shop him because it could invite a petrol-soaked rag through their letterbox in the middle of the night, or because they're involved in similar dodges of their own. All you can do is send up a private prayer of thanks for not living next door.

Eventually, the man switches off his drill with buffer attachment. He looks round. There's a hint of the hate and fear in his eyes I saw in Nick's. He thinks we're from the council, social security or Inland Revenue. When we produce our cards, it's clearly a relief to him; we're the least of his worries.

'Mr Hewitt?' I ask.

'Eh?'

Guessing he's been deafened by the din he was making, I repeat the question.

He repeats his response. A snaf; all I need. In police circles, they used to be called snafus – Sub Normal and Fucking Useless. Like everything else, it's been shortened.

I'll rephrase it. 'We're looking for the family of Nick Hewitt.'

The snaf jerks his head at the half-opened back door. 'His old lady's inside.' He doesn't follow us in, merely switches his buffer back on. Visits like ours, I suspect, are routine.

I knock, call, then push the door open. The kitchen is in a worse mess than C&D's office. The floor is covered with folded-out newspapers, all of them the *Sun*. A small, wonky table is piled with laundry, cracked sink with plates, all dirty. A cooker has almost as much congealed fat among the four rings as black enamel. A dog's water bowl is empty.

Sounds flow through another door and I follow them into a living-room, if you can call it that. A TV is running an old *Star Trek*. Below the set is a new video recorder.

Toys, some expensive, but none of those canvas reading books my kid adores, are scattered on a stained carpet. A sideboard is stacked with junk. A camp bed with a blue nylon bed roll is against one tea-stained wall.

On a couch not much of an improvement on C&D's lies a flabby woman, flat out, smoking and watching the screen.

'Mrs Hewitt,' I say, quite quietly, so as not to alarm her; a waste of time because she doesn't hear me, and I have to repeat it, louder.

She looks across a plump shoulder of her purple dress. 'Eh?'

At the third time of asking, she says, 'Er.' She thinks, then adds, 'Was.'

'We've had to arrest your son, I'm afraid,' I tell her.

'Which one?' she asks, undisturbed.

'Nick.'

'What?' Now her round face does register surprise. She leans sideways to stub out a half-smoked cigarette in a saucer on the carpet. She begins to pull herself up.

'We're going to have to search this place,' I continue.

'What for?'

'Evidence.'

'No, for fuck's sake,' she growls throatily. 'What's he inside for?'

'Impersonating a policeman.'

She swings her legs off the couch. Her bare feet are dirty. 'He is a fucking policeman.' She thinks again for a second. 'Was.'

I head back for the door. 'We'll start with his room.'

She stands, rather woozily. 'You'll find fuck all.'

I must be a prude, certainly a hypocrite, because my language in full flow on nights out with the boys and on the golf course can match hers, but I don't like to hear women using the worst of obscenities. My ears are inclined to filter them out and I start to delete or modify expletives that come with her every sentence.

I gesture to the door. 'Upstairs, is it?' I don't wait for an answer, and lead the way up carpetless wooden steps. Bare-footed, she begins to follow on, chuntering, behind Bill.

The front door bursts open. In crashes the dog chaser who turns out to be a girl with cropped blonde hair. She is dressed in a singlet and trousers with shredded turn-ups that curl beneath her sand shoes.

'Get it?' the woman calls.

'No. The fucking thing,' replies the girl, sulkily.

Nick's mother lumbers heavily down the stairs, cuffs her sharply on the side of the head. 'Well, get it and give it what for, pissing all over the place.'

Why is it, I think sadly, that families like this always get dogs for Christmas, not cats which can fend for themselves or, better still, piss off.

The girl goes out again, slamming the door which sends a judder right through the house.

Puffing, the former Mrs Hewitt joins us in a small back room with two single beds and only a yard of space between them.

It's as though an invisible line has been drawn down the centre. One bed is neat, with personal effects on a dusted shelf above it. The other is a tangle of sheets and blankets with soccer posters, scarves and woolly hats attached to the wall.

'Which is Nick's?' asks Bill.

'Can't you tell?' She nods to the bed that's been made with military precision. For the second time within the hour we hear that we're making a big mistake.

And, for the second time, we're rudely asked what we're looking for. We can't say a cudgel-type weapon that's been used in a murder, or money stolen from a eunuch transvestite, so we say nothing.

She tries to second guess. 'If it's money you'll find nowt.'

It's a long, very detailed search, in and under both beds, through a built-in wardrobe that has reasonably smart clothes one end and tat at the other.

She talks most of the time in a very rural accent. Nick, we learn, is the only son of her second marriage.

The half-brother who shares the room is older, from the first marriage. Somewhere the half-brother has a kid, but she doesn't disclose if he's come back home after a marriage break-up or was ever married at all. 'Hasn't had a proper job in years.'

Yet, it soon transpires, he can still afford to follow Leicester City home and away every Saturday which explains his current absence in London.

Going to matches these days I've noticed how many foul-mouthed yobs sit in expensive seats. Most of them are five years either side of thirty. They look and act unemployable, never having outgrown the halcyon days of hooliganism a decade ago. Sitting among them, I wonder how many drugs were pushed and videos and computers stolen to fund their season tickets and away trips.

Nick is not married, we're informed. 'No girl I know of.' He'd got such good GCSEs that he'd been accepted in the army at seventeen and had done seven years. 'Serve your country and this is the thanks you get.'

'Where?' I ask, merely to break the flow.

'Aldershot, mainly.'

A hazardous posting, that, I think, amusing myself, as I return to the shelf above his bed. 'Why did he leave?'

'Got fed up with all the bull.'

'Not because he's medically unfit, then?' I pick up a box of pills from the shelf and shake it.

'There's no drugs there,' she snaps.

'For upset stomachs,' I read out loud from the label.

'Ah, yer.' Her temper subsides. 'A dicky gut. That's all.'

Into the desultory conversation Bill drops a name I haven't heard before. Nick's mother has never heard it either; eliminating someone he's come across in his thus far unfruitful research, I presume.

We move into the front bedroom, the former Mrs Hewitt trailing behind, watching over us to make sure we don't plant anything. 'You find nothin' 'cos we've got nothin'.'

We start to search in and around double and single beds, both unmade, a chest of drawers and a wardrobe, me wishing I'd

117

borrowed forensic gloves, so badly soiled is some clothing. Get this over fast, I decide.

Nick had been on demob leave for a month, then got work with C&D this week, his mother says. 'First job he tried for,' she adds, rather proudly.

'What as?' asks Bill, sounding as bored as me.

'Driver-guard-escort. What he's trained as. Only a week. Then he's off. Special job.'

'Where?'

'All over.'

Now that is interesting and I slow down the search. 'Abroad?'

She shrugs a Don't Know.

'What for?'

'He's not going to miss the trip, is he?'

I haven't found his passport or any insurance or health certificates and point it out. 'Where are they?'

'At the office, maybe.'

'Why?'

'Well.' She shrugs. 'The trip's work, ain't it?'

'So he's going travelling for C&D Security?' I ask.

'He's not going to miss it, is he?'

Again it's an evasive answer, but I'm not going to push it yet. 'Dunno,' I reply honestly.

'''Cos there's good money and he's going to settle what he owes afore he goes.' For board and lodging, she means.

'Can't tell you yet,' I say. 'What's this job all about?'

'Dunno. Delivering, that's all.'

'What?'

'Search me.'

All three of us move downstairs. Among the junk on the sideboard I find twenty pounds' worth of tickets for tonight's National Lottery, a lot for a house with no money, and I fret about how much of Treasure Bottom's collection has already been spent.

As casually as I can, I pick up the questioning that had lapsed coming down the stairs. 'When's he supposed to be going on this big trip?'

'Tomorrow. Late. Can't he have bail?'

'Getting back when?'

'Dunno. But he'll look after us, he said. Help with some bills.'

She yanks her head towards the debris on the sideboard. Among it is a disconnected green phone.

'He's a good lad, never no trouble.' Her expression is suddenly very anxious. 'Can't I stand bail?'

No is the honest answer to that; too much of a risk all round. From her point of view, her son is about to depart, overseas for all she knows, probably never to return. From our point of view, we'd be hard pushed to claim our surety out of a household with no money.

I may need her again, so, 'We'll see.' Then, 'How did he land the job?'

'His brother recommended him.'

'Does he work for C&D as well?'

'No, but he knows the boss.'

'Gerry Sutton?'

A heavy nod. 'He offered him the job, but he couldn't take it.'

'Why?'

For the first time, she doesn't answer.

'Too busy with his football?' I prompt.

'Not him. The one after Nick. Brian. The second youngest.'

'Where's he live?'

'Here, when he's home.'

'Where's he now?'

'Don't you know?'

Both Bill and I shake our heads.

'Welford Road.'

Every local calls HM Prison, Leicester, Welford Road. 'What for?' I ask.

She sighs. 'They reckon he was carrying drugs, but he was set up, had 'em planted on him.'

They all say that, missus, I think.

The snaf comes in through the back door, wiping his hands on a towel before he's washed them; not that he's adding much dirt. 'Find anything?'

'Ner,' says the former Mrs Hewitt gloatingly. 'They never do.'

Driving back through the estate into another oasis of green, I change my mind. Urban deserts don't grow organically. It's

119

genetic. And I fear for that stick-waving little girl, see no hope of escape for her.

Bill stops in a road we have not previously entered, explains he wants to double-check something and gets out, leaving me in the passenger seat. He's only gone five minutes.

He starts up and pulls away. Mal's cleaner lives there, he explains. He gives me the same name he dropped into conversation back at Hewitt's house. She didn't know Nick or his family, he adds.

I don't know whether he's done it to get Prim off a potential hook or to impress upon me that he's learnt a lesson from first thing this morning.

Progress, I think, contentedly.

15

'Good news,' blurts Prim when I'm only half-way through the door, leading Bill into the incident room. She looks anything but good, more agitated than outside Soar View last night.

I sigh to myself. She doesn't mean good news as in major development. She means Good News as in Goodman.

'In his office.' She gives a tiny wave in no specific direction. 'He wants to see you as soon as you come in.'

'What for?' I ask, not sitting down.

'Not sure,' she says.

'Doc Service tipped him off about Nick Hewitt.' Williams speaks from behind his screen with absolute certainty.

'What the hell's going on?' I demand, anxiety rising.

They sit at their keyboards and answer as a duet. The identity parade had, indeed, been a breakthrough. It had been swift and easy to organise. They'd waylaid a bus taking three student teams to a rugby game. There were plenty of tall, blond, fit young men for the line-up.

Both Mr Norris, the neighbour, and the pursuing patrolman

had picked out Hewitt. 'No doubts from either,' adds Williams. 'One hundred per cent.'

I'm becoming calmer, quite cheered.

Half an hour later, she says, the custody sergeant phoned. 'Your prisoner is rolling about in his bunk in agony.' In accordance with standing orders, the sergeant called out Service. The doctor spent half an hour in the cellblock. The next thing they knew was that Goodman turned up unexpectedly.

'What makes you think the doc tipped him?' I ask.

When Goodman popped his head round the incident room door, Williams replies, he said he'd been summoned because of a medical panic over the new Mal murder suspect. 'It wasn't the custody sarge. I've checked with him.'

'Then,' adds Prim, 'Mr Goodman asked for you.'

I can't claim to be surprised. I've been half expecting Good News to intervene since I quizzed Service when I got back here yesterday. 'What was the outcome of all this panic?'

'Oh . . .' Williams beams. '. . . the doc gave him some jollop and settled him down, passed him fit for interview and further detention, if necessary.'

That's better news, I think, walking out again.

'Ah,' says Goodman as I enter a warm, wood-panelled office that's bigger than the incident room. 'Here you are.'

He turns away from gazing through fawn blinds down on the southern end of Charles Street towards the railway station. This is my domain, he seems to be telling me already.

Having stated the obvious, he turns his back on me and bends slightly to pour whisky into tumblers on a tray on a polished table.

He walks a few paces to hand a glass to Dr Service who sits in an armchair close to a clothes-stand on which hang two heavy outdoor coats.

Goodman returns to the table, picks up another tumbler and offers it towards me. I shake my head.

Sizeable shot in hand, he strolls on thick blue carpet to a tan-coloured high-backed swivel chair behind a huge, empty glass-topped desk.

121

Goodman is in grey flannels and black blazer. There's a badge I can't make out on his bulging top pocket. Above it is the clip of a bleep. When eyes go to the badge they'll also see the clip and get the message: Never off duty, this hard-working hero. Like so much about him, it's bullshit, of course.

Service is more casually dressed in green tweed trousers and a thick polo-necked sweater that's cream, almost white, and highlights his very dark skin.

Goodman gestures to a chair directly opposite him. When I sit, Service is at right angles to both of us. 'Cheers,' says Goodman, tipping his glass towards Service. 'Good health, John,' responds the doctor with an ingratiating smile.

Uses Goodman's first name then, I note; something I've never done.

Both sip their drinks. Goodman transfers his attention to me. 'I'm surprised to see you still here.'

More than surprised, I suspect; annoyed, especially when he found my car in his parking slot. I say nothing.

He sips again and works his lips. 'At the weekend, I mean.'

I'm weekend duty officer, I point out.

He forces a weak smile, glass to mouth. 'How's your hijra?'

'Hanging on; just.'

'Got a name for him yet?'

'Got a passport.'

Now his smile is genuine. 'That just about wraps it up for you, then?'

I shake my head slightly. 'Thus far his details don't check out in Bombay and I don't want to give the Complaints Authority a bum name.'

'No, that would never do,' Goodman says rather sarcastically. 'Tell me, did your prisoner . . .' he shoots a quizzical look at Service.

'Hewitt,' the doctor responds helpfully.

Goodman begins again. 'Is the current theory that Hewitt killed Mal or was it your hijra, do we think?'

We? He hasn't got a single thought about the case in his head, hasn't made any input.

Still, I caution myself, be careful here because police chiefs are notoriously territorial (me, too, to be honest). 'Well, Hewitt is Constable Williams's prisoner and Mal is Inspector Chand's inquiry. We're liaising because there's some overlap in our separate investigations.' He doesn't look very convinced, so I go on, '. . . and because you told us to.'

An uneasy laugh. 'Hope my department isn't going to foot the entire bill.'

Tight-fisted sod, I fume. Fancy thinking of cost on a murder. 'Have it all on my department's budget,' I say, airily.

He gives me a sour look, clearly offended, and takes a longer sip.

'My interest in Hewitt concerns a call at Mr Mal's home on Thursday,' I go on.

'What's that about?'

He was so busy golfing and socialising with the Chief yesterday, all for free, that he hasn't sought a progress report, I realise with mounting anger.

I brief him on the witness statement from Mal's neighbour about a caller claiming to be from CID. No record existed of an official police visit to the house. My inquiries have been to establish if an officer had called and not logged it: a possible neglect of duty rap.

A satisfied smile now. 'So, if that caller was this Hewitt, everyone in the force is in the clear and case closed as far as you are concerned, eh?'

I nod. 'That aspect of it, certainly.'

'Are you going to interrogate him?' he asks.

Again I have to be cautious. 'I plan to ask him about the allegation of impersonating a policeman and Inspector Chand will quiz him about the Mal murder.'

I want Service in on this chat, so I turn to him. 'If that's OK with you?'

'Perfectly, as far as I can tell.' He's hardly touched his whisky. 'I have given him a thorough going-over. No need for hospital. Stress-related abdominal pains, I'd say. Nothing serious.'

'Was he swinging the lead?'

A thoughtful pause. 'Hard to tell. He claims to have had stomach trouble for a week or so . . .'

That checks out with what his mum said, I privately acknowledge.

'. . . I'll look in on him before I go, to double-check, when his solicitor has finished, but everything should be all right.'

123

I hardly hear the tail end of his sentence. 'What solicitor?'

Service looks at Goodman who says, 'Julian Perkins.'

Bad news, the worst possible. 'Who sent for him?'

'Hewitt's employer.' Goodman relates how he bumped into Perkins in the courtyard as they both arrived. Perkins told him he'd been asked by Sutton of C&D Security to represent Hewitt.

'And you let him see him?' I say.

'Why not?' Goodman looks at his watch. 'He's been in custody for some time. We can't deny him representation overlong.'

Disgust must be filling my face, for he adds, 'There's no objection is there?'

'Yes, there is.' I am barely holding on to my temper. 'I wanted Hewitt ID-ed first, his home searched and for any brief to know nothing until we can hang him out to dry.'

'You . . .' There's scorn in his tone. 'Representing the Complaints Authority, as you never cease to remind us, objecting to a prisoner being granted his civil right to legal representation?'

Cleverly, he's turned the tables on me. All I can think of in reply is: 'The timing is important.'

'May I remind you that the most important aspect here is the murder, not an incompetent or bogus policeman.' With a sharp clink, Goodman puts his tumbler on his desk in a gesture to tell me: I mean business.

So do I and I need to find out what Goodman's doing here. In this mood, there's only one way, point blank. 'What brings you in?'

He leans forward, not reclaiming his glass. 'And may I also remind you that this is my police station.'

We sit for a second or two in simmering silence.

It's Service who eventually answers, stirring uncomfortably in his seat. 'My fault, I'm afraid.' His face is very apologetic. 'Sorry if I've created trouble for anyone.'

'No, no, no.' Goodman closes his eyes briefly, trying to compose himself, and waves him silent with a hand. 'It's no trouble. I was near by.'

He glances at me. 'Down at Welford Road.' He means the rugby stadium, not its near neighbour, HM Prison. From the looks of his smart, sporty dress he'd have watched the game from a hospitality suite, I think acidly.

'No trouble at all, Dill,' Goodman finishes.

124

Dill and John, I note. My, my. They are chummy.

Service comes back, giving the impression that he owes me some explanation. 'I only alerted him . . .' He flicks his head at Goodman. '. . . because I thought it was his case.'

So he would, I have to concede, from witnessing Goodman issuing orders and giving the media interviews outside Mal's house on Thursday night.

'And so it is,' says Goodman with a steely expression. He has made up his mind. 'Get on with talking to Hewitt then and if he solves the mystery of the caller at Mal's house, it's back to HQ for you.'

Not quite, I think. There's the outstanding question of confirming Treasure's ID. I've still got an excuse for being here. All I have to do is to tell Prim to stop chasing Bombay police.

Why bother? I ask myself, getting up and walking out of his office. Why should I care?

It's all I can do not to walk straight out of the station and the case.

Christ, I mean to say, all this work, all this plotting and scheming to get to the facts, the truth, and it's in danger of being buggered by an arsehole of an ACC.

In the sound-proof interview room, the twin tape machine is on, the formal introductions completed, the caution repeated for the record.

Four of us sit around a green baize table as if about to start a game of cards.

I've already decided on a strong lead and place my elbows on the table. 'You have been formally identified as a motorist who, at about noon last Thursday, called at the home of a Mr Ravid Mal.' I give the full address and describe the C&D car.

Hewitt looks across his shoulder at Julian Perkins, sitting at his side. Perkins inclines his head, the barest of nods.

'Yes,' Hewitt says, quite quietly. 'That's correct.'

I can't hide my surprise. 'So you admit it?'

'He accepts it,' interjects Perkins like a teacher correcting a pupil. He's wearing his cords from this morning but has changed into a pale yellow shirt, plain brown tie and check jacket.

Though taken aback, I decide to stick to our prepared script, still addressing Hewitt. 'A witness says that you told him you were from the CID.'

'No,' he replies positively.

'He claims that you posed as a policeman . . .'

'Not true.'

'When asked who you were, you replied, "CID."'

'No. C and D.' Hewitt emphasises the 'and'. 'I don't remember it, but that's what I must have said. I work for them. What's wrong with saying that?'

'Our witness insists you said "CID", thereby seeking to give him the impression you were a plainclothes police officer.'

'I was in the firm's uniform.' He pinches his black leather bomber jacket. 'This.' He shakes his head. 'It must be a mishearing.'

I'm already getting the feeling that someone has taken a peek at the hand I'm holding. 'What were you doing at that address?'

'Following orders from my boss.'

'What were his orders?'

It's a long answer, prompted only by an occasional question for clarification. Sutton, he begins, had given him the address and he'd been assigned to escort a customer during the transportation of an undisclosed amount of ready cash from his home to somewhere in Soar Valley. 'Separate cars. Just follow and observe. Routine, really.'

He entered one end of the driveway as a Mazda hatchback drove out the other. He didn't see the man at the wheel, only the back of a silver head, wasn't sure if the car belonged to the customer. 'Its driver could have been another visitor leaving the house for all I knew.'

He pulled up and knocked on the door. He got no reply. He came to the belated conclusion that the Mazda must have been the customer's and that he had been waiting for Hewitt to arrive, then pulled out of the drive, expecting to be followed.

With the red hatchback now out of sight, he ran across the road to ask a man backing out a car opposite if he'd seen which way the Mazda had gone.

He knew there were two routes to Soar Valley and hoped to catch up on one or the other and then follow in convoy. The neighbour hadn't seen the hatchback and didn't know which way it had gone.

Every so often Hewitt looks sideways at Perkins who nods sagely, either in approval or encouragement.

He took pot luck, he continues, and drove towards the A607 and A46, hoping to catch up.

Got him, I think. 'A police patrolman has also identified you as being behind the wheel of a C&D car which was driving very slowly. Why was that, if you were hoping to catch up with the Mazda?'

Hewitt gives his answer some consideration. 'I was hoping he might have stopped at a shop for a newspaper or filling station for petrol.'

He's sharp, I think.

On the A607 he came across a crash. He didn't stop to help because the police were already there and didn't recognise the mangled wreck as the vehicle he was seeking.

It's coming out fluently, almost glibly, so I attempt to break the flow. 'Who was with you in the car . . .'

'Nobody.' He jumps in, far too quickly.

'. . . when it was parked in the driveway outside the house?'

'Nobody.' Slower.

'Our witness states there was a passenger in your stationary Escort.'

'He's wrong about CID and he's also wrong about that. Maybe his eyesight is as bad as his hearing.'

He smiles to himself, but snaps it off when Perkins gives him a stern look of blatant disapproval.

'You see . . .' I smile back, about to play my best card. '. . . we've checked with your office. They have no written record of anyone at that address ordering an escort to go anywhere on that day. Explain that.'

'Well.' A puzzled pause. 'Mr Sutton gave me the job. Maybe it wasn't entered up. Our receptionist is a bit dozy. You'd best ask him – or her.'

My best card trumped, I sit back, hoping my expression is poker-faced, doubting it.

Prim takes over. 'You called at that address at about noon. Correct?'

'Correct.'

'An hour either side of noon, midday, twelve noon . . .' She nods repeatedly with each word to make sure he's got it, and then, for good measure: '... that very day, the occupant of that house was murdered and – '

'Yes,' Hewitt breaks in, face forlorn. 'I've heard about it.'

'How?'

'From him.' He indicates Perkins who says, 'That's right.'

I have to suppress a groan. We wanted to hit Hewitt cold with this line of questioning. Letting Perkins see him first has left our tactics in tatters; a total cock-up.

Prim stoutly battles on. 'Yet, in the two days since, despite news of that murder being widely broadcast and reported, you have not come forward with this information. Why?'

He bridles. 'I know nothing about any murder.'

'The address was in the papers. Didn't you read about it?'

'Only the headlines. I didn't know the name, because I was never given it. I didn't read down as far as the address. I've only just been told.' He motions towards Perkins. 'If I'd known, of course I'd have come forward. I did your sort of job in the army. I know how important info is.'

'Where were you bound for in Soar Valley?'

'Don't know. I wasn't given a destination. Security reasons, I suppose. The instruction was to go to the address and trail him to his destination.'

'Having lost the Mazda did you drive on to Soar Valley that day?'

'Twice, but not at lunchtime. I just returned to the office, expecting a bollocking, but none came.'

'Why did you visit the Valley twice, if not at lunchtime?'

'A different job.' The firm has a contract to do spot checks at a large house for sale, he explains.

Perkins interrupts again. 'My old place, as I've already told you.'

'What time did you go there first that day?' asks Prim.

'Ten-ish.'

'See anybody there?'

'No.'

Perkins frowns.

Doubt rises in Hewitt's face. 'There may have been someone in, but I didn't knock.'

'What was the purpose of the call then?'

'Just a presence. Preventative presence, we call it. Scares would-be burglars away.'

I come back. 'Spot checks, you said. Plural. Did you go again that day?'

'In the evening. Just to put in another appearance.'

If Perkins is coming to the view that he wasn't getting much value for money from C&D's so-called patrols at his old place, he's not displaying it.

'What time?' I ask.

'About eight.'

I sit back again, dropping out, to head off any later complaints of self-interest or personal involvement.

Prim resumes. 'We have a report from the driver of a Cavalier that a car answering the description of yours was being driven, at about that time and in that parish, in a manner likely to endanger life.'

'Sorry?' asks Hewitt, seemingly playing for time.

Perkins looks mystified and I suspect this is one topic they have not already discussed.

Prim repeats the sentence and adds, 'The car – we say it was your car – was driven at high speed in dense fog over a hump-backed bridge, forcing the Cavalier off the road.'

'Well . . .' Hewitt's head is hanging. '. . . it was foggy, yes, in patches, worst of all down by the river.'

He shakes his head as if trying to loosen a memory. 'At the bridge, I did see a car at the last minute, taking a left. And, yes, it was a near miss, I suppose. I scraped the wall, I think, but I certainly didn't hit any car.'

Now he's trumped my forensic evidence, I moan to myself.

His head comes up. 'It seemed to be going into a pub car-park.'

'That', I point out testily, 'is on the other side of the river.'

'Don't know the village that well,' Hewitt replies at just above a mutter. 'You get disorientated in fog.' He gives me a look which seems to seek support, and adds, 'Don't you?'

I give him nothing.

'I didn't hit it or I'd have stopped. Honest.' His eyes go back to Prim. 'Was anyone hurt?'

'Shaken.' Prim turns to me, her hand also played out.

We've been outflanked, need to regroup. 'That is as far as we are able to take it right now. We have further inquiries to make and . . .' I give Hewitt a steady look. '. . . we are awaiting certain forensic findings. You'll be held until those results are known.'

'What about bail?' asks Perkins over-eagerly.

'Not tonight,' I say, rising.

'But . . .' he looks up at me rather crossly, about to protest.

'Don't worry,' says Hewitt, untroubled. 'It will keep me off the night shift.'

'Not worried?' Perkins turns to him with a puzzled expression. 'No bail?'

'I'll be fine.'

'What about a change of clothes, at least?'

'I'll be all right.' A slow smiling headshake. 'I'm used to roughing it.'

Even more at home than in the army, I wager.

Outside the interview room, back against the custody sergeant's counter, Perkins says, 'Hope that was of some use.'

'Yes thanks,' I lie.

'Very docile, isn't he?'

I'm going to ask a question to which I already know the answer. 'He wasn't the guard who escorted your paintings to your new home, was he?'

'No.'

'When were they collected from Soar View?'

'Oh, they've been in secure storage for weeks. Why?'

Had the paintings been picked up from Soar View on Thursday morning, I was going to query why C&D's visit hadn't doubled as preventative presence, saving Hewitt a trip, but it's the wrong answer. I shake my head to tell him it doesn't matter.

Perkins flicks his head towards the corridor down which Prim has just escorted his client to the cells. 'Strange that he's so unfussed about not being let out. Must be all those years in the guardroom, home from home.' A tiny, tinny laugh at his own quip.

'You know him, then?'

130

'Oh, no. Got his background from him before our chat. Never met him till now.'

Sutton had phoned him at home, he volunteers, and asked him to take the case. With his partner away skiing, Perkins had suggested a couple of other criminal lawyers because he was in the middle of moving in. 'I can do without it, frankly.' Sutton phoned back to say he couldn't raise them.

'He must be a caring boss,' I put in. 'Hewitt's only worked for him a week. I thought Sutton didn't have much spare cash to throw about on legal bills.'

'We sort of bartered. I'll forget this call out. He'll forget bills for escorting my paintings and keeping an eye on Soar View. Told you. It's like a big village.' That little laugh again, irking me.

Get a smile out of this then, I think. 'I thought your new ex-directory number was on limited release.'

'Gave it to that little C&D fellow on Thursday, worse luck.' That irksome laugh again, but what irritates most is that this pair have won every rubber.

I'm not a good loser.

'Never mind,' says Jackie Jackson, Jacko's delightful and long-suffering wife, after hearing a dispirited account of the story so far over dinner that featured more *vin* than *coq*. 'Something may develop overnight.'

Some hope, I brood, not in the party spirit. I feel as frustrated as Prim looked last night. We'd had a great run all day, terrific progress, only to fall at the final hurdle.

'Look on the bright side,' says her husband. 'At least he didn't give you the age-old black dog excuse.'

'What's that – depression?' asks a puzzled Em.

'No. No.' Every police driver who's ever wrapped a car round a tree on night patrol, Jacko explains, always tells the investigating officer, 'A black dog ran across my path.'

He and the bobby whose retirement PU we're invited to next week were involved in what he calls 'a black dog situation' in their young days.

He was the world's worst driver, he recounts, should never

have been allowed on the road, but he couldn't bear the thought of pounding the beat in the rain.

One foul night, he dropped a cigarette and, while trying to brush it off his trousers, demolished a 'Keep Left' bollard.

'A black dog ran across my path,' he said when the local sergeant arrived to survey the damage.

'Did you hit it?'

'May have winged it. Why?'

'Because the inspector's wife has reported their black lab missing. You'd better make sure. It's his pride and joy. He wouldn't want it suffering. Have a good look around.'

They spent the rest of the shift poking around hedgerows in pouring rain. Only when they got back to the station did the sergeant cheerfully confess that the inspector's pride and joy was as non-existent as the black dog. 'That will teach you a lesson,' he laughed happily.

A gleam rises behind Jacko bifocals. He'll tell the tale at the farewell party. Not only that, he'll borrow a wicker basket with a lid from his local vet. He passes my prize tape recorder round the table with the brandy bottle. We all have to bark, growl and yelp into it.

Not authentic enough, Jacko decrees. Tomorrow he'll take his dog and his own tape recorder out in search of cats.

'I'll get a battery-operated vibrator . . .'

'Don't look at me,' Em butts in, loyally.

'. . . and put it in the basket to create a bit of movement inside, give the impression there's a puppy in there, not just a boring set of bowls.'

He fixed me with a bleary gaze. 'When you've cracked this tale,' he says optimistically, 'we'll call it *Black Dog*.'

'Why?' objects Jackie. 'It's got nothing to do with it.'

'So what? It's dark, sinister, nice.'

16

All that's developed overnight is a mild hangover and inflammation of the knee, the swelling so painful that I almost called in sick after breakfasting in bed on croissants and black coffee.

But, as I grumpily pointed out to a worried Em, how would that look from a departmental chief who's just started a purge on skiving? Besides, who does the senior weekend officer call when he's the only sad sod on duty?

I had a long, hot bath, tugged on an elasticated bandage and took the pills I get on repeat prescription. In rust-coloured sports jacket and fawn flannels, I limped to the front door.

Laura handed me my floppy hat and Em my raincoat and a wooden walking-stick with a curved handle and a pointed end. Fitted to it are metal badges bought at ski resorts in my bachelor days, places that will never again see me on their slopes.

With a final blown kiss, I got into the Volvo, eased it up to 40 m.p.h., stuck to it to keep knee movement to a minimum and was soon lost in thought.

The reason I'd not stayed in bed, I'd acknowledged, is that I didn't want the rumour to spread from that small incident room right round the entire force that I caved in to Goodman.

All they had to offer at force HQ when I dropped in was a domestic murder, well under control, and a free lunch at an arts festival being opened by the deputy Heritage Minister. 'No thanks,' I told the control room inspector, 'I have a date around lunchtime.'

Now I'm cruising south down the A46 by that roadside hotel with white plaster and black beams at Six Hills. To the west is Burton-on-the-Wolds and the bride's home where Gupta Shama, MP, is due later this morning. Talking to him is more important than a freebie, arty-farty lunch.

I've made the right decision and I feel good about it.

'R at 6 Hills – 12' rolls out across my mind's eye like a message on the display panel of my pager in my pen pocket.

A vital loose end that, and the feel good glow fades away.

What's to the east? I glance left but see only gently folding hills beneath a low weak sun in a mainly blue sky.

Let's think this through.

You don't believe Treasure murdered Mal because of the dollars you discovered at Soar View. Therefore, robbery as the reason doesn't add up.

Somewhere to the west, hidden by hills, is Barrow-upon-Soar

133

where, you think, Mal called at 11 a.m. to collect the dollars. Was Shama present at Soar View for the hand-over? Ask him later. A gloomy moment. If he turns up, that is. Don't even think that. Think positive.

Go on. Mal and Treasure leave Soar View. Both spilt blood from some fight or assault in the red hatchback on the way to Mal's home.

In the car or at the house Mal was killed and Treasure fled. Why? Because he witnessed something? Because he was frightened for his life?

Because, you dumbo, he saw the attack on Mal and feared that he was next.

A contract killing? I grip the wheel tighter. Looked at that way, yes, it has the hallmarks of a hired hitman.

Who had the contract? Must be Hewitt, either for and on behalf of C&D Security or acting on his own. And he planted the dollars in Treasure's room to make it look like murder in the course of robbery rather than a planned assassination.

Got it. I'm so thrilled I hardly notice that I'm passing the spot where Treasure crashed on the opposite carriageway.

Disappointment floods through as the deserted Milestones depot goes by on the right. No, you haven't got it. You're getting there, but you haven't got it; you're a mile off, that golden mile away.

Entering Melton Road, the questions keep crowding in: If you're right, who took out the contract, who hired Hewitt and/or C&D Security? Why?

Must be big if they can afford to leave fifty thousand dollars behind as a red herring. What's that big?

The jewellery trade to which everyone, apart from Dr Service, seems to be linked? Or Pillars of Faith, to which everyone, except Julian Perkins, appears to be connected?

It's a religious charity, for Christ's sake, you berk. My mind goes blank in Belgrave Road. Unless, it slowly dawns, they ferry medicinal drugs out and recreational drugs in.

Mmmmm. Smuggling? Drugs or gems?

So long and deep is my muse that I'm in Charles Street before I notice the petrol gauge on the dashboard dials is touching red. Nor do I spot Dr Service until, surprisingly, he gives me a friendly toot driving out of the courtyard as I drive in.

Hanging on to her phone, Prim gives me the briefest of waves when I enter the incident room. Bill is studying a large folded-out map and doesn't look up when he grunts, 'Morning.' Williams nods more in the direction of his screen than me.

She is in a tight, thick coffee-coloured dress. They are in grey suits, Williams's light, Bill's dark; their Sunday best.

Feeling under-dressed in jacket and slacks, I sit down, stretching out my right leg beneath the desk as far as it will go.

The only fresh item in the in-tray is a pale blue form from Forensics which reports that the sample scraped from the hump-backed bridge over the River Soar matches the paintwork from Hewitt's impounded C&D car.

So what? I brood. He's offered an explanation that no court would reject. I toss it back into the wire basket.

Williams comes off the phone. 'The LRI,' he says. 'Treasure is sinking. They want a case conference in the morning. Can you be there?'

Oh, Lord, I groan inwardly. They are going to switch off with me present. And all those years ago I ducked taking my blind old dog to the vet and left it to gran.

I give him a glum nod. 'Is Hewitt OK? Not had another bout of gut trouble or anything?'

'As far as we know. Why?'

'I've just seen Dr Service leaving.'

Williams picks up the phone again.

Bill looks up from an OS map. 'Bombay confirms the passport details.'

Shit, I think. I was in such a frustrated rush to get away last night that I forgot to tell them to put that query on hold. Now I've no excuse for being here if Goodman pokes his nose in again.

Williams puts down his phone. 'Hewitt ate and slept well, the custody sarge says. He's on his bunk, reading the papers.' The doctor had been called out to examine an overnight drunk who'd been complaining of chest pains.

'Anybody clamouring to bail him?' I ask.

'No.'

Bill frowns. 'Strange that, after the way his mum raised hell yesterday.'

True, I think. 'Anything on Shama or his hired car?'

'No.'

'What about "R at 6 Hills"?'

'Still working on it.' Bill goes back to his maps.

Williams thumbs through his notebook. Hewitt, he reports, left the army at his own request with an honourable discharge: no black marks on his record.

Sutton left the prison service on a medical discharge. The only blemish on his record was an allegation that he'd badly beaten up a prisoner who'd tried to escape from an outside working party he'd been supervising. The prisoner made a good enough recovery to stove in Sutton's face with a table.

'It was left as a one-one draw because no proceedings were taken in either case,' he adds cynically.

My phone rings. 'Julian.' A cheery, fruity voice. 'Julian Perkins.'

'Ah, Jules,' I'm tempted to answer, but don't. 'How can I help you?'

'Nicholas Hewitt,' he says. 'Is bail still out of the question?'

'Why? He hasn't asked for it and no one is rushing to put themselves up as a surety.'

'Oh.' Surprised. 'I told Gerry Sutton the score last night. I thought he might have volunteered.'

'Anyway,' I sigh, 'we're not ready to let him go yet. Sorry.'

'How about a change of clothes?'

'He hasn't requested that, either.'

'Oh, come on. If he's got to spend another night in custody and has to appear in court tomorrow, he'll look and smell like a tramp. Want me to organise it?'

I don't want Perkins near Hewitt again until I've finished with him. 'We'll do that,' I offer, pleasantly.

'Good man,' he gushes.

'Switch on your screen,' Prim virtually orders from her keyboard when a long phone conversation ends.

136

I pull myself up in my chair and do as I'm told. On it appear entries from Mal's wall calendar going back thirteen months. The first weeks vanish into thin air. The scrolling stops. A white block highlights a date in mid-May: 'Mazda – 5'.

'The day Mal handed over his vehicle in memory of his wife, remember?' prompts Prim. She'd checked Pillars' records. 'The first pair to drive the new vehicle were members of his own Zoroastrian Society, both students from London.'

Why not? I think. It was a gift to honour his Parsi wife.

'They drove all the way to Sarajevo,' she goes on, not explaining what she's driving at.

Three more months disappear heavenwards and the block rests in mid-August – 'AD – 5.' 'That was a Christian crew,' she says.

I feel I ought to ask something. 'Not from Doc Service's church, by any chance?'

She shakes her head. 'They say they took the new Mazda only as far as Geneva where the old Pillars truck is now kept. They drove on in that to Bosnia.'

Again I think: Why not? Roads get rougher the further east you go. If there's any mileage left in it, they might as well run the first vehicle into the ground.

Another quarter goes by in the blinking of an eye and the block stops at 'Exodus – 5 a.m.'

My heart stops with it; not with any blinding revelation, with shame. All day yesterday and on the trip here this morning old Abe Myles had not entered my mind; not a single thought, so intent had I been on nailing down the truth about Mal – and failing. 'That, if I'm right, must have been a Jewish pair.'

Makes sense, it's a Hebrew buzz word, I think somewhat sacrilegiously. 'Haven't you checked?'

'I'm only half-way through. I want to bounce it off you first.'

Bounce what? I wonder. The screen scrolls up to last Sunday and 'Hejira – 5'. 'Crewed from a local mosque, do you think?' says Prim.

She's lost me. 'How would I know?'

Inwardly, my language is matching Hewitt's mother's. What's she telling me? That Mal made clever little jokes on his own calendar? Operation Mazda for Parsis after their God. For Christians,

Operation AD when it all began for them. Operation Exodus – God, that word again – for the Jewish crew, Operation Hejira for Muslims.

Someone who calls a cat with more than nine lives Laz after back-from-the-dead Lazarus clearly likes a bit of harmless fun with religion. What's wrong with that? It's not supposed to be all doom and damnation.

Is she questioning the fact that the members of each crew came from the same religion? Why not? Saves having to observe different Sabbaths and adding a couple of days to the trip.

Or does she see the Islamic use of 'Hejira' as clearing Treasure Bottom? We've already agreed that the entry a week ago today can't have been a reference to him because he wasn't in this country then. It's old news.

Come on, out with it. 'What are you trying to say?'

'Look at the dates,' she says.

I look, don't see anything and say so.

'Well, the Parsi students and the Christian couple say the round trip took a week. If the Hejira trip follows the same timetable, they should be back today.'

Bill looks up from his map. 'Hewitt's mum wanted him out so he could do some immediate special delivery job for C&D.'

I recall her saying, 'There's money in it.'

'Is something going down today?' Williams asks the question that's sprung into everyone's mind.

Are we on to a big criminal conspiracy? I ask myself. 'Such as?'

'There's a drugs courier in the Hewitt family,' Bill points out.

'Drugs runs involving do-gooders from four different creeds?' questions Williams scornfully.

'They may not be aware of what's happening,' says Prim patiently.

'Nothing to do with this big film première tonight, do you think?' Bill ventures.

'Let's cut out this speculation,' I order sharply, 'and collect some more facts, starting with establishing the whereabouts of this Pillars vehicle.'

'Shall I phone round the mosques?' asks Prim.

I scroll back three months to the word that was Abe Myles's last – Exodus – and ponder: Was his final wish that we should take a closer look at 'Operation Exodus'?

'Yes,' I tell her, 'and I'll take the synagogue.' First I decide, I'll go back to the very beginning.

'Nothing wrong, is there, sir?'

Same worried question at the mere mention of my department. I must have a cruel streak, because, when confronting a bent or idle copper, I get a spurt of pleasure from it.

This time it's being asked by the beat officer who arrested Abe Myles standing among the shattered glass outside his old shop.

I tell him I'm just putting the finishing touches to my report for the Complaints Authority. 'When you arrested him, you say in your statement, he was shouting something foreign-sounding. Could it have been Hebrew?'

'Could have been,' he answers cautiously.

'You, like me, don't speak it, I take it?'

'Church of Turkey, me, sir.' I doubt it, since his wife answered his home phone, but I laugh with him at an old homosexual joke.

'Is there any phrase, any word, that stuck in your mind?'

Silence. 'He did say over and over . . .' Silence. '. . . something a bit like . . .' Silence again, longer.

'Don't try to see it in print or spell it. Just try to remember what it sounded like.' Almost begging, I add, unusually for a sadist like me, 'Please.'

The rabbi answers his phone at home. Must be his day off, I assume, after working double shift yesterday.

I tell him who I am and that I'm tying up loose ends of the Abe Myles case for the coroner. He tells me the inquest has been fixed for tomorrow and, provisionally, the funeral for the day after. 'There's not going to be a delay, is there?'

'Oh, no.'

He laments how sad it all is and yarns awhile about Abe's life, his escape with his parents from Germany, his business, and his work for Pillars.

I dwell there. 'Two members of your congregation made a trip to Bosnia, I gather.'

A young couple three months ago, he confirms. They are

139

working in a kibbutz in Israel now, but they made a film and gave a show of it to one of his fellowships. 'Fascinating.'

'Did they stop in Geneva?'

'To change trucks. A Swiss supporter of the charity put them up for a night, only comfortable bed all the trip, they said.'

'On the way out or back?'

Both, he answers. On the return trip they collected the newer vehicle, then drove on to Calais, getting back home at about eight. 'I picked them up myself.'

'Where from?'

'Peter's place.'

'Sorry?'

'Peter. Abe's son.'

'Why his place?' I barely get the question out.

His Milestones depot used to be a petrol station. The garage owner, another Pillars supporter, had allowed the charity to leave the old truck there between trips after it had once been a target for vandals. 'Peter offered the same facility for the new vehicle.' He laughs briefly. 'Should be fairly secure in there.'

'Incidentally,' I say, very casually, 'what does something like "toros" mean?'

'*Tsaros* or *sorous*, perhaps?' He spells both.

'Perhaps,' I agree.

'Trouble, woe,' he replies.

A stopover in Switzerland, I muse, hand resting on the phone, international capital of smuggling because of its secrecy laws; not of drugs; of art and antiques, hard currency – and gold.

The phone rings and I pick it up to hear the custody sergeant. 'Are you going to charge Hewitt?'

With what? I ask myself. 'Why?' I ask him.

'Because if he's going to spend another night in the cells he'll need a change of clothes. He's beginning to pong.'

'He told his solicitor he was used to roughing it,' I reply. 'Is he complaining?'

'No, but I am.'

*

C&D, I muse, hand on phone that's back in its cradle again. Peter Myles ended his firm's connection with them two years ago when he opened his Milestones depot.

What possible current link can there be between Milestones and Myles Junior, C&D and Sutton's staff and Mal's murder?

Prim comes off her phone. 'We were right. Two mosque members set out last Sunday. They are due back tonight. Their priest has ordered a taxi to pick them up at the Milestones depot at eight this evening.'

All I can do is level with them. 'Something is going down, I'm sure of it,' I begin, 'so big that Mal had to be silenced. I'd like to be with you through to the end, but my problem is Goodman.'

I tell them of his orders last night and my fear that he's bound to check up that I've carried them out.

'I can make myself scarce because I've got three personal visits I need to make,' I continue. 'But if he phones up while I'm out and learns that Bombay have confirmed Treasure's passport details, I've no reason to stay.'

'We won't tell him then,' says Williams immediately.

'We could say you popped in and have gone out to see Mr Shama merely in connection with Treasure's identity,' Prim proposes.

'It's not a wise idea to mislead an ACC,' I point out.

'Oh, sod him,' growls Bill. 'All bosses are bastards anyway.'

We all laugh.

17

Gerald Sutton looks up from the receptionist's overflowing desk in the grubby back-street offices of C&D Security. 'Still holding him?'

''Fraid so . . .' I hobble up to the counter. '. . . pending further inquiries.'

'Into what?' he asks gruffly.

'Well, he says that you assigned him to escort duty at . . .' I fish out my notebook, put it on the counter, find the right page and read out the address and time of Hewitt's call on Thursday. The name of Mr Mal is not added.

He nods. Someone phoned in, a male voice, he explains, gave a name and address and asked for an immediate escort to follow his car on a cash delivery to Soar Valley.

'Nick was sitting there . . .' He motions to the battered sofa. '. . . doing nothing, so I gave the job to him.'

'Did he accomplish the mission?'

Sutton waggles his head into an emphatic No. 'Twenty minutes later he was back and said the customer had driven off and left him standing there, the duffer, in the driveway.'

'Who is the customer?'

A dumb look. 'Can't recall.'

Mine is surprised. 'Don't you keep records?'

He'd written down the details on a pad, torn off the top sheet and given it to his receptionist to process, he claims. 'She's lost the bloody thing.' He looks helplessly down on the piles of paper on the desk. 'It will be here somewhere, no doubt, but we can't find it.' He sighs discontentedly. 'I'm going to have to get rid of her. She's always fouling up.'

'So it wasn't entered in your records, the client hasn't paid for your services and you can't send him a bill, is that it?'

'Bloody useless, she is.' He relents a little. 'Not, in the circumstances, that we could have claimed much – just a turn-out fee and a few miles. Not worth the hassle of him counter-claiming that we let him down.'

Convenient and clever, I acknowledge, like Hewitt's responses to all questions last night. Somebody is fine-tuning their answers very carefully. Let's toss a spanner into the works. 'And, of course, had it been a cash payment, there'd have been no need to put it through the books.'

I'm half expecting protestations of innocent outrage, demands to know what tax matters have to do with the police anyway. Instead he gives me a sly smile.

Anyone who admits, however tacitly, one crime is often concealing another, in my experience. Sutton is in on it, I decide, whatever it is.

One matter we've questioned Hewitt about, I reveal, is an allegation of dangerous driving. I outline the circumstances at some length without disclosing that I was driving the Cavalier.

142

He doesn't interrupt to tell me his solicitor has already briefed him on the cellblock interview last night, only to ask, 'Does Nick admit it?'

'He admits he was there,' I reply carefully.

A grave nod. 'He had a job in the vicinity at the time.' He explains his firm's contract to keep an eye on Soar View.

'Tell me,' I continue, 'was Friday night's call two-handed?'

A vague look. 'What do you mean?'

'Did you have two cars in the vicinity?'

'No.' A tiny headshake. 'Why?'

'Because the driver claims he was followed to the bridge by another vehicle which didn't stop.'

'No,' he repeats. 'It's always a one-car job.'

Hewitt, I inform him, is also being held on suspicion of impersonating a police officer. I tell him where and when, then introduce the name for the first time. 'Does the name Mal mean anything to you?'

A puzzled frown. 'Should it?'

'The man who was found battered to death at the address to which you dispatched Hewitt.'

He groans. 'Is that the real reason you're holding Nick?'

I go through the motions of asking the times of Hewitt's departure and return to the office. Then: 'Why didn't you contact us when the news of Mr Mal's murder broke?'

He looks away, in thought. 'We get odd jobs like that all day and every day. You don't remember all the details, can't. If they're not written down – '

I butt in. 'But you did write them down . . .'

'Yes.' A flash of anger passes over his face. 'And she's lost the bloody note. I never realised. Honest. If I had, I'd have told you earlier. I mean, on a murder, I'd want to help. Catch the bastards and bang them up, I say.'

He looks away. 'Didn't I read somewhere you've got a man in hospital over it?'

'Ah, so you did read about it in the paper?'

'Or heard it on Radio Leicester,' he says, wriggling, trying to get over a slip.

I won't let him off. 'Yet it never occurred to you to come forward?'

'The name Mal didn't register, honest, at the time. And, with

143

the case being all over and the suspect caught, like, I didn't give it much, well, thought ... I mean...' The sentence dribbles away.

I glare down at him.

He faces up to me. 'Should have. Sorry. It just never occurred.' He switches off a sorrowful expression. 'But if it is that bloke in hospital, it can't be Nick, surely?'

'At this stage, no one is saying it is. In fact, we might let him out on bail this afternoon. Will you stand surety?'

His response is surprising. 'No way.'

'You sounded keen enough to get him out yesterday.'

'That was yesterday. Now you're telling me he's implicated in murder.'

'I'm not saying anything of the sort. All I'm saying is that we have evidence that he allegedly posed as a policeman at the scene.'

'Will you charge him?'

'Don't know yet.'

He starts to shake his head, very fiercely. 'I'm not having that. We have rules here. No pretending to be police officers.'

'We haven't proved yet that he did.'

'Yer, and if you charge him, how will that look for my business when it gets in the *Mercury*? I'll have to suspend him, pending the outcome, on pay I can't afford and sack him if he's convicted.'

'But you went to the trouble and expense of calling out your lawyer to represent him last night,' I point out.

'I wouldn't have bothered if you'd given me the full facts at the station when I asked. We don't have staff with criminal records here.'

'He hasn't got a record yet.'

'Can't afford that sort of bad publicity. He's going to have to go, I'm afraid.'

He's washing his hands of Hewitt, I think, walking out, and I suspect I know why. He's drawn attention to himself, attracted our interest. He's become a weakness in the chain of evidence that's linked to – what?

No reply to the bell at Peter Myles's smart flat, no car out front in the secluded avenue. No reply to the buzzer at the Milestones

144

depot, but there's a Volvo parked outside, white and much newer than mine.

It's a secure-looking base with high brick walls on three sides. Little of the former filling station remains. The pumps and concrete islands on which they would have stood have gone. The forecourt has been resurfaced in dark red asphalt that's gathering moss here and there.

A single-story building which must have been the office or showroom has had its windows replaced by granite stonework with a solid steel door at the centre.

Adjoining is a taller building, big enough for half a dozen double-decker buses side by side; former workshops, I presume. Now they have concertina doors in heavy black metal. In front of them is an interwoven steel grille on rails; sensitive to touch, I suspect.

Both flat roofs are edged with razor wire. Three CCTV cameras have hinged arms allowing them to turn in every forward direction. Below them are two burglar alarms each with twin green lights that dance on and off to warn that they are active.

Under them are two plastic boards which say: 'These premises are electronically monitored by Secure World.' A similar sign has been screwed to the steel door.

The intercom next to the door is pressed again. The 'Secure World' sign, I note as I wait, has a spyhole in the 'o'.

Nothing, not a voice or a sound, comes from inside and I begin to fret that something has already gone down.

I walk with some difficulty across the road, thankfully free of traffic on a quiet Sunday morning, to a big petrol station directly opposite where my Volvo is being filled and having its oil, water and tyres checked.

At a kiosk that's more like a supermarket, piped music and all, I settle a bill for more than £40, grumbling to myself: 'Hardly any margin for profit on mileage exes these days; outrageous.'

I collect my keys and car, but only drive to the side of a wide exit to the A607 and stop. Engine idling, I phone Directory Enquiries, get Milestones' number and tap it out.

'Hallo,' says a cultured male voice.

Relieved, I tell Peter Myles who and where I am.

'Oh, sorry,' he says. 'Heard the buzzer, but didn't recognise you on the monitor.'

145

Enough walking for now, I decide, so I drive across the empty road, park behind the white Volvo, get out and limp a few slow steps to the steel door.

Returning here must have taken several seconds, but I have to wait several more, listening to clicks and whirrs. Finally the door opens with well-oiled ease.

Peter Myles waves me in. He points a remote controller to a tiny black box at the door and it closes again, untouched by human hand.

His solicitor, Julian Perkins, was right. It is like Fort Knox.

He leads me down a narrow corridor with white breeze block walls into an office. A screen showing ever-changing scenes from the forecourt filmed by the outside cameras hangs from a low ceiling. A computer displaying lists of figures is on a grained table next to a companion desk.

As we walk he apologises over his shoulder for keeping me waiting. He thought I was a samples salesman, and they're not encouraged to call at weekends for security reasons.

He's certainly not dressed to receive visitors. Over an old green sweater and grey trousers, he wears a smudged cream apron up to the throat and tied at the back.

He sits behind the desk. By a telephone is a pair of thick, scorched gloves. He throws out a hand to tell me to take a wooden seat to his right.

Behind him is a long glass window. On the other side men are at work, all in aprons. One wears goggles and a yellow hard hat and holds a steel gun attached to a rubber pipe. From its copper nozzle shoots a blue flame. He is aiming an oxyacetylene burner into a crucible, no bigger than a paint pot, which rests on fire bricks that glow red.

'Adding the alloys,' Myles explains.

The burner is switched off. A workmate in gloves picks up the crucible with tongs and pours liquid gold into a round much bigger bucket caked with solid grey ash.

A third man adjusts a pressure gauge on dials between two metal bottles, one red, one blue. Then he closes a lid on what looks like a frying pan upside down. A red flame roars out of a hole at the centre of the lid towards a copper-sided fan extractor.

Around their safety-booted feet are blackened casts and moulds and scatterings of black powder.

'You always work Sundays?' I ask.

'Catching up,' he answers. He'd been off for most of last week following his father's death and expects to be away for the next two or three days.

My eyes return to the window. In front of the far wall is a long bench, covered in blue felt, at which two women sit, backs to us, heads down beneath brilliant bright lamps. Near to their hands are small vices and bevelled files, miniature screwdrivers and other delicate tools.

On all three walls, none of which have windows, hangs fire-fighting equipment. On the concrete floor several buckets of sand are strategically stationed.

I look back at Myles.

'Fascinating, isn't it?' Smiling, he motions to the screen with the figures. 'Excellent Diwali and Christmas.'

Cashing in on festivals that, strictly speaking, his own religion doesn't observe, I think. 'Your father would have been pleased,' I say.

His smile fades. 'No problem, is there?'

My reassuring expression. 'Not about your father, no.'

He leans back in his chair, relaxed.

He knows I'm from Complaints, not general CID, so I've worked out an opening on the roundabout drive here from C&D's office via his flat. 'It's in connection with an unrelated matter, but you might be able to help.'

'If I can.'

'It started, from my point of view, as an investigation into what, on the face of it, looked like a piece of questionable police work on the day of Mr Mal's death.'

He nods solemnly.

'Happily, I've ruled that out. The culprit, I think, was a guard from C&D Security.'

Recognition flickers on his face.

'I was told you employ them.'

Surprise now. 'Who told you that?'

I put on a bright smile with lips pressed together to tell him: Can't say.

He gets the message and shrugs. 'Your information is out of date.'

'I thought there must have been a misunderstanding when I

147

saw all those Secure World placards outside. Still . . .' I spread my hands in a helpless little gesture.

He could end the conversation now. Far from it, he chats on. 'We did have them for several years in dad's time. Very efficient, they were, I must say. But when we moved here we needed a far more sophisticated service.' He looks up at the ever-changing screen.

I compliment him on the standard of security and he tells me with a self-satisfied smile that I am more or less sitting on three million pounds' worth of gold.

All I see at my feet when I look down is gold-coloured carpeting.

Underground petrol tanks have been converted and extended into impregnable vaults, he goes on proudly. Their doors can only be opened on timers. 'Only what's being worked on . . .' His head jerks back towards the window. '. . . is above surface.'

Warmed up, he continues his PR spiel without the slightest prompting. I never mind Sunday duty too much. You can park outside most front doors. People always let you in. It's as if they feel sorry that you're having to work while they are not. Everyone seems to have more time for you.

Technically, of course, this is not Myles's day of rest, but he's in the friendly mood that makes Sundays special.

All the armoured vans taking out new stock from the depot to his nationwide chain of shops come in next door, he's explaining. 'Loading's when you're most vulnerable.' The fortifications at the rear of the building are even more formidable than at the front, he concludes.

I put on my impressed face. 'Foolproof.'

His is modest. 'Simple, really. It only came to me when this place was put on the market. It was a garage, you know.'

I keep my head still.

'I'm surprised no one thought of it before.'

'When was that?' I ask.

'Two years ago.'

Two years after he took over from his retiring dad, I calculate.

'The previous owner wanted out because he was getting on and a big national outfit set up right across the road. A bargain, really.' He gestures in no particular direction. 'So, you can see for yourself, it's all a bit beyond C&D's capabilities.'

I'm going to float an easy question. 'Do you know one of their employees called Nicholas Hewitt?'

Since Hewitt's only worked for C&D for a week, I expect an immediate 'No.' Instead, 'Why?'

'He's under suspicion of posing as a policeman.'

Finally, the expected: 'Can't say I do.'

'But you do know Gerald Sutton?'

'Very well.' He modifies it. 'Used to, that is. Haven't seen him for some time.'

I put my mental calculation to him. 'So he worked for you for two years after your father's retirement, but not in the two years since?'

'Correct.' There's not a trace of anxiety on his face or in his tone.

'What's he like?'

'Ran a tight ship. Dad was sorry I didn't keep him on when we moved here, but, like I told you, he hasn't got the necessary expertise.'

'He doesn't employ cowboys, then?'

'Not in his days with us, certainly not.'

'OK,' I say, 'you've been very helpful.'

Still, he's not keen to bid me goodbye. Instead, he tells me about the opening of the inquest on his father tomorrow. I assure him that the proceedings will be a short formality which won't interfere with the funeral arrangements. Then I add, 'Terrible tragedy about Ravid Mal.'

'Yes,' he agrees mournfully.

'Did you know him as well as your father did?'

'Hardly at all, sorry to say.' His face is very open. 'But I liked what I heard about him from dad and others.'

'Are you involved in Pillars of Faith too?'

'Marginally. We continued, the company that is, with dad's financial contribution and, naturally, will go on doing so.'

'Ever been on a mercy mission with them?'

'Too busy.' Suddenly his face is closing up on me. 'If I can't help any more . . .' He stops there, a broad enough hint that I'm being asked to leave.

'Thanks,' I say, rising.

He walks me back down the corridor. At the door, he says, 'Sorry if you've had a wasted journey.'

149

Wouldn't say that, I think, heading for my car as the door glides shut behind me.

He'd almost boasted about business. He'd frankly shared his knowledge on C&D, apparently holding nothing back. He'd talked of Mal without awkwardness. He'd given the impression that he'd have been happy to chat on those topics all morning.

But when we touched on Pillars of Faith, he couldn't bustle me out fast enough.

All that he'd mentioned was carrying on his dad's charitable contribution. Not a word about continuing to garage the truck for them.

Why? Because he has something to hide.

Something is going down all right. Here. Tonight.

18

A relaxed feeling eases through me as I draw up in front of the elegant home of the bride's parents.

Standing on the smooth black driveway close to the pillared entrance is a silver Saab with the name of the rental firm in the rear window.

Only one Indian murdered on Thursday then, I think, chirpily; excellent.

In daylight, the house reveals itself not as an old barn or two at all, but several cottages merged into one rambling building. The stonework is so weathered that where it hasn't honeyed with age patches have crumbled away and been replaced with small red bricks. It should look a botch-up. It looks lovely.

Undulating lawns sweep down to low shrubs that do not screen views of the rolling Wolds from its many windows.

Nothing impresses me more than that car, though. At least one half of the duo who jetted in from Bombay will be going home.

The mother of the bride, in a green silk sari with gold borders, opens the door, smiling warmly. 'Welcome,' she says, bowing ever so slightly, but not holding her hands together in that prayer-like greeting you see in films like *Passage to India* – the nearest I've ever got to India or ever will, I suppose.

I don't attempt it, either, just smile. 'Nice to see you again.'

Now she does gesture with a cupped hand moving to one side. 'He is expecting you.' Pearls in gold jewellery dangle from her ears. She has a centre parting in glossy black hair which is clipped into a plait that curls over a shoulder. There's a mustard-coloured spot on her forehead.

Must be the daily's day off, I think, as I follow her across the tiled foyer. Carpets hanging on the walls minimise the sound of my heavy walk. The sweet scent of meat gently roasting floats towards me. The daily must be in the kitchen, I decide.

I'm led into a large conservatory that smells and looks enchanting. Exotic flowers, white orchids and golden lilies predominant among them, and multi-green ferns grow strong and tall out of scores of elaborately patterned earthenware pots.

For a moment, the colours of the bride's mother's sari make her blend into the background.

Coconut matting cuts a path through the dense foliage to a clearing where two men are already rising from cane chairs.

Through the glass behind them I can see where the lawn, much bigger than at the front, has been flattened and yellowed over an area the size of a bowling green. The marquee where the wedding guests ate and danced must have been as big as a circus big top. On the skyline beyond, Beacon Hill is caught in a sunburst.

The bride's father wears sharply pressed brown trousers and a collarless cream shirt. His companion is in a powder blue suit, buttoned all the way up, again no collar, the sort that Nehru used to wear.

The bride's mother introduces Gupta Shama. His handshake is strong. He's fifty-something, stoutish and about my height – five-ten. He has a very round face, not as dark as Dr Service or as light as Prim. He has twinkling, almost black eyes and a smile that displays a gap in his front teeth. There's more grey than black in his thick hair. I can't see why Prim described him as handsome.

'We will leave you,' says the bride's father, bending over a low table to collect a pile of Sunday papers, all broadsheets, business sections on top, and a pair of black-framed spectacles. 'You will want privacy.'

'Thank you,' I say.

Papers under his arm, he saunters in front of his wife down the coconut corridor. At the far end she stops, turns and calls, 'You will stay for lunch.' It is almost an order.

'Sorry, but I can't,' I call back.

'It is roast lamb.' A disappointed tone. 'English.'

I laugh. 'I am booked in for a curry.' I won't tell her how it came about. Just before I left the incident room Prim suggested a hot take-out instead of sandwiches, anticipating we could be working late tonight. 'I fancy an Indian,' piped Bill, oblivious to what he was saying, like me talking to Em on Thursday night. Straight-faced, she took our orders and collected our fivers.

'Pity,' says the bride's mother. 'I'll send in tea.'

'A charming couple,' says Shama watching her go.

I nod. They have style and class, an inbred politeness and wonderful command of a language that's not really their own. They put to shame incumbents of some even more stately homes, who think they bought the divine right to rule with the deeds to the Lordships of their Manors. 'Indeed,' I agree.

He waves me to sit in the chair his host vacated and sits himself. 'I gather you have bad news for me.'

I slip the passport from a side pocket. 'I believe the holder of this is in hospital critically ill.'

He takes the passport, opens and studies it, frowning, thinking. 'How did it happen?'

'He was driving a vehicle belonging to your friend Mr Ravid Mal which crashed. Some six hours later we found Mr Mal dead at his home. Murdered.'

'Ghastly. Truly ghastly.' He blows out air that makes a trembling tune on his lips. He fingers the passport. 'And you believe she did it?'

She, I observe. 'I'm seeking your help in order to answer that, one way or the other.' I get out my notebook. 'I have several questions.'

'Please,' he says with an inviting flourish of his hands.

He'd been a friend of Mal and his brother for years. He saw Ravid infrequently, occasionally here, more often in Bombay. The last time was during his three-month stay after the death of Mrs Mal.

152

Yes, he confirms, Ravid was an international dealer, buying and selling on commission, mainly medical equipment and supplies.

Having spent part of his youth in Uganda, Shama was also a long-time friend of the bride's family. When General Amin expelled Asians in the early seventies, his family returned to Bombay, his host came here to start again from scratch.

He looks about him. 'He's done rather well in the quarter of a century since, don't you think?'

I nod.

Shama himself struggled for a while until a photographer used him in a mail order catalogue as a model for men's clothes. Bollywood soon beckoned. Bit parts became bigger roles, never the star. 'Mostly the villain.' A toothy grin. 'The man in black.'

At parties to which actors were always being invited, he met many businessmen. He started recommending to them the services of both the Mal brothers and the quickly expanding business of the bride's father over here.

Shama had always had a passion for politics. He tired of Bollywood. 'The movies are so trite and repetitive and, of course, I was getting no younger.' He changed careers. He'd been an MP for five years now. 'It is even easier for a movie actor, even a villain, to get elected than a star cricketer.'

The way our lot are performing so embarrassingly badly on their winter tour they would lose all their deposits, I reflect, but silently, because I don't want to talk cricket.

Three months ago he received the invitation to the wedding. He phoned to accept on his behalf but declined with regret on his wife's. 'She doesn't travel well,' he adds, making her sound like rare wine.

The bride's mother mentioned over the phone that her daughter had expressed a wish to have a hijra dance at the wedding. 'As a child, she had seen them perform at a cousin's nuptials in Bombay and was rather taken.' He gives me a quaint look. 'Of course, you don't have them over here.'

Operated-on transsexuals, yes, crudely castrated dancers, no, as far as I know; so I shake my head.

'At home they are somewhat despised as nuisances. Their performances in bazaars and the streets can be quite lewd and their begging demanding, threatening even. If they think the tip

153

is too small, they will not only deliver curses but lift their clothing and expose themselves . . .'

Not, I hope, while you're eating your favourite dessert – banana and two scoops of raspberry ice-cream.

'. . . so stall and householders pay up to get rid of them,' he continues.

I motion at the passport still in his hand. 'Khazana, which translates as Treasure . . .'

He beams a 'well done.'

'How did you get to know, er . . .' him or her? I ask myself frantically '. . . Treasure?'

He smiles at my stumble. 'Originally, because she had appeared as a dancer in a movie musical. It was not hard to trace her. They live in small communes. Normally they work in bands of about half a dozen.'

He shrugs slightly. 'Of course, it would have been too expensive to bring them all. In any case, one dancer on her own might be better behaved and she is . . .' Pause. '. . . as hijras go, regarded as respectable.'

He'd dispatched a clerk to put the proposition to the guru, head of the commune. After much wrangling a fee was agreed. Then came the problem of the passport. To obtain this, his assistant had to go into Treasure's background.

He'd been born to a poor, very large Hindi family near Poona. In boyhood he displayed feminine traits and became such a butt of jokes that he seldom went out. 'Impotency, the failure to procreate, is much frowned on, particularly in a rural society,' he explains. 'A deep shame on his parents, so they sold him.'

'Sold him?' I query with almost a gasp.

'To the commune when he was thirteen. They put their mark on a piece of paper to make it official. We have seen it.'

Just like that? I think. Surely not. 'Aren't there any laws against that?'

He shakes his head, not in denial, more in sadness at my ignorance. 'We do not have your welfare state. In any case, he was an outcast at home. He had seen hijras dance in his village and had followed them around, entranced. He wanted to be one. It was his ambition. He was happy to go; likewise, his family for her to go.'

Him, her. I'm getting confused again.

He lived at the commune on a kind of probation for two years.

154

They fed, clothed and taught him to dance. 'He had a much better life than would ever have been possible in his village, food, shelter, companionship while learning a profession that would earn his keep.'

I'm going to sort this out. 'You sometimes call Treasure him and sometimes her.'

'Dancers when they are fully prepared are called she. Accompanying musicians are he. By tradition, she took the name of the guru.'

Again I gesture at the passport. 'Chowde is not her natural family's name?'

'She has not seen them since they left her.' He stops for a second, then plunges on. 'After a probationary period and training came the operation, of course.'

Not so fast, I secretly object, thinking of the hospital doctor's description of the operation as being an emasculation. 'Who performs them?'

'Other hijras with a razor in an initiation ceremony with blessings and dancing. Oil is used to help the healing process. A straw is inserted so the waterworks are not blocked.'

I must be wincing because he looks directly at me. 'Before you ask, yes, there is a law against it and there have been court cases, but, if there's consent and no complaint, what action can the authorities take?'

Like unreported crimes of rape here, I concede. 'And, after the op, he becomes she?'

'In their eyes.'

The daily trails down the coconut corridor carrying a well-filled tray which she places on a low round table. 'Thank you so much,' says Shama politely.

He acts as mother, pouring out dark, almost black tea from a delicate, decorated pot into two matching cups. I decline milk and sugar and opt for a slice of lemon from a saucer; a good choice, as it turns out, for the taste is tangy and refreshing.

He adds both sugar and milk and holds the cup on a saucer just below his chin. He sips, savours, swallows, then says, 'She was given her first name because she is so prized. Her fees for filming were more than the whole band could beg in a couple of weeks. Most of all earnings go to the commune. So did the agreed advance fee for performing here.'

155

'Is the guru some sort of pimp?'

A hurt expression. 'Not at all. She buys the food, pays the rent. They take care of each other until the day they die.'

I recall the bedside photo with the wizened old folk in female dress.

'I am not defending the cult but, in certain tragic circumstances, you can see it makes some sort of strange sense.'

Well, yes, I mull, sipping more tea. There'd be no children and grandchildren popping round to cheer poverty-stricken old age, a bleak future. 'Are there many of them?'

'It's such a secret community it's hard to know. Fifty thousand is the lowest estimate I have heard, countrywide.'

I try not to gulp my next sip.

Treasure, he adds, signed the form his clerk made out in the name of Khazana Chowde, had her photo taken and the passport was issued. 'All perfectly legal.'

More legal, in fact, than a British MP who used a dead man's details and left his clothes in a neat pile on the beach in a plot to elope with his secretary, so I'm not going to query any of it.

Around the New Year, Shama saw Mal's brother in their club and told him of his impending trip to England. 'He asked me if I would kindly take a packet with me for Ravid whom I obviously planned to visit anyway while I was here.'

This I am going to query. 'Did he tell you what was in the packet?'

'Fifty thousand dollars.' There's a concerned look on his face that the old actor in him can't hide.

'What for?'

'I did not ask.'

'Who carried the packet on the flight here?'

He places his cup and saucer on the table with a deep sigh. He looks at it to avoid my eyes.

'Not Treasure?' I prompt.

'She would attract too much attention from Customs at either end.' He addresses the table. 'Technically, it was an illegal act.'

'Weren't you running the risk of being caught and ruining your reputation?'

He looks back at me with an appealing expression, the actor back. 'Are you going to report me?'

'No.'

156

He shrugs. 'Well, then . . .'

You don't run risks like that for nothing. He's on the take. In his favour, he didn't give me any Hearts and Flowers stuff, pretending that the cash was in part payment for medicines to combat some epidemic or for an orphanage. He hasn't tried to dump it on Treasure. So what do I care? He's not my MP. He doesn't vote for laws that I have to obey and adminster. Nothing to do with me, this. I'm here to catch Mal's murderer. 'This aspect is not part of my inquiry.'

Relaxed again, he tells how he and Treasure met up at the airport and travelled in separate classes. 'I'm afraid she drank rather a lot; one of their weaknesses.' At Heathrow he picked up the Saab that the bride's father had ordered.

'Can Treasure drive?' I ask.

'Apparently so. Her commune have the use of an old Ambassador to get to distant engagements. I didn't let her, of course.'

He'd phoned Mal at his home from Soar View on Tuesday night. Because of the wedding the following day, they agreed, the package would be handed over on Thursday.

Mal said he would drive out to collect it at 11 a.m., which, he added, fitted in with a later appointment in the vicinity.

Into my mind again pops: 'R at 6 Hills – 12.'

Shama told him that he'd have to be on the road by then, for a business meeting in Leeds at noon. 'I told him my travelling companion was not accompanying me. When he heard she was a hijra, he laughed and pulled my leg.'

'About what?'

'Many are homosexual.'

'Is Treasure?'

He doesn't respond.

'She has a nickname . . .' I flip back a few pages in my notebook. 'Chutra, which, taken together, means – '

'Treasure Bottom.' He breaks in, smiling broadly. 'It would not surprise me. She is extremely good-looking. She would be much sought after, especially among our Arab visitors.'

I'll not press this. It may be the Indian equivalent to the Turkish Navy joke. I'm not interested in whether he's ever slept with Treasure. He didn't here, because the doctor said so. At their age, it's not an offence anyway.

Nor am I interested in where Shama went after Leeds. If he

met up with an old flame and they discussed Ugandan affairs, what's that got to do with me?

Mal, Shama resumes, said over the phone that he would call anyway and collect the package from her.

'He knew the way to Soar View?' I ask.

He stops to think. 'I didn't have to tell him.'

It's his lawyer Julian Perkins's old place, of course. Odd that Mal knew the way there, but Perkins never visited his house – or so he claims.

'We agreed to meet up this afternoon at his home,' Shama continues. '"Bring your lady friend," he said.' He smiles very sadly.

I change the subject quickly. 'What did Treasure do after she danced here at the wedding?'

'Amused and, I'm afraid, abused some of the guests. They did not take offence, enjoyed it, in fact. It's their party piece. She drank too much and slept it off.' His eyes go heavenwards. 'On her own.'

They left by taxi for Soar View at about midnight. He saw her at breakfast which the housekeeper prepared. He left at about ten on Thursday morning. She was hungover, but otherwise fit and well.

'What was she planning to do while you were away?'

'Ravid said that, if she wanted, he would take her on his next appointment, though she might frighten the ladies . . .'

Ladies? I think.

'. . . then take her to his home on a roundabout route to see some of the countryside and lunch somewhere.'

'He wouldn't have been embarrassed at being seen in some-what bizarre company?' I ask.

'Oh, he would have loved it. He had a great sense of the ridiculous. Me, too, I'm happy to say.'

Well, yes, he is totally unstuffy; a throwback to his days in Bollywood, I assume, where, if they are like what you read about in Hollywood, anything goes. Pity he's bent.

'He couldn't entertain her on the Friday evening,' Shama continues, 'because he had a meeting . . .'

With the chairman of Pillars of Faith, a special meeting, I recall.

'. . . but she was welcomed at any other time to eat and watch television and he would arrange a taxi home. Also our hosts here kindly offered to lay on transport for a trip to and around their textile factory to enable her to pick out a sari or two to take home. She would have been kept amused.'

He goes silent for a second or two, his features growing graver. 'Was the money I brought the motive for Ravid's murder?'

I tell him we'd found the dollars, but not where. Then: 'But, as I understand it, there was a substantial collection for her at the wedding for her performance and all we've located of that is thirty pounds and some small change.'

He pats his wallet pocket. 'She gave me the rest. For safekeeping. It is an agreement with her guru that she pays it into their central funds. I didn't want her squandering it on drink in my absence and being damned by her guru when I get back.'

One mystery solved then, I think thankfully; only about half a dozen to go.

I give details of the conference at the hospital tomorrow, and my gloomy prediction on what the outcome will be.

He is shaking his head, not in sadness, in rejection. 'Can't be there, I'm afraid.' He must catch his mid-morning flight in order to be in Bombay for important government business. 'Can't change my schedule. Sorry.'

Desperate to pass the buck, I invoke the name of Her Majesty's Coroner and tell him that the patient in hospital has to be confirmed as the holder of the passport.

Immediately he undertakes to visit the hospital this afternoon before the film première for formal identification.

'If the patient is she, I will tell my office to visit the guru and break the sad news.'

He gives me a long and exceedingly affectionate look. 'You have been very efficient and understanding. I shall recommend that you be nominated to act and speak for them.'

Spokesman for a household of hijras, in *loco parentis* for a eunuch transvestite who's dying, I brood, feeling cursed.

19

Time for a bit of speculation, I decree back in the incident room, now that we've collected and shared a few more facts.

Prim isn't finished with facts. All the Pillars crews, including the couple in the kibbutz, have now been traced and talked to on the phone, she reports.

All had left Leicester on a Sunday at 5 a.m., in good time to catch the ferry at Dover, always the 10.30 a.m. From Calais, they used the autoroute to Geneva where they stayed overnight.

Next day they travelled through the Mont Blanc tunnel into Italy where they took the autostrada down to Ancona. There they joined an overnight ferry which landed in Split the following morning. On Tuesday they drove on to Sarajevo where they spent three days and nights working at an aid mission.

On Friday they started the return trip, that night on the boat, the next in Geneva. On Sundays, they drove to Calais and always caught a ferry that landed in Dover at 3.30 p.m. Time of arrival in Leicester was around 8 p.m.

In May, the Parsi pair travelled all the way to Bosnia in the then brand-new Mazda, Mal's gift to Pillars of Faith.

In August, however, the Christian couple switched from the new van to the old Commer in Geneva and completed the outward journey in that.

Their overnight lodgings were changed too – from bed and breakfast they picked themselves to a free, pre-booked room in a small but comfortable *pension* belonging to a new member of Pillars, their only overseas supporter.

Near the guesthouse is a motor repair shop where both vehicles are garaged when not on the road. She smooths her notes. 'I have the name.'

The Jewish crew also changed vehicles in Geneva. 'And here is an interesting thing.' There's a glint in her deep brown eyes. 'They were late arriving back here because the truck performed sluggishly on the M1, pulling to the left.'

She gestures to the phone. 'What is more they said so to Abe Myles when they saw him afterwards at their synagogue.'

She pauses. 'What do you think?'

'Gold,' pronounces Williams dramatically. 'It's black gold and old man Mal was killed because he was going to talk.'

Not a bad theory. I have to admit. 'Let's go back to the beginning. They have been doing these runs for four or five years, to Bosnia since the truce. The first few years they used a Commer van with the name "Pillars of Faith" edged round a picture of the Pantheon on both doors.'

Three grave nods.

'Mal contributes a new Mazda. They keep the same logo on both doors. It makes its first run in May all the way. On the next two trips, and presumably the current one, the crews change vehicles in Geneva.'

I look at Prim. 'They always use the same shipping lines and times of sailings?'

'P&O and Jadrolinija, Croatian-owned,' she replies, well clued-up.

I talk as I think – slowly. 'The first trip, all the way, was to say to everybody, Customs, boat crews, "Here we still are. Nothing's changed except the van." Then a new member, a garage and hotel owner, joins Pillars in Geneva and the routine does change.'

'But not as far as the P&O crews and Customs at Dover and Calais are concerned,' Prim puts in.

'Did the Christian drivers from "Operation AD" complain about the vehicle's performance?'

She shakes her head. 'No.'

'Their August mission may have been a dry run,' says Bill, catching on.

Williams takes it further, stumbling slightly. 'They had proved . . . they were so well known . . . such a regular sight on the route . . . that they could sail through Customs.'

He warms to the idea. 'Come on, I mean, Customs aren't going to rip apart a charity wagon that's been on regular, trouble-free mercy missions for years, are they?'

I imagine the headline if Customs had stripped the white van bare and found nothing: DO-GOODERS DONE BAD – and I'm minded to agree.

'But the Exodus trip three months ago was the real thing,' Williams continues, 'and the Mazda was sluggish because bullion had been welded to the chassis at the garage in Geneva while the synagogue crew was away in Bosnia.'

'Where's the truck now?' I ask.

'It should be heading for the two fifteen out of Calais,' Prim replies.

'Bloody hell, boss.' Williams's features are crestfallen. 'You're not going to give it to Customs on a plate, are you, after all this graft?'

I grant him a thin smile. 'Nor am I going to ask the Swiss police to check out the garage; not yet. We'll tip off Customs, naturally, but only to ask them to let the van through. Then we'll request every force between here and Dover to put on plain-clothes patrols to report their progress north.'

Flippantly, I add, 'We don't want these bleeding hearts switching the bullion at some motorway service station, do we?'

'Surely,' says Prim, quite crossly, 'you cannot possibly think the crews are involved? They have been far too helpful to us to arouse suspicion.'

As a matter of fact, I don't, but I'm not going to acknowledge that yet. 'We don't want them blagged by armed hijackers on the M1.'

'How about we get a search warrant for Milestones and be waiting for them?' Bill suggests.

I nod enthusiastically, spirits rising, thinking: a terrific team talk, this.

A ringing phone breaks the spell. I pick it up and give my rank and name. 'John Goodman' comes back. The ACC opens, as usual, by stating the obvious. 'Still there, then?'

No, I'd like to say, this is a recorded message. 'Yes,' I answer.

'Surprises me, that. I thought this . . . er . . . chap . . . er . . .'

Well briefed, as usual, I think, helping him out. 'Nicholas Hewitt.'

'. . . put all police officers in the clear by admitting he called at Mal's house.'

'He did.'

'So . . .' So why am I still here if there's no longer any need for a Complaints inquiry? he's asking.

I've just popped into the office, I explain, having tracked down the dying driver's travelling companion from India who will be doing the formal identification in intensive care later today. 'Should have it wrapped up soon.'

'Good.' He sounds pleased. 'How's my murder?'

My? Can you believe this? 'Dunno. You'd best speak to Inspector Chand . . .'

Prim starts to wave and shake her head vigorously.

'. . . but she's out seeing some witness. Shall I leave a message for her to ring you at home?'

'First thing tomorrow will do.'

I put down the phone. All three have bright smiles for me. I don't return them. Something is nagging. Or do I mean blagging? There's something somewhere up there roaming my mind and I can't home in on it.

Everyone has relaxed. 'It's all very interesting.' I put on my lecturing tone. 'But it's only a sideshow, a bonus. The main event is Mal's murder. Thoughts on that, please.'

'Well . . .' Williams is the first to sit up again. 'Old Abe Myles hears from his young friends at the synagogue that the Mazda van is playing up. He tells his old friend Ravid Mal. Between them they work it out. Abe is so troubled . . .'

He looks at me. 'His word, right, when he was nicked after smashing his old shop window?'

'Yes.'

'. . . shamed, full of woe, by the thought of the scandal, the blot on the good name of his family . . .' He pauses, something else occurring to him. '. . . quite apart from being gravely ill . . . that he tops himself. On hearing that, Mal calls a special meeting with the chairman of Pillars to put him in the picture. He's got to be silenced.'

'Who by?' asks Prim.

'Who profits most?' Williams responds with an expression that suggests he's barely holding off adding, 'Need you ask?' No one does. Everyone knows he means Peter, his son.

'The old man's ill,' he ventures on. 'He's becoming a nuisance in the business; more than that, a threat. What Senior knows is going to put Junior in jail for a long time.' He shrugs to say: Simple.

'Bollocks.' Bill doesn't mince words. 'That info about the van pulling hard on the M1 is three months old. If that was all Mal had, he would have exposed it before now. Yet he had the vehicle service records on top of his in-tray in his study. Something must have happened since, far more recently, some further info, for him to have been double-checking them. Something's missing.'

'Such as?' I ask.

He scrutinises photocopies of the calendars and one of his maps. 'This "R at 6 Hills – 12" for the day he died.'

He looks up. 'Mal went to a regional conference of the Zoroastrian Society a few weeks back. It was at Nottingham University. For that date, he had an entry: "ZS 10.30 – L at QMC". There's a huge hospital, the Queen's Medical Centre, on the ring road. You turn left at it to get to the university.'

I nod because I already know that. I've spent time at both – studying music at one and having my leg operated on at the other. Neither stay rated as an overwhelming success.

'Last year . . .' Bill is citing another extract from a calender. '. . . he flew to Lisbon. "Left at J10" he wrote. That's the motorway turn-off for Luton airport.'

I lean back, visualising Mal sitting at his breakfast bar, calendar in front of him, pencil or pen in one hand, wall phone in the other. He's taking down directions to somewhere he'd never been before. He wouldn't take copious notes. There's no room for them on a line-a-day calender. He'd enter cryptic half-liners – initials like 'POF' for Pillars of Faith. I think I'll buy it. 'What's to the right of Six Hills?'

'A country manor house, golf course, water skiiing and a health hydro.'

'Where ladies go.' I can almost hear Mal telling Shama about his next appointment after he'd collected his packet of dollars. And it's in the vicinity of Soar View.

'Concentrate on the hydro,' I tell him. I look around. 'Where do C&D, Gerry Sutton and Nick Hewitt fit into all of this?'

No one has an answer, not even Williams.

Maybe it was the names scrawled on the white cardboard lids – Punjabi C (for chicken) and Kashmiri P (for prawns). Maybe it was the spicy smell as we spooned our orders from silver foil boxes on to plates warmed in the canteen. Maybe it was the crackle of snapping poppadums. Or Williams wanting to know: 'Why do they call it Indian when nearly all the cooks are Pakistanis?'

But over our take-out, helping ourselves to each other's dishes, Prim has suddenly become nostalgic, homesick almost.

'They were all together once like Britain and Ireland.' She gives him the stern look of a schoolmistress. 'Before you were born.'

Bill, who'd ordered chicken this time, clearly isn't sure which side of the border she comes from or if she was born here. 'Where does your family hail from?' he asks, diplomatically seeking clarification.

She tells him a little of what she's already told me and adds that she's going home on a visit in the summer.

Gaining confidence, he asks outright if she's Hindu or Muslim. When he's told, he displays a little learning. 'So you believe in reincarnation?'

'But, of course.' She smiles at me rather shyly. 'I suppose, being a man of facts, you find that stupid?'

'Not at all,' I assure her. I stop spooning while I tell a tale about my dear old gran. Watching evening sessions of Test Matches on the television, my grandad and I would hear her washing up the tea plates in the kitchen in the police house up in the Peaks where they raised me.

Without fail, she would appear in her apron in the doorway to the living-room. 'Isn't anyone going to dry up?' she'd demand.

'At close of play, dear,' grandad would reply, never taking his eyes off the screen, knowing full well that by the end of the live transmission she would have done the job herself.

She'd put her hands on her hips. 'When I come back on this earth,' she'd say, 'I'll return as a man and sit on my bum all day watching cricket when there's work to be done.'

'"When", she always said, never "if", so you are not alone in that belief,' I add.

She gives me a delightful smile.

'What would you like to be when you've popped your clogs?' asks Williams between mouthfuls.

'Oh,' she says with a flustered little hand wave, 'an angel, I hope.'

Bill is smiling to himself but I don't detect any hint of mockery in it. I'm changing my mind about him. He may not be racist, just unthinkingly bolshie about all bosses.

Williams ribs her that she'll miss the new blockbuster at the Bollywood cinema tonight.

She'll catch it later, she says. She asks me about Gupta Shama, rather peevishly, because she wanted to accompany me.

Not wishing to destroy her illusions, I tell her he's quite handsome, then explain in my own teacher's tone why I didn't take her. 'If your dad isn't going to tell you all about hijras, then it would have been improper of us to discuss them in your presence.'

She laughs, unoffended by a playful put-down, a good sport, and chatters on about stars I've never heard of, the garish musicals they appear in, the beauty of the leading ladies, the stories of boy meets girl and how good always overcomes evil in the end.

'How's that worthy object achieved?' I ask, rather cynically.

'The villain . . .'

'The man in black,' I interject knowledgeably.

She nods. '. . . usually confesses to his mother, often on her death-bed; real tearjerkers.'

'Why's that?' asks Bill.

She tells him that no one is more loved and revered in Asian culture than the mother figure and suggests that may be why hijras worship a mother goddess, eyeing me.

I ignore her, eating on, thinking: I wonder if that would work over here. OK, Hewitt's mother isn't revered, much less dying, but Nick did come home to her from the army, so there's some bond between them.

I let my thoughts wander on. What's nagging at me, gnawing at my brain, like a dog with a bone? Something said in this team talk, I'm sure of it. What?

I'd hate a shrink to know this, but I often hold question and answer sessions with myself in my head. One is coming on.

What's C&D Security's involvement?

It's not simply that, though, is it? There's something else troubling you, something new.

True, but it's still a bloody good question.

Concentrate on that then. Sometimes working out one puzzle solves another for you.

Well, I'd also hate a civil rights lawyer to read my mind right now, but what's crossing it is no worse than that time I put my ear to a glass against a very thin wall of an interview room and heard my prisoner, who refused to talk, telling his lawyer where he'd hidden the loot he'd stolen.

A bit of fun, that. Once you've got the goods with fingerprints on them you don't need a confession. He went off to jail for three years, still puzzling over how we found it. I couldn't have admitted in court what I did. Confronted with the find, he pleaded guilty and I didn't have to give evidence anyway. That's the way it works sometimes.

You could always get official authorisation to tape.

That would mean appealing to Good News Goodman. Besides, time is running out.

There'd be hell to pay if you're caught.

Yes, but Julian Perkins doesn't strike me as one of those cute radical lawyers who'd work things out.

Do it then.

I push my empty plate to one side. 'Prim's picture-going has given me an idea. Legally, it's a bit iffy. It might get us into trouble with Complaints.'

They all laugh.

I don't. 'If you'd rather not be in on it, I'll understand.'

20

A cheery 'Good afternoon' gets a grunt in return from the snaf, only the holed soles of his shoes visible, poking out from under the engine-less banger in the driveway.

We walk through the ever-open back door and the kitchen, calling, 'Hallo.' The former Mrs Hewitt is sprawled on the couch, smoking, watching TV.

She greets us with, 'Again?' She hardly stirs.

'A decision on Nick is imminent,' I begin, Mr Nice on this visit. 'Do you still want to stand bail for him?'

'No.' Flat, final.

'You offered yesterday.'

'Changed me mind.'

Like his boss, I think. 'In that case we'll have to keep him in.'

No response, much less an argument.

'He'll need some fresh clothes,' I go on.

A response this time, deeply offended, and I start to sift out the expletives. 'Who says so?'

'His solicitor.'

There's sharp surprise on her face. 'Has he got one?'

Mmmm, so she doesn't know Sutton engaged Julian Perkins to represent Nick. 'Wants him to look nice and smart for the magistrates in the morning. He was ill yesterday.'

She fidgets and frowns, worried. 'Sick?'

Did he vomit on his clothes? she really means. She doesn't know about Dr Service's visit to him in the cell either. Sutton has deliberately kept her in the dark. 'Tummy trouble.'

'Had it all week.' She works her bottom deeper into the cushions, taking another long pull on her cigarette.

'Come on,' snaps Bill, slipping into Mr Nasty mode. 'We haven't got all bloody day. We've got places to go, a murderer to catch.'

She blows out grey-blue smoke. 'What am I supposed to do about it?'

'Pack a bag, that's what.'

Resentfully, she rolls off the couch, cigarette in mouth, and plods bare-footed out the room and upstairs. We don't sit on the couch in her place.

I stand, watching a film about a lovable shaggy dog on the Disney Channel, uninterrupted viewing, because there's no small child or unloved puppy dog about the house. I wonder if yesterday's chase is still on.

Upstairs, she is banging drawers and mouthing oaths, searching for a change of clothing that, I anticipate, will be no improvement on what her son's been wearing for two days. The lavatory flushes.

She can't have folded whatever she'd found or packed very neatly because she's coming down in two or three minutes.

Cigarette-less now, she enters the room carrying a smart blue and white sports bag, Leicester City's colour; borrowed from his still-absent half-brother, I guess.

She offers it towards Bill who doesn't take it. 'Come on,' he repeats.

Her expression rests half-way between bemused and blank. 'Where to?'

'Get your coat and shoes.'

'Why?'

'You're going to take it.'

'I'm not.' Huffily. 'Not me.'

'We're not going to run the risk of you or some silver-tongued lawyer saying we planted evidence on him.'

'His solicitor will want it this way,' I add, quite pleasantly.

She curls back her bottom lip in a thought that suddenly makes her round face burst into a beam. 'Rightee-o,' she says, obediently.

Scruffily shoed and coated and in the back of the car, she wants to know what Nick is to be charged with.

'Impersonating a policeman for starters,' says Bill in the passenger seat.

'What do you mean, for starters?' she objects fiercely.

Bill looks ahead through the windscreen. 'There's also the matter of that murder on Thursday.'

I turn slightly, talking over my shoulder, one eye still on the road. 'And the smaller matter of trying to kill me on Friday.'

'Nick? Him?' She forces a harsh laugh. 'You both need your heads examining.' She launches into an obscene tirade against the police, concluding. 'A good lad is our Nick. You'll get nowt on him.'

'Busy, certainly,' says Bill drolly, eyes front.

Approaching Charles Street, she starts to worry about how she'll get back.

'We're not bloody chauffeurs,' moans Bill. 'We've got to go to Soar View straight after we've dropped you.'

I assure her a squad car will see her home.

My prize tape recorder has been retrieved from the interview room in the cellblock where it had been hidden among a pile of

Good Housekeeping and *Practical Gardening*, collected up by Prim in the certain knowledge that the former Mrs Hewitt would not thumb through them as she sat and waited.

All four of us have chairs drawn around my desk. I press the buttons for rewind, then play.

From it come childlike, extremely bad imitations of dogs yelping, crying, growling and barking and adult laughter, male and female. They all join in.

'Sorry,' I say. 'Testing.' I press fast forward.

Their smiles fade at the sound of a door opening and the custody sergeant saying, 'Five minutes.'

'What you doing here?' Nick's voice, getting closer.

'Brought these, like your solicitor said.' Her tone is warmer than I've heard it all weekend.

'Been on to you, has he?' He seems surprised.

'No, but your boss has.'

'Wh – '

'Don't worry, he says.'

'When?' Nick finally gets out.

'This dinner time.' One-ish, she'll mean, after I'd called at the C&D office this morning.

'What's he say?'

'If you're released, don't worry about tonight.'

Someone unzips the bag. Nick laughs lightly. At something his mother has packed; not a teddy, I assume.

'I'd have stood bail, Nicky, but . . .'

'I'm bloody narked Sutton hasn't already, letting me rot in here.'

'Better off in here, he said. Leave well alone, he said. Give tonight a miss. They've got a good sub. Thought I'd pop in, drop off some clobber and pass the message. Not to worry.'

Worried, she asks, 'Does it mean you'll still get paid?'

'Hope so.' Anxiety there, too. 'Did he mention anything about the delivery job?'

'Not to me.'

'I'll sort it.' He brightens. 'Won't be here for long.'

'That's not what the fuzz made out. Searched the place high and low.'

'They'd find nothing,' he says confidently.

170

'They reckon you pretended to be one of 'em. Told 'em you was one in the army.'

Nick laughs. 'It was just some old git getting it round his neck. I've already explained it to 'em. You know what they're like. They don't listen to nowt.'

'Today they're on about that murder.'

'Nowt to do with me. Wasn't there when it happened. I killed nobody.'

'What happened, then?'

Everyone round my desk holds their breath.

'Forget it,' says Nick sharply.

Everyone lets their breath go.

'But that cop . . .'

'What cop?'

'The one in charge. The one who drove me here.'

'In a Cavalier?'

'Don't ask me.' Suddenly she seems exasperated. 'He reckons you tried to kill him.'

'That's him, the bastard.' There's a thinness about his tone. 'It was foggy. It's always bad this weather by the Soar.'

'That's where they've gone.'

A puzzled silence. 'Who?'

'That cop and his shithouse of a sergeant.'

Bill smiles to himself.

'Where?' asks Nick.

'Soar Something. They said they were going when they dropped me off.'

A longer silence. Then: 'They'll find nowt.' This time there is such doubt in his voice that I wonder if our search was thorough enough.

She sighs deeply. 'What's that little bastard Brian got you into?'

Prim shoots me a quizzical glance. 'Younger half-brother' is all I have time to say.

'It's real tasty. Sweet and simple.'

'Drugs again?'

'Nar. Not me. That's a mug's game. This is foolproof. No one will ever know.'

'You're best out of it, if you ask me,' she says.

171

'I'm not out of it. I dug 'em out of it on Thursday, right enough, saved it coming apart. I'm already owed plenty.'

Annoyingly, she asks no more about Thursday and jumps a day. 'You're in the clear over that cop?'

'It was the fog. Nobody was hurt. They can't prove nothin' if everybody tells 'em nothin'.'

'So you're all right then?' She sounds genuinely concerned.

'Out tomorrow at the latest. The panic will be over by then. The beaks will give me bail even if these bastards won't.'

'Your gut trouble, I mean.'

'Yeah, yeah. Home tomorrow.'

'Reckon so?' There's a note of hope in his mother's voice.

'My lawyer', says Nick rather self-importantly, 'will fix it. You'll see. We'll still get our share. You see if we don't.'

'You'll be all right now?'

'Sound.' A confident tone. We listen for but don't hear the sound of a kiss. 'See you tomorrow.'

'Take care.'

Prim asks for a rerun. I hardly listen, can't believe what I've already heard. The gnawing at the brain that disturbed my lunch has gone, completely vanished.

Jesus. What a scandal.

I'd already suspected that Hewitt had to have an accomplice in radio contact when he ran me off the road. The vehicle behind that didn't stop must have been on look-out at Soar View and followed to pin-point my approach in fog to the bridge. I've accepted since yesterday that I'd eventually find the answers at C&D Security.

But, Jesus, him! He's in on it too. The black-hearted villain.

I'll not share it; not yet. Not until I've got bona fide evidence I can use in court.

Williams's head comes up first after the tape has been played again. 'Something is going down tonight.'

'Yes, but what?' asks Bill. He repeats what we've heard. 'Real tasty . . . Sweet and simple . . . No one will ever know.'

172

'Doesn't sound like a blagging,' William agrees. 'There'd be armed cops, road blocks, the media. Everybody would get to know.'

Prim chips in. 'He hints at knowing something about Mal's murder, even if he didn't witness it.'

All three look at me, but I'm too absorbed in my own secret thoughts to take the lead.

Prim replaces me. 'Let us try to work things out. He is in with Sutton on some job that's got nothing to do with drugs and is not going to make the headlines. His arrest means he's being substituted. He fears that is going to diminish his cut. Any panic associated with the job will be over tomorrow.'

'Which means it's taking place tonight without Hewitt,' William insists. He pauses, but not for long. 'Could be that Sutton has hired a gang of blaggers to do the golden shipment.'

Bill asks what he means.

His old job in the prison service would have brought him into close contact with armed robbers, Williams points out. 'He could have tipped someone off about the gold for a sizeable cut.'

'How would he know?' Bill queries. 'He hasn't worked for Myles for two years. This smuggling scam wasn't operating then.'

They dry up.

I come out of shock. 'Well, then, let's flush 'em out.' I look at Prim. 'Has Hewitt ever seen you?' She shakes her head. 'Got a change of clothes in your locker?' I ask. She nods. 'A sari?' Another nod. 'Put it on, will you, please?'

Colour, in my view, is a resource to be used sparingly. I wouldn't send her to a National Front rally. Neither would I assign myself to the annual general meeting of the Yardies. Horses for courses, I say.

Nick Hewitt, an ex-military policeman, will be looking behind him for a tail, but he won't be expecting a shadow in a sari. If he leads her down Belgrave Road, she'll be lost in the crowd on a sunny Sunday afternoon; perfect cover.

I turn to Williams but nod towards Prim. 'When she's ready, bail him without charge in his own recognisance.'

Both get up and leave.

Bill grumbles, 'We haven't got a clue, really, have we, what to expect tonight?'

I'll give him one. 'You weapon-trained?'

A slow nod.

Prim reappears in the incident room, looking like a leading lady in a Bollywood musical. Her sari is lemon and gold. Her shiny hair and lower face are covered by a thick lime green shawl that drops over her shoulders and down her back.

She has to partially unwrap herself to show us where she's hidden an ear-piece and a throat mike.

It's such superb cover for surveillance that I'm annoyed I've never thought of it before. But, like Bill, I'm working with an Asian woman officer for the very first time.

'Heading for London Road on foot, sports bag in hand,' Prim reports over her concealed throat microphone.

Not Belgrave Road, I think; the opposite direction.

Curses.

'Customs, Dover,' says the caller over the phone. 'Gone through on schedule.'

'At the railway station, bought a return to London,' Prim whispers. 'Next train is the four twenty-nine. Do you want me to catch it?'

No, I tell her. I'll get the Met to meet and follow from St Pancras. 'Just make sure he boards, then come back. Don't change. I may have another job for you, just the way you are.'

'He's getting out of it, whatever it is, running scared,' Williams sneers. 'His guts have finally given out.'

Hope mine don't in about three and a half hours' time, I privately pray.

174

21

A right turn at the bottom of a downhill slip road, then under the A46, another right following a swinging sign in a stylish wooden frame and the health hydro comes into view.

It's an astonishing place, like a brick castle in the middle of nowhere. Battlements run the entire length of the vast building. A Victorian folly, I presume. More recent extensions have cleverly copied the same crenellated pattern and there's no added-to look about them.

We enter a foyer restfully panelled with dark wood and report to reception, as requested. More than a hundred guests are here, Bill had been told over the phone, each doing their own thing – treatments, workouts, swimming.

On the whole, I think, glancing into a peaceful lounge where two women in white robes sit in comfortable armchairs, I'd prefer to be doing what they're doing – dozing.

White 'Visitor' labels are stuck to our lapels. We split up – Bill indoors, me outside.

The sun is fading now and the air is much colder. Groups in tracksuits stroll in gardens alive with white snowdrops, yellow crocuses and multi-coloured primroses that border beds of red-berried cotoneaster and pink hazel.

I yearn for a week here myself, doing no more than pottering about in grounds with breathtaking views of the Wolds to the west and the Vale of Belvoir to the east.

I feel tense and drained, my knee so swollen that I'm finally using the alpine walking-stick that's been in the boot of my car all day.

Everyone I meet, I stop and ask, 'Do you know a Mr Ravid Mal?' No one does.

By a fish pond, flanked with heathers, amid moss-covered rockery stones, the pager in my pen pocket cheeps to trail the message, 'On M25, heading north.'

The bleep disturbs a middle-aged man in a blue anorak sitting on a garden seat. He looks up from reading the *Sunday Times*.

I sit wearily beside him, ask the same question, get the same reply.

I look at my watch: almost five thirty. Time is running out, along with every drop of energy.

I'd never realised how much tiredness must be etched on to my features until he remarks, kindly rather than jocularly, 'Try the stress management talk while you're here. You look as though you need it.'

Stress? I think bitterly, on the verge of snapping. What do you know about sodding stress, you boring old anorak? What does anyone who can afford to stay in this sort of luxury know about poxy pressure?

My blood always approaches boiling point when I hear or read about businessmen and sportsmen complaining of pressure.

Pressure is a rupee-less parent with a starving family to feed; not a temporary dip in profits. Stress is a hospital team trying to keep a patient alive, not a couple of poor results.

That's pressure, I want to shout.

Starting out ... when was it? ... two, three days ago? I'm losing track ... seems weeks ... starting with a routine car crash in a police pursuit, seeing it escalate into murder and bullion smuggling, suspecting armed hijackers are about to spring an ambush, watching that clock ticking towards the showdown and not being able to find the thread that pulls them all together.

This is fucking pressure, I long to scream.

Stress is coming face to face with a sawn-off shotgun. Stress is drawing guns back at the station and stepping out into the unknown. Pressure is what you put on your trigger finger in the split second that decides whether you or someone else is to live or die.

I hold on to myself, force a weary smile, 'Maybe you're right.'

With a struggle, I lever myself up and head slowly for the foyer to find Bill. I'll pat him on the shoulder, tell him 'Good try' and return to Charles Street where there's still lots to do.

Prim and Williams have to be briefed and dispatched to the county border. They'll go in separate cars that won't look much of an improvement on the snaf's immobile fleet, but under the bonnets will be engines to match mine.

One will sit close to the exit from a service station. One will wait on a slip road from a junction roundabout. They'll be in

176

radio touch with each other, Control and me. They'll take over where the Northamptonshire plainclothes patrol breaks off.

They'll leapfrog each other – so neither spends too long on the tail of the Pillars truck – all the way to the Milestones depot.

Bill and I will take up observation in the filling station opposite the depot and just watch and wait.

Finally I face up to what really ails me and my heart fills with dread.

Bill and I are definitely going to have to sign out guns; no alternative. Oh God, how I hate guns.

'Meet Mrs Kleine,' says a relaxed Bill, escorting a woman to a marble-topped table in the garden room where I'm sitting among potted plants drinking coffee, giving high fibre Ryvitas a miss.

'She knows of Mr Mal,' he adds, 'and, it turns out, she is a long-time friend of Mr Myles Senior.'

The link, I think. He's found the link. He's also used the present tense, I spot, so she doesn't know yet that either is dead. He's left that miserable task to me.

I half stand and shake hands. She's mid-fifties and in goodish shape. Her face glows without make-up. Damp grey hair matches her jogging bottoms and sweat shirt. A hard back book is tucked under one arm.

All three of us sit. 'Found her in the gym on the treadmill,' says Bill.

Aren't we all? I think, my depression beginning to approach black dog proportions.

'Anything wrong?' she asks with a mystified little smile. 'You see, I'm rather out of touch.' She's been here since Monday avoiding all newspapers and TV, reading mainly. She slips the book from under her arm and puts it on the table. The latest Rosamunde Pilcher, I read. 'Just to get away.'

She declines my offer of a drink and a health food snack.

I put on my sad face. 'Mr Abe Myles, I'm deeply sorry to say, has died. Suddenly. On Monday.' I'll tell her the rest when she asks, I decide.

'Oh.' Her small mouth drops open as if she's been hit. She fidgets in her chair, almost squirms. 'How terrible.' She begins to recover some composure. 'I knew he was unwell, of course,

177

but it's ... my, my ...' She fans herself with a tiny hand and puffs out healthy cheeks. '... it's a shock.'

She had known him for twenty years. Her late husband had also been in the jewellery trade. 'Great friends.' Abe had attended her husband's funeral, she Mrs Myles's, both at the synagogue. 'I saw him quite often at services.'

I move her on. 'When did you last see him?'

'On Saturday, Not yesterday. Last week.'

'At the synagogue?'

A brief nod. 'And at his home afterwards.'

She'd remained a major shareholder in her family's business, was still active in the Golden Mile Guild and represented traders on various national and local bodies.

'Several shopkeepers came to see me to express concern over a drastic fall-off in trade. They were all very worried about a poor Diwali ...'

She breaks off. 'The Hindu festival of lights, you know ...'

I nod.

'... and Christmas. Bargains are fair enough, they said, but one rival was discounting to such a ridiculous extent they couldn't compete.'

'Milestones,' I say matter-of-factly.

A hesitant pause. 'They didn't want to make it official, institute a big inquiry or anything, only for me to have a quiet word with Abe, that's all. He's ...' A sorrowful expression. '... was very much respected by everybody.'

'And Abe, you hoped, would have had a quiet word with his son Peter?'

A nod. 'He said he would, yes.'

'Did you and your colleagues discuss how Milestones were able to offer such unbeatable bargains?'

A determined headshake. 'It was left unsaid.'

I push her. 'But the inference must be cheaper gold.'

Another nod, ultra-cautious.

'Smuggled gold?'

She sighs deeply. 'No one made that specific accusation. It would seem like sour grapes from rivals. They had no evidence. But, yes, that would have been at the back of people's minds, certainly.'

'What was Abe's reaction?'

178

'Furious. Not with me. With his son. He saw the obvious implications immediately. He said it was not only illegal, but dishonourable. I remember that word. You don't hear it very much these days.'

I smile.

'He said that this country had been a haven to his family – and many others like them – in times of danger and, therefore, they had a special responsibility to pay their dues. He would point this out to Peter in no uncertain terms, he promised.'

'And that was the last time you spoke to him?'

She shakes her head sternly to correct me. 'Saw him, I said. He phoned me on Monday morning, just before I set out for here.'

'Did you ask if he had spoken to Peter?'

'Yes, but he didn't go into much detail. Only that Peter had been very offhand. It was a short conversation. He just asked if I'd meet a friend of his and repeat to him what I'd told Abe.'

A slight shrug. 'I said it was difficult. I was coming here. He said his friend would visit at a day, place and time of my choosing. I suggested Thursday at noon here. He asked directions so he could pass them on.'

'And you told him, "Right at Six Hills – 12 noon"?' says Bill, grabbing his moment of glory.

She smiles faintly, impressed.

I press on. 'Did he give you his friend's name?'

'Mr Mal was all.'

'Do you know him?'

'Of him. The charity chap. Never met him. Still haven't. He didn't turn up.'

I tell her now, as gently as I can, that Mal didn't turn up because he was murdered an hour either side of noon on Thursday. 'Oh, no. What on earth . . .' She leaves it there, wearing a look of sheer incomprehension.

'To save you hearing this second-hand – ' and I tell where and how Abe Myles died.

She screws her eyes shut. 'Oh, no. Dear God, no, no, no.' All the stress that brought her here has returned, doubled, trebled, more. She rocks back and forth in her chair, like some mental patients. I take her hand. She grips it. 'Was it because of me . . . oh, no . . . because of what I said?'

'No, no, no.' I'm trying to talk quietly, soothingly. 'He was very ill. You know that yourself. Our doctor confirms it was only a matter of time.'

I don't know if the Jewish faith has a down on suicides like the Christian Church certainly used to, so I add, 'The funeral is on Tuesday. Your rabbi is very understanding.'

'I shall go,' she says promptly.

'But, promise . . .' I am gripping her hand tightly now. '. . . please promise me that you won't get in touch with Peter before then or repeat anything we've just discussed. Other lives may depend on it. Send him a condolence card if you wish, but – '

She breaks in, face set. 'He does not merit such a thought.' She looks directly at me. 'You have my solemn promise.'

Driving back down the A46, the will to work returns. I slip into a reverie and start missing all the landmarks.

So Abe Myles was tipped off that his son was suspected of smuggling gold. He tackled Peter. His pleas for fair play fell on deaf ears.

The young 'Operation Exodus' crew had already told the old man that the new truck had under-performed on the last leg home. Abe had been in the bullion business all his life, long enough to know how bullion smuggling is pulled off. He'd have worked it out.

What does he do then? Approach his old chum Mal. 'A shocking' – no, he'd use dishonourable – 'thing is happening,' he'd say. 'My son is smuggling gold into this country in the very truck you gave in memory of your wife to the Pillars charity.'

Now these are two caring, giving gentlemen of the old school. What would they do? Report it to the charity trustees, they'd agree, declare their interests and leave them to decide whether or not to involve authorities like Customs and us. Mal called for and was granted a special meeting with the chairman for last Friday.

Mal wanted to double-check Abe's information. He dug out the vehicle's service record to see if there was an explanation for its malfunctioning. He'd asked Abe to fix up a meeting with his informant, Mrs Kleine.

Abe was left in mental turmoil. Maybe it was the realisation that he had begun the process that would eventually jail his own son. Maybe it was Peter's betrayal of everything he stood for – fair competition, pay your dues, act with honour.

The latter, I favour, because he snapped, symbolically smashed the window of the shop where his own father had started the business and shouted, '*Sorous*.'

He was arrested, locked in the cell. Imagine it. Almost seventy. Sitting there, alone. Never been in trouble in your life, respected, God-fearing. Your good family name, a reputation you have worked for, given for, prayed for, about to be destroyed. And on top of that you're gravely ill; dying perhaps. 'Exodus,' you write.

I'll never know if he wrote that sacred word to speed his departure or to tip us off.

Right now, at this very second, I personally feel just a little of that *sorous*, that trouble, that woe, that shame. I was going to write off his death in a couple of pages.

'On the . . .'

'Just had the Met . . .'

Back in the incident room, Prim and Williams start talking together.

She stops to let him go first. Not so much out of politeness. She's learnt that to try to talk over him is pointless.

'The Pillars van has just joined the M1,' he goes on. 'All patrols report that it's travelling very sedately.'

I look at Prim. 'The Met's been on,' she says. 'Our target has booked into a hotel down Gray's Inn Road. He's used his own name and his mum's address. He's putting himself about the bar; very visible, they say.'

Nick Hewitt is establishing an alibi, I conjecture, to put himself in the clear if anything goes wrong up here tonight.

'Seems Dickie Williams was right,' says Bill as we walk down the long corridor to the armoury.

'Mmmm' is all I can manage as I come out of yet another reverie, trying to anticipate what could go wrong and where.

'About Peter Myles being our man,' he adds.

'Mmmmmmmm,' I repeat, longer, non-committal.

22

Eight o'clock.

Agonisingly, everybody is late, apart from Bill and me. We have been sitting in a room marked 'Service Reception' for half an hour. Hardly a word has been exchanged between us.

Bill's car is in the forecourt, bonnet up, awaiting a non-existent repair man.

Under my floppy hat, sou'wester-shaped tonight, is a light grey headset; under loosely tied scarf, a mike. Beneath my brown mac and jacket, blue ribbed body armour fits tightly over an even tighter heart. A .38 Smith and Wesson is in its holster at my left armpit.

Bill wears his armour and gun under a long, almost white raincoat that gives him the appearance of a lawman in a Clint Eastwood western.

We must look odd, like a stand-up comic and his straight man who have broken down on their way to concert night at a working men's club.

The sparse room has red plastic chairs, well-thumbed motoring magazines on a small table, a hot and cold drinks machine in one corner and a window with a view across the road, a perfect observation post, but for the piped music which sets my teeth on edge. No one else is waiting so we don't have to indulge in idle chit-chat, just sit here with our own thoughts and fears.

Oh, for Christ's sake, I sigh to myself, let's get on with it.

Now that the traffic heading for the Bollywood première has died down, Melton Road is quiet.

Opposite, at the Milestones depot, CCTV cameras nod and the green lights on the alarms wink. All is very peaceful, apart from my rumbling gut.

At last, action of a sort, I think, as a dirty blue taxi draws up in front of the concertina double doors with closed grille.

My eyes follow every move as an Asian driver gets out, leaving his door open and the engine running. He walks to the steel door and raises a hand towards the intercom.

He stands, looking idly around him, then lowers his head to speak and cocks an ear to listen to something.

Someone's in there. Good.

He turns, walks back to the cab, climbs behind the wheel and moves away slowly.

Good or bad? Can't make up my mind.

He drives beyond the steel door, half turning towards us, and stops again beside the high boundary wall.

Good or bad? Still can't decide.

Probably he's been told to wait, but not where he had originally stopped because he was blocking the Mazda's way inside. And he is waiting, because his mullah at the mosque has ordered him to, and you don't mess with mullahs.

He doesn't know it, but there's going to be a twenty-minute delay. The Pillars van has just come off the M1 and is in the western outskirts, clocking no more than forty miles an hour with traffic beginning to build up behind, Prim and Williams somewhere in the convoy.

Bad, I finally decide, my bloodstream beginning to bubble. It's bad to have a potential hostage and getaway vehicle just sitting there ready to be snatched when the shooting starts.

Should I order Bill to collect his car, drive across the road, tell the cabbie to get lost and take his place? Trouble is I'm not sure of the range of those cameras which have been nodding in our direction for more than forty minutes.

Could have done with some of Friday night's fog, I lament. If they've picked up Bill's car with bonnet up and nobody working underneath it, Peter Myles or his look-out will spot trouble when he tootles blithely across the road.

Some wise man, most likely my grandad, once said, 'When you don't know what to do, do nothing.'

Wait, I start to tell myself, already about to change my mind.

Prim breaks up these wavering thoughts. 'A C&D car has joined the convoy between Williams and me.'

Now what? I think with a start.

'It just pulled out of a side street,' she adds, 'and into the line of traffic between us.'

Wait. Think. First things first. I try to slow a mind that's now racing faster than my heart.

We don't believe these Muslims or any other Pillars of Faith crew are in on this, do we? No. So, if the hit is here, you and Bill are going to have to get across there and somehow protect them anyway. Pull the cabbie under your shield at the same time. Right?

It's still a bad situation you should have thought through earlier, but not that bad, and certainly better than breaking cover now. Wait, I decide with more certainty.

Now. Move on. What do you make of a C&D patrol tagging on? Maybe it means the ambush is going to take place before the gold shipment gets here.

Shit. We could be in the wrong place, I think, my blood beginning to freeze.

'Entering city end of Belgrave Road,' reports Williams.

At this end, the cameras nod, the green lights blink and the taxi waits.

'C&D car still following. Driver, white, appears to be talking into hand-held mouthpiece. No passenger.' Pause. 'That guy we saw when we nicked Nick.'

Tommy Keyworth, I realise. And he's sending out a location report like someone did on Friday to pin-point my position in the fog.

We are in the wrong place. I know it.

And Prim and Williams are a mile away, unarmed.

A hot spring surges through my stomach.

'A hold-up.'

'What?' Bubbles of panic within me are about to break surface.

'Sorry. No. Sorry.' Williams, hyped up, almost babbling. 'A traffic hold-up.'

184

A traffic hold-up? I ask myself. The road's been quiet since the film première started.

'I'm two vehicles behind,' he goes on. 'Can't quite . . .'

Prim talks over him. 'The C&D car is overtaking a line of stationary vehicles.'

Williams again. 'Ah, we're moving ahead again. No. Wait. The Pillars van is taking a right.'

'Where?' I snap.

'At the Melton Hotel.'

I picture the location of the local used by Sutton and Perkins. 'Why?' I almost shout.

'A diversion. Someone in uniform has coned off the main road and is pointing down the side street where C&A has its office.'

The ambush. And I'm in the wrong place.

'Not a cop at all, but dressed a bit like one,' says William softly. 'Peaked cap. Black uniform. White. Six foot. Thirties. Never seen him before.'

He's guiding the Pillars crew into a trap. Half of C&D Security seem to be in on it. 'Don't go down there,' I command.

'Too late,' replies Williams easily. 'Inspector Chand's gone.'

The bitch. The bloody bitch. I'm running this show. 'I said, and this is an order – '

She comes on. 'It's OK. OK. The C&D car drove on the wrong side of the main road past three or four vehicles and into the lead down the side street. The Pillars truck has followed. Then a couple more vehicles, then me. I am tucked well behind. It's OK. Don't worry.'

'I'm right behind you,' adds Williams, for Prim's benefit.

Don't worry? I want to bellow. 'Now listen, both of you . . .' I say slowly and very sternly.

Prim interrupts. 'Another blockage.'

'. . . on no account are either of you to get out of your vehicles. Observe and report. Bill and me are on . . .'

She won't let me finish. 'Moving again.'

'Is the Pillars truck OK?' I demand.

'Yes, sir. On the move.'

What does it mean? I can't fathom it. Are the Muslims in on it, after all? Have they switched crews? 'Did anyone get in or out of the Mazda when it stopped?'

'Not that I saw,' says Prim calmly.

'Or Sutton's office?'

'Ditto,' adds Williams. 'That Escort got ahead of everyone. It held up traffic behind to back into a parking place in front of the office. Passing it now. Confirm one occupant only. Definitely Keyworth.'

They must have switched crews, I privately fume, and they missed it. Tomorrow it's back to Community Relations for Chand and Fraud for Williams.

Or, on second thoughts, have the hijackers bottled it and aborted. Good or bad?

Good in that there'll be no gunfire. Bad in that I wanted it to go down to catch Mal's murderer. I know who it is, but need confirmation to be sure of a conviction.

Bad, on the whole, then. It's a verdict with a rider of relief, sheer relief, that I haven't had to draw my gun.

Soon Prim reports: 'Left.' Then: 'Left again.' And finally: 'Right on to Melton Road.'

All they've done is a detour around a block of one-way streets at the behest of a phoney policeman. It makes no sense. They must have switched crews, must have, and they failed to spot it, failed.

'Prepare for high speed chase,' I instruct.

'It's still dawdling along,' responds Prim, sounding puzzled.

The white Mazda van comes into view, indicating a left turn. It pulls off the road into the forecourt in front of Milestones and stops in front of the concertina doors.

Prim and Williams don't follow, but carry on northwards, as briefed. 'What now?' asks Williams as his car crosses our line of vision.

'Park up anywhere that's close but concealed,' I say, preoccupied, watching the taxi driver open his door and lean out. A white-capped head emerges from the van's passenger window. They seem to call to each other.

Above them the cameras keep nodding, but the green lights on the burglar alarms stop blinking. The grille slides sideways. The double doors fold slowly together, casting an ever-widening carpet of pale golden light across the forecourt.

The van drives slowly inside. First the doors close, rolling up the yellow carpet, then the grille.

186

'What now?' repeats an out-of-sight Williams.

How the fuck do I know? I want to reply. When you don't know what to do, do nothing, I repeat to myself. 'We wait awhile.'

Ten more minutes of indecision.

All that's happened in them is that two figures came out of the steel door. They were wearing white smocks as well as caps and carried rucksacks over their shoulders. They walked to the taxi, threw their luggage into the back and clambered in after it. The cab pulled away.

All this cranking yourself up, all this adrenalin running wild and it ends like this. Anger mixed with disappointment flows through me. Might as well execute the search warrant and pinch Myles Junior, if nobody else.

'OK.' I clear my throat, then stop when a C&D car drives into the petrol station from the right, bypassing the pumps, draws up alongside the verge to the wide exit, stops and switches off his engine.

Keyworth is at the wheel.

'We're gonna wait a little longer,' I announce.

Ten more impotent minutes.

Nothing.

Just Keyworth in the C&D car staring fixedly across the road through his windscreen, drumming the steering wheel.

Suddenly, the green lights stop blinking.

And, for the first time, the cameras stop nodding.

Inside, my brain screams out. They've got someone inside who's knocked out the security system. It's on, definitely on.

'Get that driver,' I shout at Bill.

He's off his chair and out the waiting-room before I've risen and managed a few stiff steps, aided by my stick. He's beyond the pay desk, startling the cashier, before I've reached the still-swinging door.

His gun is drawn before he's outside, terrifying a motorist

walking from a car at a pump to pay his bill. His opened raincoat flutters in his slipstream.

'Armed police,' I hear him holler from some distance away.

Keyworth is lying on his side. Both hands cup his head which rests on the passenger seat. The driver's door is opened. Bill, crouching, has his gun trained inside.

I lower myself through the opened door and lean across Keyworth's body, feeling it roughly, up and down, down and up. 'You armed, you little bastard?'

'No, sir. No, sir. No.' He is jabbering.

I look sideways through the windscreen. The grille is sliding open. Two-handed, I grab the neck of his leather jacket. When he's sitting upright, I free one hand and point across the road. 'Is the plan for you to drive in there?'

'Yes, sir. Yes.' I can feel him shaking uncontrollably.

'Right.' My freed hand opens a rear door. 'Let's do that then.'

'But – '

I draw my gun and back in, curling myself into a ball, clutching the gun at my groin. 'Let's do it.'

'But – ' he stammers.

'Now,' I shout. 'Go.'

Bill is stowing his gun.

'Recall the other two,' I tell him.

'To do what?' he snaps, understandably pumped up.

'Follow on foot.'

From the outside, Bill slams front and back doors shut.

Three turns of the ignition, two splutters and finally the engine catches hold. The car jumps forward. Gears grind.

It crosses the road so slowly that a city-bound vehicle flashes its lights to warn of its approach, then slower still over the golden carpet being laid by the folding doors.

Light is all I'm aware of. Too much sodding light.

The car stops so suddenly that Keyworth's head jerks forward and stays there, engine idling.

I look over my shoulder beyond crooked knees. 'PILLARS' is written in capitals on the top half of a semicircle. The grey dome

188

of the Pantheon stands out against a sky blue background. Its columns and 'OF FAITH' can't be seen from this position. We've come to a stop alongside the Mazda van.

I raise myself up on one elbow, turn my head and peer out of the offside passenger window.

Figures. Two of them. One has his back to me. One is in a position not dissimilar to mine – horizontal on a concrete floor, knees crooked, facing a bare brick wall.

There's no cover, no hiding place, between them and me. I'm exposed, totally exposed. Oh, shit.

Colours are all I'm aware of. The standing man – from the top – blue helmet, narrow white band beneath it, black broad shoulders, arms that stop at the elbows which means his hands are in front of him. The prone man – grey and green.

A rushing sound now, like a mains bursting, above the noise of the idling engine.

The standing man turns slightly to his right towards the prone man. A orange spurt shoots away from him at hip height. The prone man wriggles soundlessly.

A sawn-off, my brain screams – and he's used it. Mercilessly. He'll have one barrel left.

I pull my gun from my groin, crook my knees, yank open the door and yell, 'Armed police.' I am on my stomach across the back seats, arms extended, gun in both hands.

Index finger goes from guard to trigger. The pressure is about to be applied.

'*Don't, boss!*' thunders from somewhere inside a billowing white cloud in shadow to my left.

My wrists unlock fractionally, then jerk all the way to my shoulders in the recoil as thunder and lightning bounce around the bare walls.

Another spurt, rich blue this time, from the hip of the man in black. The prone man writhes.

Oh, no. Oh, God. I blotted it, deliberately missed. And he's killed him. Oh, God.

23

The off-white cloud settles into the shape of Bill. He's kneeling, arms extended, gun in two-handed hold. 'Turn it off,' he shouts.

The blue flame goes out at the hip of the man in black. His back has stiffened. The sizzling sound stops.

'Put it down,' says Bill, quieter. 'On to the floor. Slowly.'

The figure in black bends. There's the clink of something metallic on concrete. 'Come away from it,' says Bill, softer still. 'Slowly. Towards me.'

Sagging now, the figure walks a few steps, shoulders drooping, arms hanging, like an ape. On the concrete floor, in front of where he'd been standing, is a silver oxyacetylene torch attached by rubber pipes to two miniature cylinders, blue and red.

Christ, I shudder, trembling. A fraction of an inch more with my finger, an ounce more of pressure, and I'd have shot a man armed with only a burner in the back. Oh, Christ.

'On your knees,' says Bill, rising from his own. The figure loses half its height as he kneels. 'Flat out, face down, arms above you,' Bill continues, calmly. Hands in thick gauntlets go above the captive's head, palms down on the concrete.

Bill calls to me, 'Got him covered, boss?'

I crawled forward, head well out of the back seat and manage, just, 'Yes.'

Bill walks towards the flat-out, face-down figure, holstering his revolver. He takes handcuffs out of an inside pocket of his cream-coloured raincoat.

He steps over him, treading very carefully. With a foot each side of his body, he pulls his gloved hands down behind his back and snaps his cuffs. 'OK.'

I scramble all the way out of the back of the C&D car. Heavy-legged, I walk alongside the Escort to Keyworth's door and open it. His head rests on one side of the wheel, eyes tightly shut. His hands are gripping the wheel at ten to two. I manacle one wrist to the wheel and whisper in an ear, 'Don't move.'

He doesn't.

I retrace my steps round the boot of the car and walk on to Bill, standing over his prisoner. He bends forward, tips the blue helmet off his head. It rolls on the floor.

Slowly, a cheek turns. In profile is a protruding forehead.

Gerry Sutton.

A lemon, gold and green shape is at my left shoulder. I glance over it at Prim, still colourfully dressed for surveillance. Williams is a pace behind. 'What was the shot?' he asks, wide-eyed.

'A close-shave,' I mutter, hardly able to breathe. Too close, I think. I could have, would have, shot him in the back if Bill hadn't hollered.

Christ, that on your record and your conscience. God, I shiver, self-loathing welling inside me at my panic, my incompetence.

Williams walks on to the prone figure in green and grey, trussed by three bands of wide black tape – at the ankles, round hands behind his back and over his mouth.

The gag is stripped away first. 'Ow' is spluttered. Williams turns him over.

Peter Myles is looking at him, face glistening; difficult to tell from here if it's sweat or tears.

'Don't bother to untie him,' I say wearily. 'Just bring your car in and bundle him into the back. Get the doctor to have a look at him at the station before we interview him.'

I turn to Prim. 'Stay here.' Gun in hand, safety catch on, I walk back to the Escort intent on doing something I don't want her or anyone to witness.

I stoop inside the opened door and hold the nozzle of my gun against Keyworth's temple. He tries to bury his head into the steering wheel.

'Right, you little bastard,' I hiss. 'Did you follow me from Soar View in the fog on Friday?'

'Yes,' he whimpers. 'Yes, yes.'

'And radio my position to Hewitt?'

'Yes.' A whisper now.

What I'm getting, of course, can't possibly be used in evidence, but such admissions are more difficult to deny later at the station on tape.

191

There's another reason, far more ugly. Such is the shame, so overwhelming the feeling of ignorance and incompetence when I've cocked something up really badly, like nearly shooting an unarmed man in the back, that my immediate reaction is to take it out on someone else.

He looks sideways at me. There's terror in the one eye that's visible. 'That was supposed to be my lot. I'm only here because you got Nick.' Now there's a tear in his eye.

I walk back, stowing my gun, and nod Prim's attention towards Keyworth. 'Take him in and ask the Yard to rearrest Hewitt.'

Bill and I each hook a hand under an armpit and pull Sutton into a sitting position with his back to the wall. He promptly sags, finished with his chin resting on his knees. He, too, is crying.

Prim and Williams have gone, taking their prisoners. I'm sitting shoulder to shoulder with Sutton, backs to the wall. My throbbing right leg is stretched out on the cooling concrete.

Bill strolls back from a brief inspection on hands and knees under the Pillars van. 'A few smallish bricks under there smeared with grease and dirt.'

'Well,' I sigh deeply. 'There's a thing.'

A stream of abuse comes from Sutton, his disfigured face working from side to side on his padded knees, then silence, then sobbing.

Bill stands over us, looking down.

Sutton looks up, not at him, gazing ahead into the distance, seeing the future. 'What now, eh? A working over.' He snorts. 'While trying to escape? To get me to talk.'

A flashback to his prison service days, I realise. He may have got away with it, but I don't think we'll try, I decide, more at peace with myself.

'Or a slip and head first I go into that hot pot on the firebricks.' He flicks his head behind him towards the office.

Confirmation, I note, that he had Myles in there, under duress, turning off the security system. Confirmation, too, that Myles has the crucible ready to melt down the bars, reblock and renumber them in case the VAT man called.

192

Gold-plating would only improve Sutton's looks so we won't do that, either, I decide, my mood improving all the time.

'Well.' He pulls himself back against the wall. I'm together again, he's demonstrating. 'I'm saying nothing.'

In the initial trauma of capture, they all say that. Invariably, in shock, most of them do talk; can't help themselves. You just have to be patient.

There's a long silence.

He begins to shake his head slowly, sadly. 'Perfect. It was perfect.'

He points with his chin towards the open door out of which Myles had been driven. 'He wouldn't have reported it. Daren't. You would never have known.'

I nod solemnly, accepting that he's probably right.

Myles would have been found eventually, still trussed up. He wouldn't tell us, 'I've been robbed of bullion I've just smuggled in.' That would have put him behind bars.

He'd complain that someone must have sneaked in while he was admitting the Pillars truck and crew into the workshop. He'd spin a yarn of masked gunmen stealing bars he'd brought up from the vaults to work on.

Good News Goodman would have roped in the Muslim couple and the taxi driver. Anything for a quick arrest to announce to the media. He'd give them a hard time before releasing them. And they'd go away – three more innocents from an ethnic minority with a burning hatred of the police that would stay with them forever.

Meantime, Myles's insurance company would pay up and he'd make good any shortfall by sponsoring a couple of extra runs to Bosnia via Geneva.

Yep, it was perfect. We'd never have got to the truth.

Time for a little complimentary comment. 'It was clever. Did you roll under the Pillars van from a car parked outside your office?'

His answer is to look down on his black all-in-one outfit, thick and fleecy, with padded elbows and knees, like something for skiing. I think of his gloved hands behind his back – to save him from being burned on the hot exhaust pipe on the short trip from the C&D offices to here. I wonder if some prisoner escaped in similar fashion in Sutton's days as a warder.

'No masks, see.' Sutton waggles his chin to make me look at his face. 'No weapons. No need. Because he wouldn't have reported us, see. Got it? I hope you're going to say that.'

I've got it, but say nothing.

'You're not going to say I was armed, are you, or torturing him or something?' There's distinct alarm in his face. 'You're not going to try to cover up that shot that just missed by claiming that, surely?'

I stay silent.

'You could have killed me. I heard it go past my ear.' He looks round and up the brick wall behind and above us where the bullet will be embedded. 'You panicked.'

I smile, sickly, because it's not untrue.

He looks up at Bill. 'If he hadn't have shouted, you'd have shot me in the back.'

I smile sincerely now. 'I think that deserved a thank you, don't you?' I gaze up at Bill. 'Thank you, Bill.'

He beams down. 'Any time.'

'Wish you had,' mumbles Sutton. 'It was perfect, perfect. Sweet and simple. But, no, you have to stumble on it. You should have come to me. I'd have cut you in. No one would ever have known.'

Not being much of a medallion man, I'd like to think I'd have passed on that.

'Knew it. I fucking well knew it.' His forehead comes down to his knees. 'Should have called it off.'

He stretches himself up higher again. 'You are going to say I was masked and armed, aren't you? That torch was to cut away the bars and the goggles to wear while I was doing it.' He nods urgently towards them on the floor. 'There's more bars in a sealed panel inside.'

I smile quietly, thinking: That's why the van pulled to one side; the load wasn't evenly distributed.

'But you are, aren't you?' Sutton gabbles on. 'To explain that shot. To save yourself looking a fool in the witness box.'

There's desperation in his eyes. We are talking here of the difference between, say, five years for robbery without much violence and fifteen years for a terror raid; a long time, when you're locked up with prisoners you once guarded.

'I don't mind looking a fool in court,' I say, quietly. 'But I shall want something in return.'

'Like what?'

'Who tipped you off?'

'What's the charge this time?' asks an irritated Julian Perkins bustling up to the custody counter, not at all laid back tonight.

'Illegally importing £700,000-plus worth of gold, thereby evading Value Added Tax at seventeen and a half per cent,' I reply, very formally.

His stride slows. A frown forks up his forehead.

'That's a fraud of £40,000,' adds Williams, chirpily.

'Twice over,' adds Bill laconically.

'Eh?' Perkins's rounded vowels have suddenly flattened, like his expression. He leans a leather-patched elbow of his brown hacking jacket on the counter, as if in need of some support.

'Once, tonight,' Bill says, 'once, three months ago. A hundred kilo bars each trip, seven grand a kilo, and still counting.'

'Look.' Perkins breathes in sharply. 'This is a bit too heavy for me.'

'Peter Myles asked for you,' chimes the custody sergeant.

'Maybe so. Maybe so.' Perkins wags his head distractedly. 'This is just damage limitations till my partner gets back tomorrow. This is more in his line.'

He straightens. 'My advice to him will be to say nothing until then.'

'Suits me,' I shrug. I've got the gold. The Swiss police have raided the motor repair shop in Geneva. What more do I need?

'I mean . . .' Perkins seems keen to explain why he's about to hide his client behind the right to silence.' . . . it's not quite the same as yesterday; far more serious than impersonating a police officer. Hewitt wanted to co-operate.'

Not half as much as he's co-operating now, I think joyfully, having just heard edited highlights from the Met team of his interrogation at St Pancras nick.

In fact, the only dark cloud overhead is that somewhere, at Milestones or the garage opposite or in a car back here to the station, I've mislaid my waxed bush hat, my daughter's Christmas present.

Not to worry, Prim had consoled. I'm booked into her spare bedroom; no chance of going home tonight. Tomorrow, if it doesn't turn up, we'll nip into the Army and General and buy a replacement. At her age, Laura will hardly spot the difference, she pointed out. Even so, I'm deeply unhappy about it.

'When you've finished with Mr Myles,' I go on, still formal, 'Gerald Sutton of C&D Security requests your advice.'

'What about?' An impatient expression.

'Attempting to steal the said £700,000-plus worth of bullion from Milestones,' says Bill, deadpan, enjoying himself.

'What?' Horror wipes impatience clean off his features. 'Impossible.'

'Fact,' says Bill, gesturing to me. 'We were there.'

'No. No.' Perkins is shaking his head. 'I mean, there's a conflict of interest here. My firm can't possibly represent the alleged robber and the alleged robbed.'

'That's your decision,' the custody sergeant puts in.

Given the choice between a small, bankrupt security firm and a jewellery business that will bounce back, it's not hard to anticipate Perkins's decision. 'You'll have to tell Mr Sutton I can't see him.'

'He's asked for you,' huffs the sergeant, going by the book. 'You'll have to tell him.'

Perkins gives me a harassed look. 'Nothing else, I hope?'

'Not for the time being,' I reply, smiling.

Dr Service walks into the incident room without tapping on the door. 'He's in shock, but getting over it. No need for hospital. He's with his solicitor.'

He walks up to my desk and places his black bag on it, alongside my right leg which is stretched out towards the telephone.

'Thank you,' I say. I nod to a chair across the desk. 'Sit down.'

He stays standing. 'The custody sergeant says you want me to see someone else.'

Again I motion at the chair.

A thin smile. 'Who?'

Prim, sitting beside me, repeats, 'Sit down, please.'

He still stays standing. 'Who else is sick?' He glances down at my leg. 'You?'

'No.' I shake my head. 'You.' I pull my leg back a little way and screw my bottom into my chair. 'You are a sickening disgrace to your Hippocratic oath.'

He gasps, then blurts, 'How dare you.'

'You came in here, six nights ago, a servant of the State . . .'

He breaks in, threateningly, 'Don't you dare.'

'. . . to examine a dying old man who had suffered a brain-storm. You listened to everything he had to say – the whys, the wherefores of his conduct, a full explanation.'

I flick my head towards Prim. 'You knew she was concerned about his mental state. You could and should have transferred him to hospital. But you didn't want him repeating what he'd told you to another, more honest doctor, did you?'

Service leans forward, placing the tips of his fingers on my desk. 'I'm warning you.'

I go on, 'To hell with patient-client confidentiality. You had a better idea. All that Myles Senior told you about the shame he felt over his son's gold smuggling and how it was being done . . .'

Service hammers the desk with clenched fist. 'Preposterous.'

'. . . was repeated to Gerald Sutton, your old colleague from his trips to the cellblock here in his prison service days.'

'Ridiculous.'

I smile brightly. 'He's downstairs in the next cell to Peter Myles and he's talking.'

Service lowers himself on to the front edge of the chair opposite. He's ageing before my eyes.

I go on, 'Instead of transferring that disturbed old man to hospital – and letting him die in dignity in, God knows, a short enough time – you kept him in here and didn't order a suicide watch.'

'Genuine medical decision,' he tries to protest.

I wave a hand dismissively. 'You told all to Sutton.'

He opens his mouth to say something else.

I hold up a hand. 'But you'd reckoned without Abe Myles having already confided in Ravid Mal.'

There's as much grey as dark brown in Service's face now.

'Mr Mal phoned you on Thursday morning to cancel the

197

following night's symphony concert. He told you he had to go to a special meeting he'd called of Pillars of Faith.'

I'm approaching a bit of speculation and hurry into it. 'Since you are a medical adviser to the charity, he may even have told you why he'd called that meeting. Panicking, you suggested lunch that day.'

He spots I have no corroboration here, can't have. 'Pure fantasy.'

I continue to theorise. 'He told you he couldn't make it because he had to complete some business at Soar View and then go on elsewhere to confirm the information his friend Abe Myles had intended to present to the charity trustees.'

He tones his criticism down to 'Conjecture' so I know I'm near the mark.

'This bit isn't, though. You turned up at Soar View, just as Mal and the hijra were in the porch, locking up, about to leave. You followed them to the red hatchback. You asked, begged, Mal to hold off exposing the gold smuggling old man Myles had confided to both of you. "For just a few days", you pleaded. By then you'd have your hands on the gold. You offered to cut him in, anything to let Sutton's perfect plan go ahead.'

He sits back. 'How could you possibly know that?'

'He turned you down, out of hand, threatened to report you, too. So you struck him again and again from behind. And when the hijra tried to help him you hit out yet again.'

He folds his arms. 'Someone's making it all up.'

'Trouble now – two bodies in the hatchback. You phoned Sutton. He dispatched Nick Hewitt, his right-hand man on the operation, an ex-military cop, cunning.'

He works his shoulders, huffily, trying to tell me he's not listening.

'Hewitt told you to use the hijra's porch key to plant the dollars in her room and where to get rid of the murder weapon. You drove your car back into the city, he following. Then you got in his C&D Escort and you both went back to Soar View.

'You drove the red hatchback to Mal's house, Hewitt following again. You used Mal's own key to get in. From previous visits you knew that the alarm outside was just a shell, non-operational. You got Mal up to his study and went down again.'

He crosses his legs. 'I'm not listening to this.'

'The plan was to dump the hijra out of the rear window. It would look like he'd robbed Mal at Soar View, gone with him to his home where Mal discovered the cash was missing. The hijra killed Mal and then met with a fatal accident trying to make a getaway. The dollars in her bedroom would convince us.'

He sighs, shoots Prim a long glance, trying to look bored.

'But, surprise, surprise. When you went down to the front door, the hatchback was pulling out the drive because you hadn't hit the hijra hard enough.'

Sullenly, he shakes his head at Prim.

'You didn't know which way the car had gone. She wouldn't have much of a clue herself.'

He smiles weakly.

'A strange vehicle in a strange country. Her only hope was to find help, try to get back to the house where she'd danced at the wedding.

'Hewitt ran across the road and asked a neighbour who hadn't seen which way the car had gone. He took pot luck. Somewhere he dropped you off to make your own way to your car. Driving around, hoping to pick up the red Mazda's trail, he came across the crash. A street lamp had all but finished her off for you.'

Arms folded, legs crossed, he leans forward. 'And how, pray, do you think you know all of this?'

I nod at the phone. 'Because Hewitt is telling us all, everything you told him.'

He stares, disbelieving, at the phone.

I'm not going to bother to tell him this but Hewitt has also admitted to the Met detectives that Sutton ordered him to run me off the road in Friday's fog – just to put me out of action for a couple of days.

Only Service knew I was using a Cavalier that day. I made a joke about pinching the ACC's slot. Only to him had I hinted at my interest in the then-unknown caller at Mal's house. Inquiries into that represented a huge threat to the plot.

When we arrested Nick Hewitt, he gave his workmate Keyworth the message about the medicine to pass on to Service via Sutton. Hewitt wanted Service to coach him on how to handle our questions. And a good briefing it was, too.

Service tipped off Good News Goodman about my continued presence here, still meddling, in a second attempt to get me sent back to HQ.

He was desperately buying time until the gold arrived. It was a never-to-be-repeated opportunity. Had Mal fixed the Pillars of Faith meeting for, say, tomorrow, he wouldn't have had to have been killed. By tomorrow they'd have had the bullion and they'd have all been away, leaving only Hewitt behind as the fall-guy.

Belatedly realising that, Hewitt took off to London to establish an alibi. Now, like Sutton, he is telling all to talk himself out of life for murder. They all do in the end.

It was only this afternoon that I began to work the chain of evidence back to Service. I've Good News to thank for that. He saw Perkins arriving at the station yesterday. Perkins hadn't spoken to Hewitt then. At that stage he knew nothing. Only Service could have told Goodman that Hewitt had cleared up the mystery of the caller at Mal's house.

Why was Service so anxious to see me off the premises, run me out of town? I'd asked myself.

I don't think I'll put that bit in my report, a two-hundred-pager, bound to be, for the Crown Prosecution. I don't want Goodman to get a single mention, one gram of glory out of this case.

Ironically, Hewitt is still insisting that he never posed as a policeman outside Mal's house. Given C&D Security's methods of illegally using traffic cones and setting up phoney diversions and its police-style livery, I'm still inclined to accept the word of the Neighbourhood Watch man. Somehow I don't think it matters much now either.

Service pecks his head at the phone. 'He's lying. To save his own skin.'

I shake mine, smiling. 'Our scientists have just completed a search at Soar View. Guess what they found in the garden bonfire which, unfortunately for you, was too wet to burn?'

He unfolds his arms and cups one hand in the other.

'The murder weapon – the blackthorn walking-stick you took from the porch at Soar View when you followed Mr Mal and his friend to the hatchback. Guess whose fingerprints we'll find on it?'

I switch off my smile and let contempt fill my face. 'The murder apart, I could perhaps have understood this if you'd dreams of funding a medical project back home but – '

'Back home!' he exclaims. 'This is my home.'

He wrings his hands and tightens one knee over the other. 'Servant of the State. You smug, self-satisfied bastard.'

He rocks forward. 'Know what my family name was?'

I'm so startled by his outburst that I don't reply, not that he's giving me much chance.

'Servicewalla, imposed on us by you colonialists. Know what walla means?'

'Worker,' I attempt uncertainly.

'Man.' Prim offers, more positive.

'Servant, slave labour for your Empire.' He is almost spitting. 'And when I get my qualification and come to this motherland of the free you sing about at the Proms, what do I find?'

His face is screwed with hate. 'A job in the armed services – service again, to you lot. Servant of the State. No promotion. No good postings. Not for me. Years of athlete's foot and VD. And afterwards, no health trusts or private practice. Oh, no. Drunks and junkies. Why?'

With the fingers of both hands, he paws his greyish brown cheeks.

I don't really know how to reply.

'Do you think . . .' Prim does, and she's speaking very softly and slowly. '. . . that the answer to that might possibly be that, as events have proved, you are no good at your job?'

Oh, how my heart sings. I've always wanted to say something like that to the many malcontents and incompetents who whinge week in, week out about discrimination and reverse discrimination, whites and blacks, male and female.

But, in this company, it sounds so much, much better coming from her.

24

When England have their backs to the wall they can be more tedious to watch than India, and the evening session is becalmed with five maiden overs in a row.

There's so little action that a flock of pigeons has settled and is feeding, undisturbed, on the outfield as flat and as green as a billiard table just inside the boundary.

From our railed balcony in the hospitality stand, Jacko and I have been watching the Test Match all day, freeloading for most of it in scorching sunshine; courtesy of a drinks firm keen to land a contract to supply all police social clubs.

He's dozed off now in a cushioned chair beside me, twitching his nose and occasionally sighing contentedly.

My eyes go to the pigeons and rest on one that's sleeker and more nimble than the rest with a grey coat that shines. I think of grandma and wonder if grandad is somewhere high up in a tree by the river, cleaning out their nest, grumbling at being left alone with all the chores, and I smile to myself.

And, in the way my mind works, I think on to Treasure.

We went, Prim and I, the next morning to the hospital where all the necessary documents had arrived by fax from Bombay.

They explained that every test had failed to find signs of brain activity.

We were led into a curtained-off cubicle in intensive care where she lay. Ever since Shama explained that dancers were shes, I'd come to regard and accept her as female.

She was on her back, eyes shut, breathing – just. She wore a cream unisex nightgown up to her neck. Her cheeks were smooth and shiny. Her arms were outside a sheet that came up to her midriff. On either side were monitors, some with leads attached to her, some that bleeped faintly.

A very kind nurse in crisp blue uniform, fair hair turning to grey, addressed most of her remarks to Prim. 'We're not asking you to do anything, just be here,' she'd said. 'She's in no pain.' Then she smiled sadly and, oh, so very tenderly. 'Her spirit left her some time ago.'

We sat each side of the high bed and took a hand. The nurse busied herself behind a curtain at the head of the bed. Doing what, I wasn't sure; adjusting some controls, I assumed.

Not wanting to listen to the bleeps fade to nothing or watch the shallow wave on one monitor level out, I lowered my head and privately acknowledged what a comforting way that nurse had put it. If everyone paid their dues, I thought, there'd be tax revenue to engage more like her and have more hospitals like this.

And I lower my head now when I think of the tax-deductible booze I have downed today.

We were at her bedside for ten minutes, no more, and then the nurse said, 'She went very peacefully,' and led us out, me with an arm round Prim who was weeping.

She wept again at a funeral service at the crematorium. Bill and Dick joined us for a ceremony I didn't fully follow – lots of mantras and chants.

The bride's parents came, the mother wearing a long white sari, as did Prim, and they brought friends, wedding guests, I supposed, so the place was quite full.

Last week Prim went on leave and flew off to see her family. With her she took the urn with Treasure's ashes – to scatter on the Ganges, their sacred river.

I look down again at the pigeons and wonder what Treasure came back as. Not one of them, I'm certain. All look too fat to fly a couple of hundred yards over the Trent, never mind thousands of miles from the River Ganges.

I hope she's not a vulture. Not that I've anything against them. After all, one sleeps at my side and I'm sure his mates did a thoroughly hygienic job on Mr Mal at the Towers of Silence.

But I'd prefer her to be one of those tropical birds you see on TV nature programmes that hover and dance in mid-air, gorgeous colours and a lovely singing voice.

All I hope . . . oh, come on, face up to it. I pray that, wherever and whatever she is, she is happy.